Sapphire's Grave

DOUBLEDAY

new york   london   toronto   sydney   auckland

Sapphire's Grave

Hilda Gurley-Highgate

PUBLISHED BY DOUBLEDAY
a division of Random House, Inc.
1745 Broadway, New York, New York 10019

DOUBLEDAY and the portrayal of an anchor with a dolphin
are trademarks of Doubleday, a division of Random House, Inc.

Book design by Nicola Ferguson

Library of Congress Cataloging-in-Publication Data

Gurley-Highgate, Hilda.
Sapphire's grave / Hilda Gurley-Highgate.—1st ed.
p.   cm.
ISBN 0-385-50323-7 (alk. paper)
1. African American families—Fiction.   2. North Carolina—Fiction.   3. Women slaves—
Fiction.   4. Sierra Leone—Fiction.   I. Title.

PS3607.U55 S36 2003
813'.6—dc21
2002073871

and I saw the cemetery in my dream
or my back yard
I cannot tell which

there was no marker I just knew
and forgave myself
my sins

          at the cross at the cross
          where I first saw the light at
          Sapphire's grave where the burdens of my
          heart
          rolled away

it is easier to be angry than to hurt

I done give up cryin'

Sapphire's Grave

prologue

> *The thing that hath been, it is that*
> *which shall be; and that which is*
> *done is that which shall be done.*
> —*Ecclesiastes 1:9*

she was a fierce woman—the kind they did not bother. No, the captain said, raising one hand to stop the advance of several of his crewmen. This one is hostile. She may be violent. The crewmen stopped short, and backed away from her silent, smoldering ferocity. She was black—blue-black, as the crewmen described her—with several stripes carved into each of her glossy cheeks, and wary, narrowed eyes. She did not scream or cry in anguish as did the other women. She had been trekked to the coast from inland, where it was said that the women did not cry, for internment until the ship set sail. Silent and resigned, her angry, level stare had warned of a latent wrath, barely held in check, dreadful as hellfire. The captain was intrigued by her kind. He would have her for himself.

Long after dark they came to retrieve her from the bowels of the lumbering vessel. She was not asleep, but staring expectantly at the opening to the hold. She had seen the captain's lechery, and had known that they would come. She was prepared to do what was needed.

The captain's quarters were illuminated by a strange glow from a covered receptacle. As her eyes adjusted to the eerie light, she sensed him moving behind her, smelled his alien stench as he came slowly, cautiously toward her. She turned to face him. He was shirtless, with strange, gossamer hairs on his chest that made her skin crawl and her lip curl. He raised a hand as if to fend off an attack. She did not move. Slowly, he lowered his hand. Her eyes followed it to his crotch as he began to speak, softly, in his alien tongue, his eyes moving across her bare breasts, the plane of her belly, the curve where her waist met her hips. Inwardly, she crouched as she waited, marking his steps, measuring the distance between him and herself. For a moment, she was distracted by his phallus, now exposed, pink and erect and defenseless.

She had steeled herself to face the unknown, watchful and alert for opportunities to escape. She had suffered, patiently, indignities not inflicted upon an ox, things that she must never mention. But she would not suffer the further insult of bestiality with this creature against her will. She would destroy him, and be destroyed.

He quickened his measured pace, suddenly, and she sprang upon him, her ankles locking around his body, her fingernails digging into his back as she sank her teeth into the flesh surrounding his jugular. He cried out in pain and surprise, beating at her back in a futile, pathetic defense. He bellowed again, but she held her grip, willing him dead, he and all of his kind who had come uninvited from some unknown hellish place to destroy her and hers.

Men poured into the room, some shouting in horror and shock, others too frightened or stunned to move when they saw the blue-black woman and their captain, locked in a macabre embrace, his hoarse cries dying as she held his neck in her jaws, his blood dripping from her chin.

It took several men several minutes to detach her, their captain's agony worsening each time they pulled at the woman, who tightened her death grip, digging into his shoulders yet more deeply, with each tug at her waist or legs or arms, and each blow to her back.

But when she was finally yanked away from him, she did not fight, only stood quivering with rage, not looking at her captors or struggling against the shackles with which they bound her.

Had they killed her, she would have won. The captain understood this. He pondered this blue-black woman quaking, he felt, with vengeance and an awe-inspiring and mystic power, as the crewmen tended his near-fatal wound. It had been her intention to kill, and then to be killed. He would see that she lived, in a misery that she could not yet imagine.

He gave the crew an unconventional order: This devil-witch was not to return to the hold. She would be bound, hand, torso, and foot, to the deck, to be sold not in Charleston but in Santo Domingo. He knew of a trader there who would see that she got her due.

But a violent tornado prevailed against the great ship, gathering so suddenly and with such might that it took the crew, resting on deck as the human chattel lay secure in the hold, by surprise. The winds seemed to blow in all directions. The ship rocked dangerously as violent waves engulfed the deck and overtook the crew.

Their bodies were washed ashore days later at the Cape Verde Islands, to the alarm and delight of other crews who waited shipless on the shore. Replacement hands were hastily dispatched to rescue the floundering ship, which lay a day's journey, it was guessed, from the islands.

At first the blue-black woman shackled to the deck went unnoticed, lying quietly and still, sunbaked, desiccated, and barely alive as the excited new crew examined the ship's exterior. When they finally boarded the vessel and found her bound hand, torso, and foot, they speculated as to the reason for her cruel isolation, and the extreme measures that had been taken to bind her to the deck, measures ironically responsible for her survival. She was nursed to health and, exhibiting no signs of aggression, returned to the hold. She would fetch a good price in Charleston.

And indeed at Charleston she brought a handsome sum at auction, touted as a breeder and field servant, her corded arms and strong back, her slender fingers fit for cotton-picking. No mention was made of a violent temperament or rebellious spirit. No one knew that she possessed a power that had brought the wrath of God upon a great vessel.

Had they known that she was pregnant, she would have brought an even greater price. But they could not have known. Her pregnancy was barely apparent even at the time of delivery in a rice field in Charleston, some ninety days after sale. Her child, it was said, would not—could not—survive. The tiny girl child, nearly embryonic in appearance, could barely muster a cry when they drew her, a silent and reluctant arrival, into the new world, an ocean away from the place of her conception.

But survive she did, to grow strong and slender as a reed, blue-black and smoldering with the promise of hellfire in her narrowed eyes. People were frightened by the woman and her child. By the time she was five years old, the girl had become obstinate and sullen toward her masters; and so she was sold away to St. John's Parish. She would never see her mother again.

She came to be called Sapphire for her blue skin and flaming, fearsome beauty, alien and frightful and exciting a terrible awe in all who saw her, drawn in spite of themselves.

At fifteen she received word of her mother for the first time in a decade; her mother—dark shadow of a memory who had instilled in Sapphire a sense of oneness with a God whose nature she could not recall. Her mother, Sapphire was told, had succumbed to a fire of her own setting in Charleston. That part of Sapphire that believed this relinquished its faith in her mother's God. Her mother had been the only person who had ever loved Sapphire, and even in separation, that love had sustained her—until now.

She was courted, briefly, by a young man from Cuba called Neptuno, a boxer traveling with his master in the local prizefighting circuit. He was killed during a match in Stono. Sapphire bore his child several weeks later, a premature infant, brown-skinned and green-eyed, whose hair would grow long and straight as sugarcane. Her violent and early arrival caught the attention of the local veterinarian, a young man of Greek descent and gentle disposition. He had been visiting with the livestock when he heard Sapphire's tortured screams. His compassion drew Sapphire to him. Her glowing black skin and feisty spirit drew him to her. Their affair lasted nearly a year and yielded another girl, this one pale and amber-eyed and, by Sapphire's calculation, nearly six weeks early.

Sapphire shared a cabin for a time with a field hand recently imported from across the sea. She was given to him to distract him from the memory of his homeland, to assimilate him and make him feel at home. But after giving birth to their daughter, a dark girl who brought to Sapphire the clarity of her own mother's face, Sapphire was taken from him one night upon the whim of the Master's son, who shared her with his friends at a party given on the occasion of his impending marriage.

Rejected thereafter by her former husband, Sapphire moved to a cabin of her own with her three daughters. She began to receive visits—first a succession of white strangers, usually teenagers from nearby plantations who accosted her in the fields or en route to her cabin at dusk, their hands groping and awkward. Then, overseers and their friends, supposing that she enjoyed, rather than merely endured, their lewd attentions. Eventually, slave men began to take liberties with her, accusing her of disloyalty and asserting their right to exploit as white men had. And she began to give in to them in a desperate attempt to salvage some approval from the enslaved community in which she was forced to live; and when this effort failed, she gave in to them because she had nothing to lose.

When she discovered that she was pregnant, and horribly alone, Sapphire gathered all the faith that she could recover, and God sent her an angel of benevolence.

Concerned about the rising rate of infant mortality among the slave population, and the consequent loss of wealth, a neighboring planter had purchased a midwife—an African woman trained in the handling of difficult deliveries, and hired out to neighboring plantations. Sarah was her name.

Sapphire, with her history of premature deliveries, was a suitable candidate for Sarah's care. Such care involved a diet of fish and beans, onions and dandelion leaves, and a regimen of herbal concoctions. It stopped short of relief from backbreaking labor in the rice paddies. Sapphire and Sarah developed a comfortable friendship. Some said that they even looked like sisters. Sarah felt this kinship in her heart; but Sapphire could not truly trust in the kindness of others. Sarah understood this, and maintained a comfortable distance.

But there was trouble: Sapphire had become coddled, the overseer reported, and was refusing to work. She complained of fatigue, headaches, and swelling of the extremities. The Master of the great house nodded his agreement. On two occasions, he had nearly taken a whip to her himself. He had feared that the care of a midwife might spoil the gal. By the time Sapphire's child was born—another girl, small, but sound—he had decided to fix Sapphire. He would make an example of her that the others would not wish to follow.

And something in Sapphire would die, imperceptibly but certainly. The luxury of human weakness would die for Sapphire. She would be imbued with a hardness and tenacity born of hardship that exceeded the limits of human tolerance. Without understanding the import of his deeds, the enslaver would create the beginning of a legend.

chapter 1

WARREN COUNTY, NORTH CAROLINA

MAY, 1863

> *One generation passeth away, and another*
> *generation cometh.*
> —*Ecclesiastes 1:4*

at first, the people did not believe; not when they were gathered to-gether, the music of their whispered prayers, their plaintive sighs, silenced; hoes in hand, their faces expectant; their feet caked with the red mud of the field, the lush, May grass beneath them, they listened but did not hear the message, the messenger, through lies and deceit, having lost the faith of the congregants many decades ago. They could go, or they could stay—it was up to them entirely. The people stood stunned, the messenger thought, into a silence of incredulity and joy. But it was only the silence of disbelief, and the fear of deception kept their feet frozen to the grass. The fear of lashing and the loss of children, limbs, bound their feet to the muddy soil, and flattened the grass of a fine spring day, when freedom came four months late to taunt them, pitiless and unkind.

It was not until they were dismissed, by the nod of the messenger, his face crimson, his eyes afraid, that they turned en masse to return to the fields, the stables, the kitchens, and parlors of their labor. In these, their places, they resumed their work—the mindless, often backbreaking toil that blunted their senses and made possible the breaking of their spirits, that part of them which might have otherwise been free. They would not believe. They set their faces. They would not believe until God himself said it.

Sister, too, did not believe that she was free; not when she ventured alone, with caution, to the edge of the field, unsure whether she was seen, then wandered back to the high, dense tobacco field, feeling foolish and sweating, her heart beating wildly. She paused for a moment, her hoe in hand, and placed her free hand on her pounding chest. No one spoke to her. No lash came down on her back, the onerous heat her only oppressor, the silence of the people a void resounding. *You may go, or you may stay.* Sister would stay. She would wait until a sign came.

She had not thought of liberty. She had not thought of bondage. She had worked, her mind numb, not daring to confront the betrayal of a god who had enslaved. She had been offered this god. She had not received him. She did not think of him. But alone in her cabin, alone in a room filled with others—others numb to all things except the fear of an unknown almighty—she closed her eyes and allowed herself, briefly, to peer into heaven with anxious eyes, eyes fixed on the inner, the eyes of her heart, not her mind. Eyes that *heard*—freedom whispered. And in the field of her labor, freedom whispered. It did not shout. It did not come.

chapter 1

WARREN COUNTY, NORTH CAROLINA

MAY, 1863

> *One generation passeth away, and another*
> *generation cometh.*
> —*Ecclesiastes 1:4*

at first, the people did not believe; not when they were gathered to-gether, the music of their whispered prayers, their plaintive sighs, silenced; hoes in hand, their faces expectant; their feet caked with the red mud of the field, the lush, May grass beneath them, they listened but did not hear the message, the messenger, through lies and deceit, having lost the faith of the congregants many decades ago. They could go, or they could stay—it was up to them entirely. The people stood stunned, the messenger thought, into a silence of incredulity and joy. But it was only the silence of disbelief, and the fear of deception kept their feet frozen to the grass. The fear of lashing and the loss of children, limbs, bound their feet to the muddy soil, and flattened the grass of a fine spring day, when freedom came four months late to taunt them, pitiless and unkind.

It was not until they were dismissed, by the nod of the messenger, his face crimson, his eyes afraid, that they turned en masse to return to the fields, the stables, the kitchens, and parlors of their labor. In these, their places, they resumed their work—the mindless, often backbreaking toil that blunted their senses and made possible the breaking of their spirits, that part of them which might have otherwise been free. They would not believe. They set their faces. They would not believe until God himself said it.

Sister, too, did not believe that she was free; not when she ventured alone, with caution, to the edge of the field, unsure whether she was seen, then wandered back to the high, dense tobacco field, feeling foolish and sweating, her heart beating wildly. She paused for a moment, her hoe in hand, and placed her free hand on her pounding chest. No one spoke to her. No lash came down on her back, the onerous heat her only oppressor, the silence of the people a void resounding. *You may go, or you may stay.* Sister would stay. She would wait until a sign came.

She had not thought of liberty. She had not thought of bondage. She had worked, her mind numb, not daring to confront the betrayal of a god who had enslaved. She had been offered this god. She had not received him. She did not think of him. But alone in her cabin, alone in a room filled with others—others numb to all things except the fear of an unknown almighty—she closed her eyes and allowed herself, briefly, to peer into heaven with anxious eyes, eyes fixed on the inner, the eyes of her heart, not her mind. Eyes that *heard*—freedom whispered. And in the field of her labor, freedom whispered. It did not shout. It did not come.

When freedom came, its name was Prince. On loan to a nearby farm, where he had sired a brood, he had not heard until his return. People saw him running, 'way out across the field. Some took off their hats and stopped to watch him, their hands shielding their eyes from the sun, from whence there came a more acceptable messenger, his shirt loose and flapping, his arms flailing.

He arrived to stand before them breathless, his eyes dancing, his face aglow. He smiled, displaying the empty spaces where there once resided three teeth kicked out by the boot of a Negro overseer; and God spoke in the voice of a fool.

"We free!" he shouted.

The people stood stunned in the silence of incredulity and joy.

"We free!" he repeated, and tilted his head in puzzlement at their silence. Sister set down her hoe. She leapt into his arms, her skirt entangling her legs. He spun her around, chanting. "We free! We is free!"

She lost her hat. Her knees were exposed. She did not care. Freedom had come.

They were married the next year, on an April day, beneath an elm. Sister wore a crown of hibiscus and juniper. A garland draped one shoulder and encircled her narrow waist. Barefoot in a gown made of bleached white sacks, she felt like royalty beside her Prince as they recited their vows in the setting sun, beneath the elm.

They came back to make love there when the guests had dispersed and the sky had grown dark and starry; and again on the night of their first anniversary, and the next year and the next.

Until the babies became children, and her life an uninterrupted blur of domesticity and toil. An overtime schedule of parenting and hard work made the frivolities of youth an indulgence she could no longer spare the time for, much less the energy. Besides, they had moved to town for a time, and the pebble-strewn dirt road to the elm made for an inhospitable journey. And so it was *honey let's just do it in the yard it's more convenient;* and then *honey let's just do it on the floor;* and then *honey I'm tired let's just do it tomorrow;* and finally, they did not do it at all or talk about doing it or, eventually, even think about it.

But when he was gone, she could think of little else: his hands his mouth his breath and his eyes, wide with wonder and excitement when he came.

Sometimes, she recalled the smell of hibiscus and juniper, on a dew-soaked April morning, beneath the elm.

And there lived in Sister the memory of things horrid to recall; things she had lived in her own time; things passed to her from her mother, and her mother, who had received them from hers. Sister chose not to recall. She would not cause her daughter to recall. They would be free of this memory, and pure. The former days were past, carefully interred, and securely, she thought; and all things had become new.

LICKSKILLET, WARREN COUNTY, NORTH CAROLINA

SEPTEMBER, 1873

There had been a time when life was new, and love untried; when love, in fact, had filled these very rooms. That had been when she was young and thoughtless. She had assumed that things would always be this way. Never had it occurred to her that he was not "future-minded." The too lavish gifts during the early days of their marriage, she had accepted eagerly and with appreciation. He was a good man, hardworking and devoted. Maturity, purpose, and a vision for their future would come later. She had been sure of it, as she squeezed his large brown hand, dry even in the sweltering summer heat. She had envisioned growing old together.

But not so soon, and not like this. She could not recall just how or when the fabric of their well-woven love had become frayed at its edges, the delicate porcelain bracelets and carved figurines becoming relics of a long past and foolish time of extravagance. The babies had come in rapid succession, leaving her strained and impatient, as cruel, cold winters, scant meals, and past due debts ushered in a harsh reality.

They whispered of her Sunday mornings, supposing that she did not hear: *He be wit' his woman on Thursday nights, while she prayin'.* Straight-backed, steely-eyed, Sister brushed past these women in their severe white dresses and, one child's small hand held tightly in each of hers, she lowered herself stiffly onto a pew, all the while staring straight ahead at the mammoth cross that lent a calculated austerity to the otherwise humble schoolhouse, which on Sundays doubled as the Bull Swamp Methodist Church. Thus seated, she would squeeze her eyes shut against the hot torrent of tears that pushed past her lashes to stream down her carefully powdered cheeks. Always, she thanked God first for her height and carriage. They communicated a haughtiness and indifference that she did not possess but needed desperately to convey, enabling her to disguise her pain as piety until it subsided, finally, mercifully, if only briefly.

And after a time, she would no longer wonder about his paramours, about who, how long, how frequently, or how many. These questions, like most others, would cease to matter. Gone—the artless girl of so many hopes and unspoken pleas ago; gone, her eyes would tell him each time he looked at her, to some distant place where his touch no longer melted her and his tears no longer moved her and his words, thankfully, could no longer hurt her.

This morning, as on many others, she rose before dawn to begin her washing. But this time, she paused in the doorway of her shotgun hut, squinting at the darkness that stretched ahead, listening, but hearing only the breathing of her sleeping children.

Last night, she had dreamed an indecipherable dream of yellow-eyed witches and devilment, and things unspoken, unheard of. She had dreamed of pirates and thieves transporting human treasure stolen from another continent; of loss and sorrow and heaviness too awesome to bear; and of a broken heart, and contrite spirit. She had dreamed of a great black bird, its wings spanning an ocean. Without understanding, she had nodded and said: *Yes, Lord. Thy perfect will be done.*

Neither do I exercise myself in great matters, or in things too high for me. Surely I have behaved and quieted myself, as a child that is weaned of his mother: my soul is even as a weaned child . . .

LICKSKILLET, NORTH CAROLINA

MARCH, 1874

> *I cry in the daytime,*
> *but thou hearest not;*
> *and in the night season,*
> *and am not silent.*
> —Psalm 22:2

This night Sister did not pray. She had deliberately not prayed for weeks now, taking care not to whisper thanks in the mornings or before she ate her meals, as had been her custom; not leading the children in prayer as she tucked them in at night. They looked at her curiously, and she felt all the more the glaring omission, the absence of God in her daily routine.

But she had felt God's absence from her heart for some time now. She was angry. *Mama is angry at Daddy,* the children thought. *Or at God.* She kissed them lovingly, the boy a replica of his father, handsome and sly; the girl a reddish brown, testament to a Cherokee ancestor whose name was not recorded in the family bible. Another child, a burnished boy with blazing eyes, had succumbed to cholera in infancy. She wondered if that loss had been the beginning of their end. Her eyes closed for a moment as she queried God for the thousandth time. Then she reminded herself, as she blew out the lamp and closed the door against the puzzled expressions on the faces of her children, of her own resolve not to think on such things, to not think or care or *feel,* and above all, to refrain from prayer, from the thought that anyone would hear her if she prayed. Faith involved risk, and she lacked these days the fortitude to believe.

Night after night she steeled herself against the need to vent, to cry and labor before God as she had been taught, to unburden herself and fall to thankful, restless sleep. She was angry.

For a decade, she had done all things correctly, a soldier of faith and humility, her citizenship celestial, her allegiance to her man and her God—not the god of her oppressors, but the God of her longing, her prayers. And *him*. She had withstood his self-indulgences and insults to her personhood, his myriad small betrayals, those countless accumulated injuries. She had been the obedient servant, mopping up his messes, both literal and figurative, defending and excusing his transgressions, stopping just short of calling him Lord.

She had been studious and attentive to God's will, careful to select a God-fearing man, and *still*, he had turned suddenly, it seemed to Sister, into someone else; someone who could leave her behind as offhandedly as a man changing his clothes, discarding her as soiled laundry, yet another mess for her to clean up: the wreckage of her own visage to tidy up and hide, again atoning, her own blood covering his sins; the malady of her own spirit to heal alone, unloved, and untouched.

Wearily she lay down and blew out the single candle that gave light to her room.

My God, my God
why hast thou forsaken me?
Why art thou so far . . .

Slowly, she succumbed to sleep, and a woman appeared quite suddenly, either in a dream or in the backyard. Sister was not certain. Intrigued, she rose to her knees to better view the scene outside the small, square window that faced the backyard. The woman, slight but muscular, with an oddly cunning, almost insane look about her face, was kneeling on a dirt floor strewn with straw. She was quite dark, with striking features and a muslin scarf askew on her short, tight locks. Sister could, she felt, almost reach into this other world, both real and surreal, and touch the bony, earnest face, trace the outline of the bulbous lips the color of raisins that moved silently. The woman leaned over suddenly, doubled over with her face to the ground. She appeared to be praying. Then, she sat up resolutely, and Sister noticed for the first time one small breast exposed by a savage tear in her dress, one ashen knee scraped bloody, and ten broken, dirty fingernails as the woman brought her hands to her face and cried. Touched by the woman's distress, Sister searched for words of comfort. A slight movement not six feet from the woman caught Sister's eye; and there, on the dirt floor, lay a tiny bloody mass of human flesh and exposed bone, gasping desperately and hopelessly for life.

The woman vanished with all of her surroundings.

Sister awoke with a start.

Each morning thereafter, Sister awoke with an aching jaw and grinding teeth, surprised to find how tightly they had been clenched throughout the night. Her back began to give her trouble. Her hair fell out in clumps.

And a spirit came to rest upon her. Subtle at first, it went unnoticed as she went about her tasks: *Aloneness*; then Sadness followed. Before she knew it, they had settled comfortably, growing sturdy and rotund.

The others, Anger and Worry and Death, also flourished unnoticed. Each day began to blur into the next as Sister slowly came undone, detaching herself from her children, her surroundings, her miserable reality.

Before long, her absence from the pews at Bull Swamp caught the attention of the overtly righteous: Those who with practiced eye sought out and discovered opportunities for public displays of charity and compassion. This vanguard brought the following disturbing report to the Bull Swamp Motherhood Board and Missionary Group Number Two: Sister had been feeling poorly. Her usually tidy home was in disarray, and the children needed tending to. Certain of their heavenly reward, the women determined that they would visit Sister at home.

And so they came with covered heads, outfitted in white and carrying their bibles. They opened steaming covered dishes, fed the children, and saw that they bathed. They set the disordered house to gleaming, tactfully not mentioning or alluding to the wayward husband's conspicuous absence.

Finally, silently, the women joined hands in prayer. It had become apparent to all present that their reserved Sister, whose snooty arrogance had often occasioned their annoyance, was in a much more sorry state than they had first imagined: Her sickness was one of spirit, not flesh, and her ailment was of the heart.

As they began to pray and leap and shout in earnest, they noted that their formerly pious Sister did not pray, but instead stared glassy-eyed ahead, an expression of serene patience on her heretofore expressionless face. One by one, they fell silent.

And within each one of them, *godness* stirred, moving them to compassion. Mother Hedgebeth moved to take Sister's hand.

"Baby, we don't know what it is, but it ain't go' do you no good to hold it in. 'Taint no secret what God can do if you jes—"

" 'Taint no God." An audible and collective gasp was followed by a hushed astonishment in the small spotless room, and Sister smiled contemptuously at the cadre of stunned believers. "Betcha didn't know that," she added.

SHOCCO CREEK, WARREN COUNTY, NORTH CAROLINA
JUNE, 1874

There shall not be found among you any one that maketh his son or his daughter to pass through the fire, or that useth divination, or an observer of times, or an enchanter, or a witch.
—Deuteronomy 18:10—Exodus 22:18

Thou shalt not suffer a witch to live.
—Exodus 22:18

It was June. The merciless heat and the endless outpouring of anger, sorrow, and hurt had taken its toll. *No more today,* she thought. She feared that her power was waning. Wiping the sweat from her brow, the sorceress sat heavily in a cane-backed chair. She sighed, releasing a gale that whistled faintly as it moved across the barely furnished room; wove its way through the rows of candles arranged on small, rectangular tables of varying heights; and settled against a wall covered with gilt-framed mirrors. She caught a glimpse of her own reflection in the dwindling, late-afternoon light that peeked through the small round window above her head. The skin was becoming sallow. Small bags were forming beneath the eyes. She was weary.

But there would be more.

The warm evening sun beckoned the choir from its stand at the holiness church across the road. Hearing their voices, the sorceress opened the whitewashed door and moved onto the porch of her clapboard house. She watched them file down the three steps of their rickety house of worship, fanning themselves with their slender brown hands, to stand in a ragtag semicircle, their plaintive, mournful song drifting across the road. Sensing a presence nearby, the sorceress glanced to the right of the house. A young woman, perhaps in her late teens, was approaching, her jet black hair shining in the setting sun. The sorceress moved to meet her at the door.

Brown, timid, and fragile in appearance, the young woman's lip trembled. Her hand shook slightly as she introduced herself—Queen Marie was her name—and pressed a crumpled dollar bill into the sorceress' hand.

The sorceress glanced once more across the road and led the young woman inside, watching closely as Queen Marie's eyes adjusted to the darkness of the room, then gestured toward a battered chair. Queen Marie sat, glancing eagerly up at her hostess, an imposing figure over six feet in height, her hair concealed by a white cotton head wrap. For several moments, neither woman spoke.

"Watcha want, Chile?" The witch's voice, melodic and sweet, belied her ascetic appearance. She was a yellow woman, large and square, with broad African features and slanted amber eyes. When she spoke, her lips barely moved, and Queen Marie doubted that it was, in fact, she who had spoken. She fidgeted, uncomfortable beneath the gaze of the all-knowing yellow eyes. She could not answer.

Once, she had written a poem.

A wandering soul . . .

It had been before she met Prince, but she had known that she would, someday.

The man of my heart is a wandering soul

She had known that he would be troubled, and elusive, a challenge to love.

from path to path

and from door to door—

See?

She lifted both hands to reveal the horizontal scars that embellished each wrist.

I have tried to stop him

She had assumed that the sorceress could hear her words. The yellow eyes confirmed that she did.

Like the memory of a tryst long laid to rest

he is present

yet absent/he is

as sand in the fingers of a child

never tarrying long

always leaving

my longing heart enveloped

in the billowing dust of his departure . . .

The poem had ended there. Now, she sought the words that could describe her desperation and obsession. It had become evident, very early on, that she could no longer hold his attention. She was bested by his memory of a love that was dead, yet remained, a miraculous hope, in his heart: Someday, some way, he believed, his wife would look at him in that *way* again, that worshipful, adoring way; and all of Queen Marie's efforts had failed to distract him from this confidence.

The girls outside the lone small window sang of God's amazing grace and o! how sweet the sound; and of how they had come to stay, Lord, until they died. The girl sobbed. The sorceress looked away.

"Go, Chile."

Queen Marie looked up in surprise. The small, hot room was suddenly cool. The sorceress' eyes seemed to sparkle with—insanity? "Go," she repeated. "You have your wish."

The girl sat frozen, too frightened to move, yet afraid to disobey, determined not to leave this place without accomplishing the purpose for which she had come. "He—," she began, then faltered under the burning gaze of the sorceress. "He has forgotten his wife?" She choked on the words, having voiced her desire without first forming the conscious intent to do so.

The yellow woman stared for a moment at the young woman. "*She* has left *him*."

An unease quite unlike any the girl had ever experienced began to creep up within her, and settling first in her stomach, it filled her to the base of her throat. For a moment, she fought the impulse to vomit. Then she collected herself and, standing unsteadily, sweating in the cool, dark room, she left the clapboard house of the evil yellow woman, closing the door softly behind her.

LICKSKILLET, NORTH CAROLINA

JUNE, 1874

> *For I the Lord thy God am a jealous God . . .*
> —*Exodus 20:5*

The door was opened slightly when he stumbled up the two wooden steps and determined that yes, this was the one: his house. The girl jumped up to hug his waist when she saw him standing in the doorway, an only slightly drunken grin making him appear adolescent and penitent, his eyes scanning the disheveled room for his long-suffering and forgiving wife. He caught the belated attention of his son, who glanced at him with his own eyes from a corner across the room where the boy sat, his back against the wall, studying a worn picture book that lay open on his knees.

The boy did not stand or greet his father. This hurt, but only for a moment. He wandered toward the back of the house, his gait casual if slightly unsteady. The room with the cornhusk mattress was empty. He saw her through the small square window that faced the backyard, sitting on the edge of a straight-backed wooden chair, her back turned toward the window. She was clad in overalls with no shirt, her shoulders hunched and thinner than he recalled, her hair longer but more sparse, hanging just past her shoulders in one thin braid. He squinted, moving closer to the window.

She was shelling peas, tossing them into one iron pot and the pods into another. She turned to find him watching her through the window, but did not appear surprised, only nodded slightly as if to acknowledge his presence. Slowly, she wiped the sheen of sweat from her brow with the back of her wrist before turning back to her work.

He sat on the cornhusk mattress to wait for her embrace or silent reprimand—he never knew which to expect. At times she was reticent, her eyes angry, refusing to look at him upon his returns from unannounced departures. She held her sensuous lips tightly shut, making them protrude from her face in a way that beckoned him. She would move about the tiny house, her face a wall between them, a closed door, making dinner, sweeping the dirt floor, braiding their daughter's hair, an open jar of lard beside her on the cornhusk mattress. Sometimes as she moved purposefully from the front room to the back, he intercepted her path, stopping her in midstride, his arms outstretched for the embrace he craved and had come home to obtain. But her icy stare quelled the swelling at his groin, and she stepped around him. His arms fell to his sides.

"Take me through, dear Lord, take me through . . ." she would croon, softly, her voice deep and throaty and compelling. He would watch her from across the room until he caught her eye, and she would look away resolutely and kneel before the window, her slender torso swaying forward then backward, her eyes closed and her face upturned, singing in her throaty voice a song of pleading and adulation.

It was at these times that he felt furthest from her. Something in her posture made him shrink from her, feeling himself a rejected sovereign, a lesser god.

At other times, joy overcame her pride and she fell into his arms, breathless with relief at his return, almost apologetic, he thought, as if it was *she* who had wronged *him*. Tentatively, she would touch his face, confirming that he was really here, had actually returned, mercifully to bestow himself upon her.

"Why you do this?" she would finally ask him wearily. "Why you go away and leave us so long? Prince Junior, he need you—he don't even know if he got no daddy. We don't hear nothin' 'bout you, don't know if somebody done cut you and lef' you fo' dead . . ."

He would kiss her gently on her forehead creased with concern. She would pause only for a moment, then swallow and continue more earnestly. "Why you stay gone so long? Why you can't tell nobody where you go? Why you make me worried all the time? I don't know what to tell people . . ."

He would kiss her again, this time insistently on the animated mouth to quiet her, and she would struggle free of his embrace to step backward and—*"Prince!"*—she would say, her chest heaving. "I'm *talking* to you, but you ain't *hearin'* me. You got to *stop* now. You's a grown man with *chirren,* and you got to stop progin' 'roun' in the street, you hear me?" And her voice would rise to a whine as he stepped toward her and wrapped himself around her, cutting off her breath with a fierce and determined kiss, holding her tightly as she struggled hopelessly to free herself, then relented, her body folding lifeless as a rag doll to the dirt floor. It was for these moments that he lived, and for this reason that he made his frequent and randomly scheduled departures: to feel her weak with surrender as he covered her body with his own; to feel her, as he rarely did, truly his.

He stood to watch her from the window. She had not moved from the wooden chair. Peas and pods fell haphazardly into their respective pots. Her motions were languid and unhurried, her posture relaxed. She paused for a moment to stare absently toward the wooded area behind their yard, but did not turn again to face him. He realized with a pang that she was not ignoring him, but was genuinely uninterested. Puzzled and hurt, he moved into the front room, where his daughter sat fussing with a yellow-haired doll.

"Daddy, look what they gave me at Sunday school." He smiled indulgently at her. His son did not look up.

He opened the door, negotiated the two steps to the ground, and walked around the side of the house with much scuffling and kicking of pebbles. His wife did not seem to hear. He shuffled on and stood in front of her. Intent on her work, she lifted only her eyes, and only for a moment.

Exasperation and fear made his smile tremulous and his words came out in a whimper.

"I don't get no hug?"

Again she lifted her eyes to gaze up at him bemused, then her face, sarcastically surprised.

"Who are you?" she asked almost sweetly, the edge on her face, rather than in her voice.

His mouth worked silently and desperately, and he stammered, finally, "I'm—I'm yo' husman."

Her expression did not change. She raised one fist over a pot and dropped several peas, then placed her hands on her knees and leaned toward him. He could see her breasts suspended and loose against the denim of her overalls. "You bastard," she said, her teeth clinched in an otherwise expressionless face. "You my *husman?*" she inquired, and laughed a short, humorless laugh. "Well. Husman. Where you been all yo' chirren's life? An' who da heifer you been sneakin' 'roun' wit' dis time? Yeah, I know 'bout ya women, *husman,* 'long wit' dis whole godforsaken town. An' I'm ti'ed of it, ti'ed, you hear me?" She paused, and smiled wickedly. His mouth had fallen open. "Yeah. Close yo' mouf. 'Cause I done got ti'ed o' foolishness. I don't need it. I don't need you, and my chirren don't need no part-de-time daddy. What you lookin' at so hard? Oh. I know *who* you lookin' *for*. Well, she gone. I don't hurt no more. I done give up cryin'. I done give up carin', you hear me? So you can go back to your *whore*"—this word carefully pronounced—"or who'es—I don't care. I don't care if yo' *private* parts lay down and don't even get up on Judgment Day. Ain't doin' me no good no way."

He had begun to back away from her, his face shocked and boyish in a way that used to move her. He stared hard into her angry eyes, not knowing this woman, or this thing that had possessed his wife. She stared back unflinchingly.

She has left him . . .

She looked away from him, finally. Again she wiped the sweat from her brow and licked her lips, almost teasingly, but with an expression of great seriousness on her face. She nodded, as if he had asked her a question, and without looking at him. "Yeah. You best to be gettin' on."

INEZ, NORTH CAROLINA

JULY, 1874

Queen Marie had learned to cope with his dalliances: the many women, wealthy and poor, black, white, and Cherokee, married, widowed, and single; even his wife, she tried to persuade herself, was a mere dalliance. Prince belonged to her—Queen Marie felt this. He had been the stuff of her teenage dreams, the loping knight in shining black armor come to save her from the boredom of chastity. Surely he would recognize the truth in time: He belonged to her, as she belonged to him.

She had learned also to wait, with the forbearance of Job waiting for his returns from these dalliances, and welcoming him every time with the affection she had quickly learned that he required. For two years she had waited in the boardinghouse upstairs from a barroom, waiting nervously and praying and hoping against expectation that today would be the day that he would come back again as he always had before, sometimes broken by his wife's rebuff, sometimes drunken and cheerful, wearing pink or red or mocha lipstick on his shirt or on his thigh as he lifted her and spun her in the air. For two years she had loved him and forgiven him, reminding herself that he would come around in time. For two of her seventeen years she had barely spoken with her mother, a dignified widow who lived in a hard-earned house not far from town, close to the white folks. Her devotion to him had been costly. She loved him all the more for this.

Her rivals were many but manageable. She had persuaded herself of this, and become almost indifferent to the myriad women whose doors he darkened; except for his wife. She had not met the bony old hag, but had heard of her piety and pride.

"I don't see what you need wit' her," she had told him more than once as they lay entangled and satiated, diagonally across her bed in the boardinghouse above the barroom. "Bet she don't do this," she had often urged while demonstrating some erotic proficiency that she had perfected under his instruction. "Or this," she whispered on darkened dance floors or in a smoke-filled billiard hall. He never confirmed the wisdom of her wager, only stared uncomfortably ahead or changed the subject whenever she brought up his wife, or questioned his reasons for clinging, as if for survival, to the hope of his coming reconciliation to her.

For he believed that it would come: the day when he would come home to find his wife compliant and ready to love him with the single-mindedness and ardor that she had never demonstrated consistently, but that he believed her capable of rendering. He had told Queen Marie of this, and others of his dreams, babbling drunk and only half-coherent, on the morning they had met at the holiness church.

She had come with Dottie, her closest friend and only ally at Bull Swamp's one-room school, where her peers had openly scorned her while they secretly envied her brilliance: She was gifted, and was going to be a poet the likes of which Negroes had not produced since Wheatley. Her mother, who took in sewing, made her bright pink and yellow dresses tied with ribboned sashes, and bound her jet black hair with bows to match. This drew the envy of the other girls, whose hand-me-down cotton dresses had been pilfered or inherited from the families of former slave masters.

The white teacher had fawned on her from the beginning, coaxing and praising her, urging the talent that, in a short time, would bring her the accolades of her elders and the envy of her peers. She had taken extra assignments in reading, writing, and public speaking, creating phrases and sentences, then finally prose, melodic and lilting and beautiful, lofty and soaring, or scathing and provocative, while the other children struggled with letters and words.

Her mother's business had become increasingly lucrative and consuming, and as she reached her teens, Queen Marie had found herself left almost entirely to her own devices. Encouraged by the teacher, she filled much of this time by reading voraciously, Trollope and Austen and the Brontë sisters, her imagination growing more and more vivid and inventive. At night, she would slip out while her mother worked or slept, and sneak into the barrooms in town. In these dark places, full of immodestly clad women, and dressed-up men bearing the wages of a week's labor in the tobacco fields, she discovered new mystery and the promise of adventure. In these places, she became aware of a peculiar power that she possessed: power that made men leer and whistle and all but drool when she passed by them, making women giggle or laugh aloud, "You betta quit foolin' wit' dat gal. She justa baby. Gal, what you doin' up in here? Yo' mama know you up in here? You hear me talkin' to you?"

But Queen Marie was gone, not wishing to suffer the humiliation of being ejected, or worse: being found out and reported to her mother. But something kept drawing her back to these places. Her stories became dark and filled with veiled passion, expressions of things she could not fully comprehend but found words in her heart to describe.

Only with Dottie did she share these stories: melancholy stories born of loneliness and boredom and anger at her peers; increasingly sinister stories, deliberately shocking or frightening and, as she began to discover the power of her own sexuality, increasingly lewd. Dottie was alarmed. "Girl, you betta stop talkin' dat stuff. You gon' git in trouble."

But Queen Marie had sucked her teeth and waved her hand. "Oh girl. I ain't gittin' in no trouble. What kinda trouble you think I'm'a git in? I ain't gittin' in no trouble." Unconvinced of this, Dottie had invited her to church, hoping to save her from the darkness of her imaginings and the magnetism of her newfound sexuality.

The service had been uneventful and uninspiring, as Queen Marie had expected, until he had wandered into the hot and overcrowded little church, world-weary, despondent, and impressionable, his gait betraying his intoxication even before he passed close enough to assault her with the aroma of corn liquor. He stood for several minutes in the doorway, his face rapt with attention. She thought him beautiful, tormented, and disconsolate, like a character from a tragedy.

Under the spell of the minister's dogma, he soon lay rigid with sorrow and repentance on the plywood floor. At Dottie's urging, Queen Marie had come to the altar, too, not in sorrow for her transgressions, but intrigued by the mystery and despair of this handsome man. Sitting beside him on the mourner's bench, she had not been able to fight the temptation to raise her skirt, ever so slightly, revealing her shapely right calf, slung over her left knee. He had blinked, but slowly, and shook his head before opening his eyes to meet hers, and they had smiled.

He relieved her of her virginity in the woods outside her mother's house that night, after a Sunday dinner marred only by her mother's inquiry as to his marital status. He had lied unconvincingly, squirming beneath her mother's disapproving stare, and disappeared before dessert, mumbling apologetically about a sick mother to visit. But her fifteen-year-old heart had been pricked by the possibility of him. She met him while her mother slept soundly, slipping out of the house in her white cotton nightgown to allow him to undress and adore her by the light of a brilliant moon, filtered by the branches of the elms.

She had asked him then if he still loved his wife, as he had this morning before their bonding. For surely, he could see now that theirs was not a passing desire, but a union spiritual and fundamental, leaving no hope for his ill-destined marriage, no future with his wintry wife.

He had been silent. Their breathing had joined the chorus of the crickets, the solo of an owl, and she had felt the two of them one with each other and with nature. And although he did not answer, she had known that as of this night, his marriage was over, his wife a mere phantom, not yet aware that she was dead to him.

Her mother had been appalled to find the muddy nightgown crumpled beneath her bed. Her baby, child of a slave and the pride of her race, a candidate for college at the age of fifteen, turned so suddenly into the brazen wench of a drunken field laborer! After weeks of disapproval and consternation, the distraught mother had finally been reduced to begging: What about her writing? What about her scholarship to Bennett, the Methodist school for Negroes, soon to open at Greensboro? But the girl had found her life's vocation: the pursuit and keeping of the man who had brought life to her life, that previously missing and masculine mystique, embodied in this bumbling man-boy, worldly but lost, heroic and precious to her. She would care for and live only for him.

Before Prince could fully comprehend the extent of her preoccupation and delusion, she had declined the proffered and much-celebrated scholarship to take a job as dishwasher in a barroom. He heard of this by chance at a roadhouse near Fishing Creek: The estimable seamstress, proud freewoman and widow of a slave, had put her only child—a student of considerable talent, with a scholarship!—"outdoors" for philandering with a married man. Smart girl, right smart you know, but forward and never quite right in the head. Um, um, um! You don't say!

Prince had tried to discourage her. Sober and apologetic, he had encouraged Queen Marie to continue her schooling, make amends with her mother, and find herself a nice boy. She had responded with much wailing and gnashing of teeth, threatening starvation, self-mutilation, and suicide. Confused and frightened by her ardor, Prince had finally withdrawn, only to find her waiting for him one night outside the roadhouse near Fishing Creek, bleeding from her wrists and begging him to give her reason to live. This stratagem worked beautifully: He was bound to her by guilt and obligation. She was pleased to have secured his attention, no matter how ill-obtained.

For Queen Marie had discovered early on that, despite the accolades of her teachers, and the envy of her peers, in her world of women so recently liberated from the fetters of forced whoredom to the men of two races, the necessity of male patronage was obsolete in theory only, not in fact, outweighing in importance all other considerations.

And if she did nothing else in her misspent life, she would have this man. Questions of right and wrong and sin and morality became abstractions to her—interesting from a philosophical standpoint but irrelevant. She would have this man at any cost.

chapter 2

> *And I knew such a man, (whether in the body, or out of the body, I*
> *cannot tell: God knoweth); How that he was caught up into*
> *paradise, and heard unspeakable words, which it is not lawful for a*
> *man to utter.*
>
> —II Corinthians 12:3, 4

sister saw the woman again on countless occasions. Bits and pieces of the woman's life fascinated and repelled her. Often, Sister's children found her sitting in the yard, tears filling her eyes, and thought she cried for Daddy. Sister's small daughter—Lilly was her name—kindhearted and always full of compassion, put her arms around her mother's neck, whispering the words of comfort that her mother had taught her, and that had often stemmed her own tears.

"Sh-sh-sh, Mama. It's awright. It's awright."

The boy—Prince Junior—looked away.

For days, it seemed to Sister, the mysterious woman remained locked in the barn; bloodying her own hands while beating the doors or walls; demanding, screaming, and finally begging to be released. At other times, she yanked at her own short hair, screaming her frustration; or walked the perimeter of the small barn muttering incoherently, pausing occasionally to fall to the floor, giggling uncontrollably and clutching her stomach. Sometimes, she shook her fist and ranted at everyone and no one in particular, uttering a stream of epithets both lyrical and vile.

But some days she was somber, lying quietly on her side, hugging her knees to her chest; or kneeling on the floor, swaying gently as she hummed a melancholy tune. Always, she carefully avoided the lifeless child whose body lay uncomfortably on the red clay floor, a trickle of blood, long dried immobile, snaking a path to the center of the barn. As hunger and dehydration began to set in, she moved about the barn less frequently and much more sluggishly. The impudent lips began to turn downward at the corners, and at night she moaned, a low tortured sound that made Sister shudder and beg for someone, something, to free her from these visions that imposed themselves upon her without warning or preface.

The woman seemed unaware of Sister's presence, unable to hear Sister's silent appeals.

"Can you see me, over here?" Sister sometimes asked aloud, squatting in the room with the cornhusk mattress, staring intently through the small square window, frightening her children, who watched her wide-eyed from the front room.

"Mama," Lilly would venture, with tears in her eyes, clutching tightly her little brother's hand. But Sister did not hear her, or see her children huddled together on the dirt floor.

"Can you hear me?" Sister would ask the space outside the window.

The woman would not respond, would only sit immobile and silent as stone, her head in her hands.

It was during one of these attempts to speak with the woman that Sister fell backward from a stool, striking her head hard on the floor. She had been doing the laundry that she took in to eke out a subsistence for herself and her children. The vacant expression on her face had been making the children uneasy, but her hands moved methodically, squeezing warm soapy water in a large iron tub through the delicate powder-blue fabric of a baby's blanket. The woman was in another of her somber moods, sitting with her back against a wall, her head bowed, and silent. Sister became aware that the woman was confused, that parts of her mind struggled to recall things ugly and grim, while other parts fought back with a fury, pushing and driving the thoughts from her mind as they fought with equal fury for entry. Sister was torn between her horror of the ugly memory and her need to know the particulars, the source of this woman's torment. She needed to ask.

She became dizzy, leaned forward and dangerously backward on her stool. The children gasped. The baby's blanket slipped from her fingers. Sister's head hit the ground with a *pound* and she was there, in the woman's body, the woman's dress being torn at her breast, her throat constricted as Sister tasted the woman's tears and pleaded, "Naw. Suh. Naw, it too soon." She was sitting on the floor of the barn, leaning backward on the woman's elbows, her legs aching and spread wide. Two women huddled horrified in a corner, one as thin and dark as Sister, perhaps slightly older, the other matronly, the color of peanuts, with a naked yellow infant cradled by her elbow, whimpering pathetically.

Sister felt a blow to her stomach that winded her. She looked down to discover a bloody mess between her knees, then raised her head in bewilderment to face the thick neck and reddened jowls of a white man, his face contorted and ugly. Sister blinked the woman's eyes. The white man's narrowed. "I'll set you uppity wenches. I'll teach ya yet. You will learn to *obey*. Do you hear? Every one of you will *obey* me, or I will make every black *whore* on this place live in *hell*. Now GIT nekkid, *whore*."

The room fell silent. The infant began again to whine. The two women did not move, only stared helpless, their eyes filled with pain for the woman. Sister could not move, could not think of moving any part of the woman's body, or of anything else but this strange, barbarous man and the hate she read in his cold blue eyes.

He was upon her, striking like a lion upon a lamb. He tore at the hem of her dress and was in her, pounding flesh against raw and torn flesh, bleeding flesh. Sister gasped, the woman's mouth frozen wide, unable to breathe; the pain, pounding and pounding, unbearable. Reason left her. She knew it the moment it departed. And the pounding and pounding went on, for a day and a night, she was later to swear, her life becoming an endless cadence of pain that she could not survive whole. She was keenly aware of his stench—the acrid stench of him, insulting her further as the pain became blurred and indistinct.

He was looming over her, withdrawing himself with ridiculous care. He studied her, his face thoughtful and almost kind. What was left of Sister regarded him through the narrow slits the woman's eyes had become.

"I will have you. You and any other wench. I will have you all at my will." He stood and raised his breeches. "And when she is a gal—" He jerked his head toward the women who stood motionless in their corner of the barn, hunched over the now-silent child. "I will have her too."

Something stirred within Sister, recalling the former days. It stood on legs that threatened to buckle. It moved toward the two women, and fell to the woman's knees. Sister heard him laughing. It spurred her on. She crawled, barely able to see through the woman's outraged tears, reaching at last the astonished women. With a burst of vigor, Sister leaped to the woman's feet, wrenching the infant from the matronly woman.

"You—" Sister began, spinning around to face the laughing man. There was a strange gurgling in her throat. The words came out in spurts, with breaths taken in between. "You. Will. *Not.*"

His laughter mocked her. The thing that had stirred within Sister found its voice, shocking the women and silencing his laughter. *"You! Will! Not!"* It raised the child above the woman's head. "You will *not* have my daughters! You will *not!*"

The next time Sister awoke, she was in a strange room; strange at first, then recognizable as a room in her parents' hut, where she had slept as a child with her seven sisters. People came, occasionally, speaking to her or feeding her gruel, or washing her hair. Loving hands braided and brushed, rubbing cottonseed oil on her legs and arms and face. Voices comforted. Faces young and old, wise and filled with understanding, hovered above hers, then disappeared, replaced by others.

Sister slept peacefully.

There was a bandage around her head. She raised both hands to touch a place near the nape of her neck where her hair, she determined, had been shaved. In fact, Sister realized as her fingers traced the back of her head, from the nape of her neck to a place half the distance from her crown, a wide aisle had been shaved up the center of the back of her head. Puzzled, she sat up in bed, and saw that she was wearing a faded pink-flowered nightgown with a ruffle across the boat neckline. Her mother's "good" nightgown, given to her by a benevolent slave mistress during the latter days of chattel servitude.

Sister remembered then, falling and striking the ground with her head, perhaps several weeks ago, and the long-running episode from which her own mind recoiled in horror.

Had that been she, Sister, transfigured and transported to an earlier time, and another place? Or had she been dreaming, a long and awful dream? Sister began to cry, soundlessly and helplessly, her hands in her lap. For seven days, Sister had learned, she had been confined with the woman's slaughtered child. She had despaired of ever returning to her own home, and her own time. Then, she had been released from her prison, only to find herself a stranger in a world where everyone knew her, but as someone else, at an unknown time in the rice paddies of South Carolina. Mosquitoes and gnats had tormented her as she stood in the marshy soil, her back aching, the menace of an overseer's whip spurring her onward as she struggled to keep up with the others.

In the mornings, and again sometimes in the evenings, she was often summoned to the edge of the woods or behind the slave houses and ordered to disrobe. The other women, probably fifteen or twenty others, Sister guessed, had avoided contact with her. They spoke frequently of her, she suspected, and rarely to her. But the woman had been a favorite of the Master and his sons; the overseers, drivers; tradesmen, neighbors; house guests, and passersthrough. The woman, it seemed, had earned a reputation as both compliant and rebellious. *She likes a good beating,* the men had said of her. *She'll give you a fight.* The woman cursed them all, eloquently, first in her own mind, then under her breath, and finally out loud; long, loud monologues of venom and outrage earning her even more notoriety, and making the men laugh, infuriating her all the more.

But now that she had murdered her infant, she had been reputed deranged, and violently so. Now, they were careful, approaching her two, sometimes three at a time; tying her to trees, or shackling her ankles to poles. Sister performed the woman's motions—mental, emotional, and physical motions through which she moved mechanically. She knew, on some level, that she had lost some vital and human part of herself, but it had been by no choice of her own. She could not afford regrets or self-pity.

The woman had other children, Sister had discovered. This knowledge renewed the tenacity of which she had been robbed during her morbid incarceration. Sister had resolved that no one would touch the woman's daughters—three small girls, all under ten. No one would bring her daughters to the circumstance to which she had been brought. She had acted swiftly and with finality before. She would do it again if necessary. She would see the children dead, their small skulls crushed or their bodies floating in a pond, before she allowed them to suffer as she had.

And so weeks passed, weeks of humiliation, misery, and arduous toil. The smirks and openly disapproving stares of her peers were acceptable to Sister so long as they were not directed toward her children. The continual and offending parade of assailants, white, black, angry, impassioned, or indifferent, rolled on.

Strange discharges, malodorous and purulent, began to stain her ragged dresses and the blanket on which she slept. At times she was feverish and suffered from headaches, fatigue, and aching joints. Round, red patches appeared on her hands and feet.

The woman thin and dark as Sister returned to nurse her, her eyes kind and worried, hugging her comfortingly, not speaking. Sarah was her name. She held the woman through sweats and chills, dabbing at her forehead with strips of cotton, or wrapping her in blankets before a fire, while the children watched terrified, a trio of varying hues and hair textures and eye colors. Sarah smiled at them, a forced grimace of a smile, and reassured them as best she could.

"She be awright. Yo' mama ain' so well right now. But she be awright. You gals go'on-a sleep, now. I be here wit' yo' mama. Go'on now." And she smiled falsely at them again.

Once, during a calm between episodes of fever, Sister had tried to ask Sarah of the woman's identity. Sarah's expression had become troubled, then patient as she kissed the woman's forehead. "Git you some rest. I be here all night. Git some rest now." And she had blown out the lamp in the musty cabin. Later, Sister had asked Sarah where they were. Sarah had looked at her strangely and patted her hand. "You's in South Ca'lin'y, Sapphi'. Saint John's Parish. Now git you some rest."

As harvest time drew near, she was sent back to the rice paddies, her odor and pallor too horrid now to escape notice. The succession of ravagers had come to a halt. The smirks and stares of the other women became more overt. The men, both Negro and white, looked away when she passed. But Sister persevered—there was nothing else she could do. There never had been.

Soon, she was again too weak, too sick to work. Her children were taken. "Don't let nobody hurt 'em," Sister begged, delirious and befuddled with laudanum or whiskey. "Don' let 'em hurt my—" her throat was hot and parched—"hurt my babies. Please don' let 'em . . ." She knew that she was dying. But she knew also that she was dead already inside, and had been dead for what felt like years. She had lived, had heard and seen and felt and acted only to the extent that was necessary for survival and the care of her children. She had been, for most moments of her recent life, otherwise dead.

Sarah, her eyes solemn and calm, squeezed Sapphire's hand reassuringly. "Ain' nobody go' hurt yo' babies. I swear 'fo' God. I'll guard 'em wit' my very life."

Slowly, Sister relinquished Sapphire's feeble grasp on life. She experienced a curious mixture of regret and relief—regret that life had dealt with Sapphire this way, and that she was of no use now to her children; relief that Sapphire would finally be free of this, her brief and miserable life, to face whatever circumstance, pleasant or ill, awaited her hereafter. For Sister had become convinced, during her internment in the barn if not before, that there was no hope in Sapphire's life for a meaningful existence, only misery and loss; and if no hope, then certainly no kind, benevolent God in the heavens to meet her at the celebrated pearly gates. She knew that Sapphire had no fear of death—no hell, Sister thought, could torture and consume her as the hell from which she was at this moment departed. Sister supposed that she should close Sapphire's eyes. But then she thought perhaps she should not, for this would impart to her passing an inappropriate finality. She did not know if this was the end, or the beginning of another life, perhaps more merciful than the one before. Surely, it could not be less so.

But whatever this mystery, this death, she would face it open-eyed, her chin raised and defiant, as if issuing a challenge to death itself:

O death, where is thy sting? O grave, where is thy victory?

St. John's Parish, South Carolina

February, 1772

Sapphire was buried in a hole at the edge of the woods. Few people mourned. Her children, timorous but instructed to be brave, moved like wooden soldiers toward their mother's inglorious grave, and the thin dark woman who had been Sapphire's only friend stared angry and appalled over their small heads as Sapphire's body was dumped unceremoniously into the hole and covered with dirt.

Some folks said that Sapphire's spirit would never rest. She had challenged God and death, making of each a formidable opponent and dooming herself for an eternity. Had she gone meekly, death might have taken her to a place of quiet and calm, her ravaged soul to comfort, her spirit laid at last to tranquil rest.

Instead, the soul met its eternal fate; but the spirit of Sapphire lived on in her daughters; three, hundreds, then thousands dispersed, bound by a collective memory of suffering and shame. Persisting against monumental antipathy, they would pass bits and pieces of their inheritance from daughter to daughter, the things that Sapphire did not carry to her vile grave: tools of endurance, a hunger for love, and a haughty, surly spirit to defend and protect them from further pain, but with dire consequences and at great expense. Sapphire would leave her daughters, also, her hugeness of heart, and a willingness to sacrifice, labor, or even kill, for that which she loved.

And long after Sapphire was buried, and few remembered her name, she would live on, her acrid presence surviving several centuries, so pitiable yet so unpitied, a vilified image never lain to rest.

The daughters had not cried. This was what was recalled of them, ages later, when they were dead and deeply buried, the memory of them hazy, their names unrecorded, their faces indistinct in the collective and deliberate amnesia of a people too ashamed to recall. Their words did not become wisdom. Their deeds were neither folklored nor memorialized in song. No glasses were raised in oblation, no altars erected in tribute. The three girls had not cried, and this the people could not forgive.

Finished. Done, or so they thought. Forgotten, except to say that they had not cried.

Their names were Ndevu. Eshe. Zoe. Collectively, their name was Life. This was what their mother had intended for them, in the days before her broken baby, in the days before she understood. They would go by other names, as would their progeny: Hagar. Sister. Sojourner. Diaspora, as they took their leave of one another. Other places, other circumstance would claim them. But they would remain just one. Many lives. Just one.

The first one—Ndevu—the brown one, gave up. She would not live in this place. Not here. Not like this. Her sisters stared at her, but understood. The people stared, too, reproach on their faces, and in the set of their mouths as she passed. Sapphire's daughter, as surely as she was born. The smell of whiskey and honey on her voice, she laughed as wanton women laugh when carried to the gallows of popular disapproval. *I will not live as you say. I will not do as you say.* She lay supine in the fields, her arms spread, awaiting their wrath. Praying for it. Surrender was her name. Triumph was her name. The tether came down on her chest, her belly. *I will not do as you say.* She smiled drunkenly, or perhaps insanely, doing instead what they had come to expect, and bearing the scourge they had come to enjoy. Her mouth worked silently in a tongue no one understood.

Only her sisters heard.

I am my mother's daughter, and the daughter of her mother.

With the power of her mind, she had discovered, she could cross the waters, become royalty, warrior. Zhenga. Amira. Nzingha. But she would never become theirs. She would not live in this place. Not on their terms.

Neither would she flee this place, as cowards flee their captors. They branded her nevertheless. The green eyes laughed, defiant. Bloodhounds sank their teeth into her flesh, and when this did not move her, they used lye to turn her back to Hades, home of the dead. Her flesh swelled, exuded pus and contagion, her back a welcome sign for Death.

The daughter of her mother.

No one knew what else to do with her.

They hanged her by her apron strings. Brown, melting flesh dripped like whiskey and honey when they set it aflame. The hair long and straight as sugarcane curled as it burned. The people sniffed the air. Her spirit far away, she never flinched.

The daughter of her mother's mother.

Zoe: the secret revealed. Sarah had seen it in the yellow eyes. This child would not soon die. Patient, Zoe bided her time, did as she was told. Yas-suh. Yes, Ma'am. The yellow eyes were lowered so they could not read them. But Sarah saw the Evil. Zoe glanced up at her, knowing, wondering if Sarah knew, shadow of a smile dancing at the corners of her mouth, the eyes grim. They were not the eyes of a child, a girl. They were the eyes of death, the grave, and infernal places, of memory aged as soil and vengeful as the sea. They were eyes that held the knowledge of death, and therefore of life.

When they came to her at night, she turned the burning yellow gaze of death upon them.

They never came to her at night again.

Zoe had no children.

They would kill her if they could not subdue her, make hell of her flesh if she laughed. She had seen this, the dark one, Eshe, daughter of her mother, sister of Ndevu. Disconnected from Godness, she lacked her grandmother's power. She lacked Zoe's knowing superiority, Ndevu's re-solve. She learned to adapt. The daughter of her mother. She lay down, but only when directed to—no antics in the field; and she did not smile.

She flinched when they raised their fists. She cried only when she was alone, when she was sure that no one heard.

No one ever knew.

Only Eshe had learned to cry. Beg. Retreat. Somewhere along the way she lost sight of her Self. She survived, barely, not for herself, but for her children. She was her mother's daughter.

They gave her children, and her grandchildren, nice names. Lilly. Jasmine. Mercy. Grace. Comforting, nurturing names. Still, they were too dark for the big house. Lovey. Sister. These girls fought back their sadness, had angry, tearful rages, but later, among themselves. Eventually, they seasoned their discontentment, fried it in cornmeal and chicken fat, consumed it as it consumed them. Their cheeks grew round, their bodies fat and greasy. Peaches. Big Dessa. They called them "healthy," these women who ate their anger, their grief. They called them Strong; and the women, fat with their own anger and grief, believed themselves strong. After all, they outlasted the others, had more babies, lived to lose their teeth and go through the change.

Still, as each generation succeeded the next, they missed their sisters, the ones they had outlasted, the ones who had been killed, or sold away from them to other places, other circumstance. They searched for each other in sullen, shackled groups as they passed through the marshes of South Carolina; along the red clay roads of North Carolina; across the bayous of Mississippi. They looked for legacies of one another in the features of the new ones brought from other places, other circumstance.

Binta?

Adero? they questioned, leaning forward to peer into uncomprehending faces.

They looked for one another in their children, in each tiny newborn face.

Nyallay? Sister? Are you there?

And in St. John's Parish, in Warren County, each first born girl became Sister. One generation, and the next, then the next bore this question, this hope upon her face. *Sister?* The eyebrows arched. *I've lost you. I so miss your face . . .*

And all this because they had not cried, only stood stoic, dry-eyed and strangely alert as their mother was returned to the earth. She was their mother, after all. It was unnatural, unreal. Who ever heard of women not mourning, women's eyes not closed in pain or fear, trembling? Little women, at that, not doing as women do? It was dangerous, 's what it was. Why, what if they had children, and they had children—girls named Constance, Courage, Njeri, daughter of a warrior; unnatural, unwholesome children, who came from dreadful places where the women never cried, not even in prayer?

LICKSKILLET, NORTH CAROLINA

AUGUST, 1874

Sister was surprised to hear that she had only been absent from her own time for six days, six days during which she had thrashed about on her mother's mattress made of chicken feathers and quilts, babbling incoherently or gyrating wildly, barely accepting small portions of water or grits. Toward the end, she was told, she had sweated and shivered and cried aloud for her children. Finally, Sister had sat upright in bed, apparently unable or unwilling to respond to her surroundings.

Word had traveled quickly: Sister Yarborough had lost her mind; proud Sister, finally driven by that Prince of hers to madness, babbling, yelling epithets, and making indelicate gestures. People had stopped by, ostensibly to show concern for Sister and regard for the family. In truth, curiosity and a need to verify Sister's plight had been the motivation. For in Warren County, proud home of robust former slaves, people were seldom on their backs, and never lost their minds. A real live crazy person was a tantalizing spectacle. People came from Henderson and as far away as Oxford to visit the pitiable Sister whose mind had so departed, leaving her unable to speak or hear or do for herself.

Prince had come, sheepish and contrite, only to be discouraged by the withering stares of Sister's mother and sisters.

Queen Marie had come, too, pretending to be a friend, but looking for further details to support the already incredible tale of Sister's demise. It was Queen Marie who had started the story that Sister had been stricken by a demon of licentiousness, had arisen from her torpor to molest poor Prince, and attempted to seduce her own unsuspecting daddy.

But Sister seemed to pay no mind to the rumors. She moved, with grace and dignity, quietly back to her humble hut, her bewildered children in tow. And again, having failed once more to destroy her with their slander, the townsfolk said that she was vain, begrudging Sister the only refuge that she had left: her pride. They would have seen that devastated, too, if they had had their druthers.

Prince's sisters, her own sisters, came at intervals to ch
her, and take the children to church. Sometimes, they made d
small talk.

"You awright?" they would ask, and smile thinly, expecting no response. They knew that Sister was not alright.

But no one knew the horror of profound loneliness that Sister felt inside, when no one saw her downturned face but her children, who grew
quiet and watchful during these periods when their mother was irritable
and intolerant of them. No one else knew the terrible burden of standing
alone against a great torrent of fear that threatened to sweep her beneath
its current; fear of failing herself and her children, who looked to her for
their livelihood and nurturing, while her own internal resources seemed
to dwindle yet more each day; fear of being forever alone, and frightened,
in a world not fashioned for her survival, no one to lean on, even for a moment, when she sorely needed comfort; fear of the ever present spirits,
some amiable, some hostile, that seemed to reign over her soul; fear of
having lost the strength of her own will; of death and hell, eternal and
more horrible than anything she could fathom, for hell itself, she had become sure, lay just beyond the reaches of her consciousness—just there,
silent and simmering, waiting for her.

At times, these fears overcame Sister. It was at these times that she returned to wait huddled on the dirt floor of the barn in Saint James Parish,
waiting for someone, anyone, to unbar the heavy door and free her from
the grief of Sapphire's sins and the consequence of her dreadful act of liberation—emancipating her child, she had heightened her own bondage.

Sister waited patiently now, knowing that what lay beyond the walls
of the barn was a prison of another sort. She waited feeling the sting of
the contempt of others, knowing that she could never redeem herself. Yet

she returned, again and again, for certain tools of Sapphire's survival were there imparted to Sister: an ever more haughty spirit, and a tongue sharp as a sword. These kept her enemies at bay.

And an energy drawn from Sapphire's spring filled Sister and made her strong.

chapter 3

INEZ, NORTH CAROLINA

APRIL, 1875

after his wife had gone crazy, he had begun spilling his semen on her sheets. No, Queen Marie thought, it was not until Sister had made a public spectacle of herself, showing up at the Fields' Good Inn, affectionately known by its faithful clientele as the Feels Good Inn. Queen Marie did dishes there, and Prince loitered or clowned, sometimes drunk, entertaining the customers and, if he had managed lately to beg, steal, or swindle enough, buying a round for the entire house.

It had been a particularly boisterous party, the whole house dancing and sweating in the darkened barroom.

But all had fallen silent when the door had opened, and Sister stood with her children, scowling as she surveyed the room. Everyone knew who she was, of course, and what had happened to Sister, and whom she was seeking. When her eyes fell upon him, she had stepped inside, yanking her children with her, holding their hands tightly. The dance had ended, the music had stopped, and Sister had surveyed the crowd with her trademark arrogance.

Tall and of regal bearing, Sister was not the ancient harridan Queen Marie had envisioned. She was shapely and unobtrusively beautiful, even *elegant* in her shabby dress and bare feet. She had walked up to Prince with her chin held high; and Queen Marie, uncertain of herself in the face of her rival, had half-hidden behind Prince; but Sister had regarded Queen Marie briefly, without envy, and with only a fleeting interest. She had stood as close to Prince as she could without stepping on his toes, and gestured toward her children.

The girl was willowy and embarrassed, her face the face of a child far too wise for her years. She shot her father a desperate look, pleading in her long-lashed eyes. But when the eyes found Queen Marie in his shadow, they hardened with the hate Queen Marie had looked forward to engendering in her mother. Defiantly, Queen Marie raised her chin and glared back at the girl, touching Prince's arm possessively. Who did she think she was, after all? These were grown folks' affairs. But Queen Marie could not help but be impressed. This child was neither dull-witted nor subtle. In time, she could prove a remarkable foe.

But it was the boy who most impressed Queen Marie. A small reproduction of his father, he had the hooded hazel eyes and bored expression of her Prince. Queen Marie fell immediately in love with this child who, unaware of his own charm, surveyed the room with little interest. He glanced dispassionately at his father, then meaningfully up at his mother. Taking sides, Queen Marie noted. She shrank behind Prince again, hoping the boy had not seen her, dreading his disapproval. She hated his mother for being his mother, and wished that the boy was her own.

"You see dese?" Sister hissed at Prince. "Know what dey is? Dey your chirren, Prince. Da ones what you ain't seen in months, and what ain't seen a dime o' yo' t'bacco money in longer even dan dat." She paused and raised one eyebrow. "You *is* still workin', ain't you?" Prince did not respond. He took a step backward, dropping his head. "Lawd ha' mercy." Sister threw up her hands. "You is just *go*' be triflin', ain't ya? It's jes *in* ya." Shaking her head in mock pity, Sister turned and walked away, her children in tow, and tossed over her shoulder one final condemnation.

"Jes hope you don't keep waivin' 'at thing 'roun' makin' no mo' o' dese fo' you to fo'get about. Niggas like you oughta be neutered." With that she opened the door and led her children out of the hushed barroom.

He had stayed with Queen Marie for several nights, making love to her with fervor. She had hoped that she could have his child—a boy. Like Sister's. But he had heeded the veiled warning of his wife, always withdrawing from her at the moment of culmination, leaving her frustrated and fretful.

"What you skeered of, Prince? I ain' try'na ha' no babies," she had lied, marveling that he should begin to be cautious just as this ambition had dawned within her. She had tried hard to distract him, squeezing her knees closed around him, holding his buttocks firmly to prevent him from withdrawing, but he was adamant in his resolve: Queen Marie would have no babies with which to obligate him. He would have no more daughters, vulnerable and eager, to hurt with his absence; no more sons with eyes like his own, condemning and cursing and finally dismissing; no more of himself, in all of his wretchedness, squeezed into a tiny vessel: a child undeserving of the burden of this uselessness and colossal failure; no more responsibility imposed upon him by others wanting and needing and expecting from him.

It was enough for Prince to immerse himself in pity and self-doubt, no sage advice to offer his son, no gleaming heroism to proffer his daughter in exchange for the adoration he read in her eyes. He could not bear the passing of this heinous and inevitable torch to yet another child.

Perhaps even more, Prince dreaded the thought of Queen Marie, her once adoring face twisted in contempt; Queen Marie, the only person in his life ever to insist upon giving without taking. He could not bear to see her transformed into an angry mother, making him painfully aware, again, of his own failings, but helpless to correct them.

Queen Marie could rant and rage, her eyes narrowed and accusing him of selfishness and distrust; but Prince would have no more children. He would have no more reasons for feeling unworthy to live.

At first she told herself that it wasn't Sister that she sought. Yes, Queen Marie rationalized, she *could* buy her cornmeal and flour at the store in Inez; but the one near Lickskillet was larger, with a greater variety of produce and sundry items that might catch her eye, reminding her of something that she needed or that Prince would like. And yes, Sister did her shopping on Thursday evenings, her children following as she moved down the aisles, the boy mischievous and given to antics, the girl giggling at his performances. But Thursday evening was also a good time for Queen Marie to shop before going to work, with Friday being her night off and a good day to prepare the sumptuous meals that Prince enjoyed.

And so Queen Marie made the four-mile trek to Lickskillet each Thursday to do her shopping, not caring, she argued with herself, whether Sister was there or not! But once Queen Marie was there, curiosity never failed to draw her, stealthily, toward Sister and her son; careful to keep sufficient distance between them and herself, so as not to draw their notice, but straining to see what curiosities might be contained in Sister's basket.

Tossed in with the salt pork and cornstarch and pepper, Queen Marie occasionally glimpsed a tin of lilac-scented talcum powder, or lavender water; perhaps a few red peppers or ground nutmeg, small clues to Sister's tastes and habits, hints at what she cooked or did or wore that made him love Sister, love her hair her scent her touch her feel her taste, the way he did not, could not, love Queen Marie.

Next she began to attend services at Bull Swamp, a hat perched on top of her head, heavily veiled to obscure her face. It was only after she was seated strategically at the rear of the building—this allowed her a maximal view of the church and its parishioners—that she would allow herself to wonder if, by chance, Sister might be here this fine morning, and her eyes would pan the small room. She could not bring herself, after being disappointed several weeks, to ask the faithful members whether Sister still attended. After all, Queen Marie reasoned, she really did not care whether Sister still attended church. That was why she was returning to her former habit of sleeping on Sunday mornings, not rising until noon. A working girl did need her rest.

Soon, she began to take walks—long walks on Sundays or in the evenings before work; walks that took her to Lickskillet, past Sister's shot-gun hut, to which Queen Marie carefully paid no mind, then back to it again on her return walk home. Occasionally, she would see Sister hanging clothing on a line or chasing chickens back into their coop. *So,* Queen Marie would think as she noted the opulent silk or satin dresses and pantaloons and shirts, *Sister is taking in laundry now;* or, *Sister is raising chickens now,* she would whisper to herself. Sometimes, the children would be playing outside, alone or together or with other children who lived nearby, and she would stop to watch them, especially the boy, with longing in her heart. At other times, Queen Marie would find the children carrying tubs full of water from the well to the house, or burning refuse in the yard.

But mostly, Queen Marie found the small house silent, its residents inside, its mystery beckoning. More than once, she had toyed with the idea of sidling up to a window and peeking inside. Just what she expected to find, she was not certain: some clue, perhaps, to the domestic environment maintained by a woman of the sort that Prince could love; her interactions with her children; a glimpse of the room he had slept in. Or perhaps she hoped to find out some habit of Sister's, sinister or bizarre, that it would give Queen Marie satisfaction to know. Perhaps Sister had a man, the husband of a sister or friend, that Queen Marie could discover if she approached with sufficient silence. Always, she dismissed the idea of such blatant voyeurism, and walked away ashamed of her own behavior. Yet something always drew her back—back to the people that Prince held dear, and their house, where he had once lived.

chapter 4

LICKSKILLET, NORTH CAROLINA
MAY, 1879

her name was Queen Marie. Daddy's girlfriend.
It had been the school's commencement day, a fine and sunny day, turned suddenly into rain, splashing red mud, and commotion as the ceremony ended.

The one-room school, run by do-gooder white folks from the Methodist church in Warrenton, was still housed by the Negro Bull Swamp Methodist Church. It only went to eighth grade, but the students and proud parents were grateful for it.

Sister was proud, in her white dress formerly reserved for Sundays, now rarely worn at all; and Lilly was proud to see her baby brother march the distance from the plywood platform, hastily erected each year for this occasion, to the makeshift podium, there to receive handshakes from kindly teachers, affluent benefactors, and the pastor of Bull Swamp.

The brassy witch had approached Lilly as she emerged from the outhouse, following the ceremony's hurried benediction. *I'm yo' daddy's girlfriend,* she had told Lilly, smiling with self-satisfaction. *I'm Miss Queen Marie,* and Lilly had wanted to gouge out those smug brown eyes aflame with wickedness.

But she had not. Lilly had been taught, by her aunts in light of her mother's backslidden state, to love her enemies, and failing that, to pretend. So she had stepped around Queen Marie, lifting her skirts above the mud as she ran to meet her mother at the front of the church. She did not mention Queen Marie as they strolled silently home.

But it was harvest time, and Lilly and Prince Junior had cotton to pick at the great field a county away. Cotton-picking was therapeutic for Lilly, a time when neighbors, usually chatty and loud, fell silent and intent on their labor. Occasionally, someone hummed a tune. Mostly, people worked, surrounded by their peers, but each alone with her own thoughts; in Lilly's case, thoughts of Daddy and Mommy and Queen Marie, and other daddies and mommies and why; confused thoughts, and painful.

She could not imagine what had made of the genuine affection her parents once shared such putrid disdain and bitterness. Her mother rarely spoke of him, and when she did, it was with contempt or indifference. For years, Lilly had pondered how she might bring them together, but had come up with no viable plan.

Prince Junior did not share her concern. But Prince Junior had been an infant. He could not remember the days when their parents had been loving and affectionate toward each other. By the time he was a toddler, their parents had become cordial. Later, their mother would vacillate between overt anger and a greed for Prince that cut into her attention toward her children. But Prince, as far as Lilly could see, never changed. It seemed to Lilly that he had always remained gentle and attentive, a near-mute teddy bear of a man who bore his wife's wide mood swings with patience.

Yet her mother had become increasingly disgusted with him, finally driving him to the likes of Queen Marie—nasty, obnoxious Queen Marie—shameless wench with no more decency than to impose herself upon her lover's family; and on what should have been a happy occasion, shared with their father.

And where had he been, anyway, on the day of his son's graduation? Prince Junior's manner toward their father, much like his mother's, had no doubt kept him away. With each birthday, holiday, or special occasion that Prince missed, the light of Lilly's hope for a reunion of their family faded but slightly. She would not hand him over to that brazen slut without a fight. On this inclement graduation day, Queen Marie had unwittingly declared war.

When Lilly cooked for her father, she felt the move of God within, a primal knowledge of calling and destiny. Everything turned out better when prepared for Prince. Fish fried firm and even-toned. Corn bread melted in one's mouth. And the flavor of turnip greens retained its edge, delicately. Chitterlings satisfied. Shortbread delighted. Once, she made dumplings from three-day old bread, and Prince, having dropped by unexpectedly, made a meal of these and squash seasoned only with butter. They had known that he was coming, those dumplings, and Lilly swore that they had set themselves right for his consumption.

"Girl, you needs you a man to cook fo'," Prince had teased. But Lilly had seen his sadness and dread at the thought.

"Oh, Daddy," she had said, reassuringly. "What I need wit' another man? I got you." And she had hugged him around his waist, the way she had as a small child unable to reach higher. Now, she was becoming a young lady, and an artist of artifice and feminine wiles. If Sister did not know how to keep her husband happy, Lilly knew how to bring Prince home.

"You don't have to cook for him," Sister once told her, breaking the silence of a still night as they had washed clothing in cast aluminum tubs, working side by side on their knees. She had meant that Prince loved his daughter, in his way, and would always return, albeit less frequently, to indulge himself in the smile of his baby girl, if not her cooking, a delight for which he lived. Recalling her mother's words years later, Lilly would understand this. But now, she regarded her mother sullenly from the corners of her eyes, biting her tongue. After all, Sister had cooked for *her* father, each year at Thanksgiving and Christmas. She had baked yeast rolls and sweet potato pies, and yams candied with brown sugar and nutmeg. Her sisters, too, Lilly's aunts, had prepared for days in advance all of his favorite dishes. And at those family gatherings, when Grandma had shushed all of the children and seated everyone around a plank that masqueraded as a banquet table, no one had spoken until Grandpa had blessed the table and taken his first bite of this, and then of that, turning his plate for easier access to each course. Then, having taken note of what was and was not on that heavily laden plate, the sisters would raise a cacophony:

"Have some of these beans, Daddy."

"You didn' get none o' my puddin'? Try some o' dis puddin."

And steaming cups and bowls of whatever and what not would surround his overflowing plate.

Prince may not have been as righteous as his father-in-law, but Lilly understood and loved him every bit as much as Sister had loved her own now departed father. Lilly would resent her mother's remark for years.

But mostly, Lilly felt protective of her mother who, despite the cutting tongue and often caustic manner for which she had become known, had a vulnerability and despondency that shamed Lilly out of her sulking resentments and small youthful rebellions. Sister was an agonized woman, and the source of her pain was a knowledge personal, burdensome, and unutterable.

Prince Junior felt this, too. They had not forgotten Sister's excursions from reality when they were both small children. And Lilly, a solemn child and wise beyond her years, had learned to be attentive to Sister's changes in disposition, watching with the tremulous expectancy of three small girls waiting for deliverance—not their own, but that of their mother held captive inside the barn.

When Sister was "low," Lilly picked up the laundry from her mother's employers; saw that it was delivered clean, crisp, and on time. She fed Prince Junior and the chickens; kept the yard swept and tidy. She even kept visitors away, engaging in pleasant conversation the occasional stoppers-by, keeping them tactfully outdoors with an apologetic smile and an explanation: Sister was feeling poorly. Yes, she was sure Sister would be fine. Jes needed a lil' res', dass all. At night, she hummed pleasantly as she combed her mother's hair before the dying embers in their darkened hut. She had learned the comforting effect of near-silence and touch; the soothing power of near-darkness—a reprieve from the stark clarity and ugliness that filled her mother's days. She understood Sister's need to be alone—almost, but not quite, alone—and to appreciate her own solace. And Lilly developed a special sensitivity to the pain of others. Pain reached out to Lilly. It spoke to her in a language understood by the truly discerning; and it brought forth the kindness of the sainted Black Woman. Mother sister burden-bearer. Counselor comforter. It evoked the quiet efficiency of a midwife; the strength and patience of a woman waiting for deliverance—not her own, but that of her mother, her father, brother, and sister human beings struggling for their own lives.

She learned to control, gently, with the unassuming wisdom of one who knew what was best for others. Friends grew to rely on her. Young men saw in her a fine, Christian wife, a capable mother; and Lilly began to appreciate her own value, to understand her role. Somebody had to have some sense around here. Somebody had to hold things together.

Somebody had to be strong.

chapter 5

INEZ, NORTH CAROLINA

DECEMBER, 1880

christmas Eve. Parties erupted along the roads of Henderson and Warrenton, dotted the countryside in Nash and Vance counties, bringing a liveliness and cheer seldom seen among the colored of eastern North Carolina. Barrooms and billiard halls had lately been packed with merrymakers throughout the night and well into the mornings. The Feels Good Inn rocked. Queen Marie felt the jarring rhythm of the live band, and on her night off, she danced a jig naked before the one small window of her room above the bar. "Come on, Prince," she cooed. "Pleeease"—turning toward him to wiggle her shoulders, her arms extended gracefully—"let's go out dan-sing," she sang, and began to chant, "A-ring-a-ring-a-ring-a-ring-a-ring-a-dem bells, a-ring-a-ring-a-ring-a-ring—"

"Queen Marie," Prince laughed, accepting her embrace. "You know you is a fool. But I got to go. Let go, now! I got to go."

"Go where," Queen Marie whined. She sat pouting on the bed, crossing her thin bare legs at the ankles. "Not to go progin' 'roun' *her* house." She paused, and when he did not deny this: "Priiince! You said you wouldn't go dere no more. You said yo' chirren didn't wanna see you nohow—"

Prince winced. "I said my *boy* didn't wanna see me." Queen Marie could see the pain of rejection on his face. It hurt her to see him hurt, and she was sorry that she had raised the issue of Prince's children. But he recovered quickly. The rift between Prince and his son was an old one, and he had resolved to leave it unmended. Prince Junior was just as well off, Prince knew, without him.

The girl, Lilly, was another matter. The holiday season always meant increased guilt for Prince. Lilly looked forward to his occasional visits. She wanted to spend time with him—like family, she had said, staring meaningfully into his eyes and grasping his hand. He had marveled at this cunning child as beautiful and manipulative as his mistress, yet, at times, as benign and full of gentle grace as her mother had once been.

Sister barely tolerated Prince during these visits. Prince Junior was always conveniently absent, without explanation or apology. But Lilly freely forgave Prince his desertion, chattering as she moved about the little house, cooking, feeding, and fussing over him. Lilly's absolution made these paternal visits endurable for Prince. "My girl—Lilly. She wants to see me."

Queen Marie sucked her teeth and turned her head to stare at the wall. Prince continued. "She my baby girl. She don' ask much. I be dere for her dis time." Prince moved toward the door.

Queen Marie sprang to her feet, her small breasts bouncing as she rushed toward the door and flung her back against it. "An' nex' time?" she asked. "Nex' time I wanna do suh'm, you gon' go runnin' off to dem and leave me by my lonesome?"

They stared at each other for a long moment, Queen Marie pouting and insolent, Prince realizing with a start, as he often did, that Queen Marie was, after all, still a child, albeit in a woman's body. He lifted her gently and placed her beside the door. She looked up at him, sadly, but said nothing as he opened the door and bounded down the stairs.

FISHING CREEK, WARREN COUNTY, NORTH CAROLINA

CHRISTMAS EVE, 1880

It was snowing when Queen Marie arrived at the roadhouse near Fishing Creek, her backside sore from the buckboard ride she had hitched with a stranger. The door was wide open despite the chill, and inside, Queen Marie could see sweating bodies flailing and spinning to the song of a local celebrity, who swung her great bulk from side to side as she belted out a half-angry, half-forlorn song. Squeezing into the small wooden structure, patched in several places with sheets of tin, Queen Marie removed her coat and shook it vigorously, holding it outside the door, and attracting the attention of several young men who stood in a cluster in the red mud outside. One of them whistled. Queen Marie frowned, squinting at them through the delicate curtain of snow that fell between her and her admirers. She did not notice the boy with the hazel, hooded eyes, younger than the rest, with a thinly veiled excitement and expectancy not possessed by his companions.

She turned to navigate her way through the crowd, refulgent in a drop-shouldered dress she had appropriated from her mother, a relic of a years-ago past but still fashionable, more than conspicuous in this lackluster gathering of the county's poorest and least refined. A young man offered to hold her coat. Another offered her his chair, and yet another brought her a drink, and another—151-proof whiskey with no ice.

Queen Marie danced, her throat burning as she fought back tears. Her Prince was with Sister, at Sister's house, probably in Sister's arms. That wench and her daughter—that Lilly—had conspired to lure Prince from her. And Prince was cooperating with them, dim-witted in his wish to be near Sister under any pretense that his wife devised.

And Queen Marie—childless after years of effort—was left alone on Christmas Eve, no child to even the score between Sister and herself, no family to entangle Prince in a web of loyalty and love and tradition during this holiday season. She whirled in the space on the dance floor that had opened for her, her eyes half-closed and her skirt billowing around her, giggling foolishly, not certain that she had a partner. She said this aloud—"Don't know if I even got a partner"—although she was sure that no one could hear her above the din.

But when she opened her eyes, miraculously, he appeared, standing just outside the door: a young man with wide, thin shoulders, and intriguing eyes; eyes that seemed to make love to her from across the room. Queen Marie blinked. This was not her Prince. Her Prince was heavier, more substantial. She began moving toward him, her eyes fixed on him, making him shift his weight nervously from one foot to the other. Delicate hairs darkened his chin, she saw as she came closer and stopped directly in front of him, staring up into his narrow face. His friends grinned at her, knowingly at Prince Junior and each other before wandering away to watch from a respectful distance.

Queen Marie barely noticed them. *Prince Junior.* The angry, hurting little boy clutching his mother's hand at the Feels Good Inn. The child she had wished could be hers. He swallowed but met her stare, uncertain of what he should say or do. She was flattered by his discomfort. It made her feel mature, worldly.

She took his arm and strolled with him down the path that led to the road, forgetting her coat. The snow had stopped, and the sky was clear and blue, peopled by stars that seemed to crowd the sky. Queen Marie supposed that they were having a Christmas party of their own.

"You gotta name?" she asked when they were far enough from the roadhouse to hear themselves speak.

"Yes, Ma'am," he replied. Sister, Queen Marie noted, had raised a nice boy. "Prince—" he caught himself before saying *Junior*—"My name Prince."

Queen Marie hesitated, deciding what to call herself if he should ask her name. "Well, dass a fine name. For a fine fella," she added, looking up at him. He blushed. She contemplated his age. Probably in his early teens, she guessed. Younger than Lilly. She took his hand and stopped walking as they reached the turn-off onto the road.

"You ever been wit' a woman, Prince?" she asked softly.

His eyes widened, almost imperceptibly, as he tried to appear unruffled. "Yes, Ma'am." Queen Marie was disappointed, and this must have showed, because he added, hastily, "I mean no, Ma'am. Not wit a *lady*, not like you." She recalled the frantic groping that went on when fourteen-year-old boys were left alone with unsuspecting girls. She understood what he meant. Without a word, she led him into the dense woods beside the path, a shortcut to an abandoned supply shed where she and Prince had often made love.

He was not as shy, or as unskilled, as she had expected. His hands moved along the length of her body, stopping at points of interest, exploring every inch of her in wonder and amazement. He had never seen a completely naked woman before, and he intended to exploit this opportunity for all that it was worth. And Queen Marie, content with her fantasy of Prince, allowed his son to stroke away the pain of his rejection.

And as Prince Junior helped her into her dress, she turned to embrace him, discarding the dress again, pulling him with her to the floor, drawn to him by loneliness or vengeance or confusion as to his identity, or perhaps some combination of these. Queen Marie knew only that there was satisfaction of a sort in the uncertain embrace of this boy-man who had not asked her name.

INEZ, NORTH CAROLINA

MARCH, 1881

> *Thus saith the Lords of hosts; Consider your ways.*
> —*Haggai 1:7*

Spring came early that year, melting the frost of winter, causing folks to accelerate the stowing and mothballing of overcoats, the consumption of canned goods, now overstocked, and the carrying out of spring cleaning: quilts hanging from clotheslines, rugs shaken vigorously in front yards. And with the warmth of spring and its attendant fever, churches began once again to compete with the forces of darkness that beckoned from juke joints and whorehouses, luring away young deacons-in-training and junior Willing Workers, emptying pews and choir stands as thoughts of a wintry and wrathful God gave way to shindigs and impromptu barbecues.

Business began to pick up at the Feels Good Inn. Queen Marie worked tirelessly, the hours of labor in the solitude of the kitchen proving therapeutic. She had had several weeks to consider her ways, and to consider their consequence, the enormity of which had begun to sink in on a tepid evening in February when Prince, always cognizant of her menstrual cycle, had made inquiries as to her health. Queen Marie had smiled innocently, lowered her lashes, and hinted at maybe being in a family way.

She had done this as he sat on the edge of her bed, shirtless and removing his shoes, the light from the gas street lantern outside the barroom, new and cosmopolitan, casting a yellowish glow on his profile. She had waited for a rejoinder, crouched behind him on the lumpy bed. For several moments he had not spoken. A chill, slight and barely stirring, had filled the room, causing Queen Marie to hunch her shoulders and pull a quilt around them. Prince had not moved a muscle.

"Prince?" She had begun to move toward him, finally, touching his broad back.

"You's in a family way," he had stated, his voice flat. Still, he had not turned to face her.

"Maybe, I reckon," she had replied softly, afraid of his posture and tone. She was not sure what she had expected. She had known that he did not, *had* not wanted this. But that, Queen Marie had thought, was water under the bridge. She would have a baby now, a boy, like Sister; and Prince would love both her and their son. Like Sister. And her son.

He had not touched Queen Marie that night. She had tried not to worry, and toyed with the idea of trying, once again, to elicit a response to her touch. But she had thought better of it. He was angry now. His contraceptive efforts had failed; but he would cool down in time.

After that night, Prince had avoided Queen Marie. She saw him once in early March, at a general store in Warrenton, buying fatback and homemade "cracklin'" corn bread. He saw her, too, watching him from the candy counter, holding a bag of butterscotch stick candies, her favorite confection, and he had looked away. When she cornered him to ask him of his plans with respect to her, he had looked at her strangely, then looked away, above her head, past the rough wood door that led to the fields outside.

"*You's* in a family way," he had said, and shuffled around her and toward the door.

She stood frozen for a moment, wondering at his words, before the intended impact of his "*you's*" dawned upon her, and a gathering began to assemble in Queen Marie's heart.

Disbelief arrived first. Then, the thought of Prince denying in this way his role in her pregnancy Shocked and Shamed Queen Marie.

Then, Doubt made its appearance. Queen Marie had had sex with two men, only one of whom had the foresight to have made feckless, undisciplined attempts to protect himself from unintended paternity. She had taken for granted, irrationally, the identity of this child's father, on no basis other than that she had wanted to; and Queen Marie had not been able to imagine things not working out, ultimately, in the way that she wanted them to.

Realization arrived disheveled, hurried, and unfashionably late: Prince did not intend to claim this child. Her jaw lowered itself slowly, her mouth opened in a horrified O.

Prince did not believe that he had spawned this child.

Prince believed her a liar and a cheat.

She watched his departing back, dumbfounded. Suddenly, she dropped her candy and ran after him, intending to take an authoritarian tone—this worked sometimes with Prince—and scold him into repentance.

"How you know it ain' yours!" she cried, all attempts at dignity and indignation lost as she began to wring her hands, something she had never done, in horror and frustration. "How you know? How you know you ain'—how you know we ain'—" she sputtered.

"Queen Marie," he said, his voice patiently condescending, as if talking to a stupid child. "I keeps up wit' yo' mont'ly. I knows yo' cycle. I ain' never touch you when you was . . . dat way."

Queen Marie stared at Prince. *Cycle?* She had no idea what this meant. She stood silent, puzzled and ashamed of not knowing this thing that she should have known. And as Prince ambled down the path that led from the store to the road, hot tears began to burn a path down Queen Marie's face.

For weeks thereafter, she sat alone in her room above the barroom. Sometimes she plotted ways to win back her Prince. She even toured the barrooms in three counties searching for him, prepared with well-rehearsed words of wit or charm or sore contrition. At times she was filled with dread of her life without Prince, now looming ahead of her, a drawn-out and unpleasant nightmare with no hope of awakening, a dark drama without the light of resolution at its end; for Prince had been both her reason for living and her life's only goal. Without him, her life was aimless and morose.

She also thought of life, for the first time since she had shared her callow philosophical musings with Dottie—those innocent, life-ago ruminations with Dottie.

She reconciled with her mother, finally, tearfully; and in her own bedroom, kept exactly as she had left it, Queen Marie found her writings from that time, untrained but promising, the germinating talent of a child soon to be thrust into a kind of infantile adulthood. And for the first time, she grieved for lost possibilities, lost newness and freedom and power—the power of Queen Marie's own mind, which had been known to take her to heights of adventure and enlightenment, weaving stories of complexity and fascination that had made Dottie shiver, her teachers gush, and her mother hug her with satisfaction and pride.

She could have been somebody.

Yet, she still loved Prince, loved him fiercely and unconditionally, and it was hard to regret the years she had spent with him, the sweetest days of her existence. She knew in her heart that given the same options, even knowing the outcome, she would spend those days with him again—every one of them. Some part of her would always live in those days, with her Prince.

Queen Marie kept working at the Feels Good Inn, harder now that she had a purpose. Her insecure future, her brazen past, the need for rectifying things—these matters concerned her now. In September she had a girl—a girl with skin the color of caramel and Prince's soulful eyes, or perhaps Prince Junior's, or perhaps it did not matter. There was business to take care of—Queen Marie's business and that of her baby, Vyda Rose, named after Queen Marie's great-great-grandma who had once held off a handful of British soldiers with a musket. What difference did it make who the father was? Vyda Rose had a pedigree to rival even that of the finest white gentry in the state of North Carolina. Why, her grandma was a successful business*woman*. She had come from a bloodline of heroines.

Lots of people came around the Feels Good Inn these days, to see this girl child of uncertain parentage. Prince, it was reported, was not claiming the child. Of course, no one spoke of this around Queen Marie, as in years to come, no one was to speak of it within earshot of Vyda Rose. This inviolable silence was forged to a wrought-iron rule, not entirely out of kindness and tact, but out of fear as well: Queen Marie had become fiercely maternal—it was her job to protect her child and, for her child's sake, her own reputation as well. And although it was rumored that she had messed around with Prince Junior, it was speculated as well that Sister had brought an abrupt end to this, and advised that the townsfolk avoid the subject. And so folks regarded the child with the sorrowful eyes, and looked away without comment.

When she saved enough money, Queen Marie bought an inexpensive headstone and secured a plot at the cemetery adjacent to Bull Swamp. She fabricated a somewhat vague but intriguing story of an itinerant father for Vyda Rose. And every year on the anniversary of his purported death, she took Vyda Rose to visit her father's grave. The trustees at Bull Swamp each raised an eyebrow at the solemnly marked but apparently empty grave.

But they said nothing. Queen Marie had paid for her plot. She could sleep in it or fill it with pig slop, for all they cared.

During these annual treks to the graveyard, Vyda Rose drew from Queen Marie whatever details of her father's life and death she could. The remaining details she filled in herself. Aside from this, he remained, for the most part, unmentioned, shrouded in a mystery that Queen Marie and Vyda Rose were happy to maintain, each comforted by her own privately invented image of a man whom neither had known.

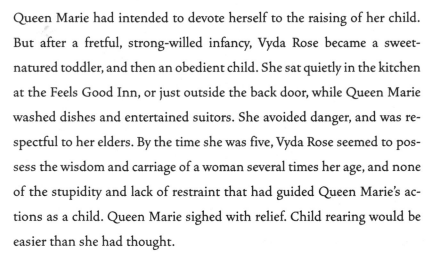

Queen Marie had intended to devote herself to the raising of her child. But after a fretful, strong-willed infancy, Vyda Rose became a sweet-natured toddler, and then an obedient child. She sat quietly in the kitchen at the Feels Good Inn, or just outside the back door, while Queen Marie washed dishes and entertained suitors. She avoided danger, and was respectful to her elders. By the time she was five, Vyda Rose seemed to possess the wisdom and carriage of a woman several times her age, and none of the stupidity and lack of restraint that had guided Queen Marie's actions as a child. Queen Marie sighed with relief. Child rearing would be easier than she had thought.

With Vyda Rose safe in her own care, Queen Marie began searching for a replacement for her Prince. She did not need to look far for candidates, for there were many men in Queen Marie's life now, suitors who wished to be lovers, even husbands: She was still young and attractive, with a few babies left in her.

But Queen Marie had trouble bonding with these men. Their love-making disappointed her—it lacked the emotional intensity of her experience with Prince—and she could not settle for less than the all-consuming love she had first had. Some part of her could not let Prince go.

Yet the steady stream of admirers continued, in and out of the kitchen at the Feels Good Inn, each disappointing her, each informed, eventually, of his deficiencies and tactfully dismissed, usually without having gained so much as a kiss for his trouble. Occasionally, she grew discouraged, wrote poetry, and cried on the large and sturdy shoulder of Fields, her employer and friend, painfully sorry to have lost Prince, even though he had never truly been hers to lose, and even though years had passed. She despaired of ever finding another to fill his space in her heart, and badly wanted him back.

Were it not for Fields, and the fact that she seldom knew where to find Prince, she would have pursued him to the end. But Fields reminded her, in his quiet, rational tone, that she did not need Prince, that her love was wasted if it was not returned.

Once, upon hearing of Prince's liaison with a dancer in a musical revue company, Fields had thwarted Queen Marie's intention to sneak backstage after the show and fling herself at his feet, confessing her sin and begging, as she had on earlier occasions, for forgiveness. Fields had held her, fighting and screaming, her fists falling upon his solid chest with a hollow *thudding* that he did not seem to feel. When she had exhausted herself, he had led her meekly home, where she had dissolved in tears, her head in his lap.

The following morning, she had made careful incisions in her wrists, avoiding the green veins that lay visible just below the surface of her skin. Fields had discovered her in the kitchen at the Feels Good Inn, as she had expected him to, and she had lain comfortably in bed for several days, composing rhymes, reading novellas, waiting for the news to reach Prince; hoping that he would rush to her side.

But it soon became apparent that Prince had not heard or did not care, her artifice transparent to him now, or her life a matter of indifference. Queen Marie rose from her bed and began to wash dishes.

Vyda Rose played quietly alone outside the back door.

Lonely, she made of her surroundings imaginary scenarios and friends, birds and squirrels who stopped to chat with her before flying or scurrying away through the woods that surrounded the Feels Good Inn. Soon, her precocity and hunger for attention began to attract certain patrons to the back of the roadhouse, where Vyda Rose was a pleasant distraction from the goings on inside.

Meanwhile, Queen Marie's relationship with Fields began to metamorphose. She began to rely upon him to comfort her, and to steer her through periods of erratic behavior and irrational decision-making. He was like a father to her, caring and accepting and wise; and although he did not evoke in her the passion she had felt for Prince, her gratitude and respect for Fields turned to something comfortable and mature and akin to love. She declined to marry. She was not certain of her love for him. It was not what she had expected.

But Fields moved Queen Marie with her daughter to a small house that he had built next to his own, across the road from the Feels Good Inn. There, Vyda Rose could have her own room, and he could spend nights with Queen Marie. He was certain of his devotion, and he was a patient man.

LICKSKILLET, NORTH CAROLINA

APRIL, 1888

> *And how dieth the wise man? as the fool.*
>
> —*Ecclesiastes 2:16*

Surprisingly, word traveled slowly, and it was not until the morning of his burial that Queen Marie heard of Prince's passing. ". . . Quietly in his home," the obituary read. But everyone knew that Prince Yarborough had died violently in someone else's home, shot in the back as he fled an adulterous scene, by a cuckolded husband unexpectedly come home.

The homegoing service was well attended. Prince had had many well-wishers. Sister appeared in black, apparently in shock. Out of respect, Queen Marie took a seat near the rear of Bull Swamp, next to Fields, hoping that Sister would not see her. And she wore a veil over her face, not wishing Prince Junior to recognize her as she followed the procession past the wood coffin. She need not have worried. Mother and son sat huddled in the front pew, oblivious to all others, his arm resting protectively around her shoulders. Lilly alone cried profusely, her shoulders convulsing as she took in great breaths and wailed aloud. She did not notice Queen Marie, who tiptoed past her relieved to have looked, for the last time, upon the face of the man that she would forever love, and to have done so without upsetting the family that Prince had loved. Years under Fields' charge had sobered her. She did not wish to cause the Yarboroughs further pain.

Queen Marie secluded herself for a week after Prince's funeral, strangely hollow and quiet inside, almost as if she had died. She waited for tears that would not come. It was not until her seventh day of unexplained absence from work that Fields finally rapped on the door of her house. He understood her need to mourn in private, but he was becoming concerned. When she did not answer the door, he opened it with his key.

He found her kneading dough, tears rolling, finally, down her cheeks. He tried to hold her, but she stiffened at his touch. He left her alone, taking Vyda Rose with him.

Queen Marie emerged the next day—Sunday. "I think," she told Fields, "that I would like to be somebody's." They were married three weeks later, with little Vyda Rose as maid of honor.

The fact of Prince's death had an unexpected impact upon Sister. She had thought herself through with him for over a decade, and had barely seen him for years, aside from those uncomfortable visits with Lilly, during which Prince had watched Sister with the sad eyes of a chastised puppy, and the uncertain longing of a soldier boy wrenched from his beloved and not confident of her loyalty. Sister had found him resistible. He had had no mercy on her when she had loved him. She would show him no mercy now.

Suddenly, he was dead. Finished. Over. Done.

The spirits that had lived in Sister had not allowed her to show compassion. She had needed them to ensure that she would not forgive. Now she wished them to leave.

They scoffed at this.

It was funny, Sister thought, how precious moments and people could become once they were lost. She realized now how joyous those early years with Prince had been, especially when compared with this vacuum of time and feeling in which she now lived. She realized, too, with no more Prince to hate, that hating him had given her life meaning, and she resented him for taking this from her. Now, her life was without purpose. She was persistently unhappy for the first time in more than ten years.

To her surprise, men began to court her. Had they been waiting, Sister wondered, for her husband to die? Sister laughed. For her to regain her sanity? For her children to become grown? She could only guess what had made her so suddenly alluring. But she hoped that their intentions were not honorable. An occasional lover, she might take. But Sister did not want another husband. She wanted contentment, solitude, and peace.

Time passed—briskly. Lilly got married—to Horace Cheeks, son of a pharmacist, light-skinned and destined for great things. Lilly and Sister knew, though neither of them said it aloud, that Horace had chosen Lilly, at least in part, for her brown skin. Lilly was an act of rebellion on his part. She would spend the rest of her life compensating, proving herself—a brown-skinned girl from the dirt poor shanties of Lickskillet—smart enough, pretty enough, clean enough, chaste enough. It beat taking in laundry, the wife of a brown-skinned laborer. Lilly and Sister wanted what was best.

Prince Junior married, too—a plump girl, not overly cheerful, from Raleigh, with citified ways. She abhorred country folks and was embarrassed by their backward behavior. But she loved Prince Junior, and he seemed to like her, too. She died six months into their marriage, giving birth to twin sons, Hardy and Grandison. Prince remarried quickly—a widow with a toddler. Her name was Suzanne. She would know what to do with Prince Junior's twin difficulties. Together they had a son, Sylvester O'Brien, and twin daughters, Linda and Laura Lee.

In a streak of gambling luck, Prince Junior acquired several acres of tobacco land; but he still found it necessary to sell moonshine occasionally, and to work the land of others. In his heart, Prince Junior knew that the land he and his family worked was rightfully theirs. His father and grandfather, and several generations before them, had worked this land for the benefit of their masters, with nothing to show for it.

He would not repeat the failure of his fathers. He would not die unlanded or poor.

He visited his mother often, and she told him stories of another time; stories, perhaps, of an ancestor whose life had been a message that Sister had failed to perceive. Or maybe she had merely seen visions, visions she could taste, touch, and feel. She talked of his father, of spirits that had once possessed her, long ago, and he recalled it had been said that his mother was insane—a long while ago, when he was a child. He remembered that she had fallen and hit her head, but he felt certain that her eccentricity had begun long before then. Yet, he could not quite believe that his mother—calm, competent Mama—was daft.

So when she said that she could see into the future, he put down the bottle of moonshine he had been drinking and leaned forward in his seat.

"What you see, Mama? You see my chirren? You see dem tobacca fields? They gon' be mine?"

Sister was silent for a long moment, and Prince Junior knew that she had never before shared the revelations she was about to divulge. A chill came over him. He was not sure that he wanted to know.

"I am cursed with clarity," Sister began. Prince Junior was startled by his mother's tone and diction. "I see things, about myself, and about others. Others cannot. They are blessed." Prince's skin crawled. He had heard of demon possession, in the long ago past when he and Lilly had spent Sundays, all day and evening, at Bull Swamp with his aunts. He had heard of strange voices, and tongues not of God, of collapsing and frothing at the mouth. But he was not prepared to see his mother possessed.

Yet, aside from the strange voice, she did not appear possessed, but calm, filled with an eerie peace. "I see visions of people who've been dead for years," Sister began again. "I feel what they felt. I feel they have a message for me, but I don't know what it is. I see a young woman, no more than twenty. She has come across the water on a vessel, in the water, in another vessel. She is tormented and oppressed, reproached, and forgotten. I see her children, burdened by the sin and violation of their mother. One of them seems to live forever. She has discovered the force of an evil as ancient and intangible as time. One of them gives up, and is consumed by her enemies. One of them survives, but barely. She lives in perpetual retreat from warfare, only one step ahead of her pursuers. She knows something of her grandmother's God, but not enough.

"She has many daughters, each carrying something of her mother, her grandmother, her aunts; each passing to her own daughters blessing and cursing, the consequence of her own choosing."

Sister paused and shut her eyes. Prince Junior watched her, fascinated. Sister frowned, as if in concentration, and continued without opening her eyes. "I see a girl with a gift. I cannot tell if she is coming or has passed. She may be two, or many. She dashes the gift against a tree. It fragments into tiny pieces. She pursues the tree, but it flees from her. She prays to it, but it does not respond. She gathers the pieces and hides them for two, perhaps three generations."

"I see another girl. She is lonely. She has no words to articulate her loneliness. She is not aware of the gift her mother has discarded. She sells herself for far less than she is worth. She has a child, but the child is—" Sister paused for a moment, and opened her eyes. "Gone. The child is gone. She may be lost. Or perhaps it is her mother who is lost. At any rate, they are separated. The child knows that something has been hidden—a creative force, a capacity for love, a connection with—with God."

Sister stopped for so long that Prince Junior thought that she would not go on. "And I see a bridge. The bridge is a girl. She is weak, but she is holding on to the water's edge. Her body is stretched to its length. Her back is sagging. She lacks the power of her own convictions. But she holds on. Another girl crosses over on her sagging back. When she reaches the water's edge, she spreads her broad black wings and is taken up by a tempest. I do not know where it takes her." Tears welled in Sister's eyes. Prince Junior leaned forward and took his mother in his arms. "But she is carrying the others on her wings," she said, her voice muffled against his shoulder. "I am afraid for them."

chapter 6

> *Neither hath Samaria committed half of thy sins;*
> *but thou hast multiplied thine abominations more*
> *than they, and hast justified thy sisters in all thine*
> *abominations which thou hast done.*
> *—Ezekiel 16:51*

sunlight woke Vyda Rose each morning in the room without windows, sneaking through the crevices of the clapboard addition to a crude brick structure. She liked it this way—no windows, no jolting awakenings, glaring and garish and rude, but gentle rays of sunlight sneaking in between the boards to brighten, but only slightly, the small narrow room. It nudged her to half-slumber, and she lay relaxed and content, not wanting to rise or to sleep, but savoring these precious moments, alone.

Usually, they were gone by morning, though she never let them leave as soon as they were through. *Stay,* she would urge, lying amorous and half-dreaming in their arms or on their chests, her fingers stroking the stubble on their faces or chins. And they stayed, more often than not, until she was asleep, then disentangled themselves, careful not to wake her, to tiptoe home to wives or mothers, allowing her the comfort of illusion: She was theirs and they were hers, if only for an evening.

The crude brick structure had originally been intended to serve as an arsenal. Constructed during the early battles of the Civil War, it was an aggregate of red brick and mortar, thrown hastily into something closely resembling a colonial-style house. After the war, squatters had come to inhabit the structure, the first residents giving life to its austere confines.

As the population grew around Warrenton, whorehouses had sprung up and competed, those with larger quarters accommodating more courtesans and attracting more clientele. The original proprietor of this particular establishment, one Zoe, had been a shrewd businesswoman with frightening yellow eyes, mysterious origins, and a reputed interest in witchcraft. She had discovered the structure soon after the war, evicted its residents, and set up shop as a madam.

Zoe had soon eliminated her competitors, her brothel having gained a well-deserved reputation for prompt and excellent service. The sparsely furnished waiting room seldom held a guest for very long. Zoe's girls were numerous as well as diverse—dark plum girls with sparkling eyes and teeth, smiling and coaxing and engaging; large-boned tan and yellow girls with loud mouths and gaps in their teeth, laughing and boisterous and lewd; long-haired mulatto girls from the coast of South Carolina, skilled and efficient, cooing and encouraging in their distinctive patois.

The brick structure had first been divided into rooms, then enlarged, in response to the growing needs of the community, by the ungainly, windowless clapboard addition where Vyda Rose now lived and entertained her clients. Vyda Rose had always felt that the addition imparted an appropriate vulgarity to the otherwise respectable, if not admirable, construction; home to the privy parts of proper society, ugly and shameful to those who beheld it, but necessary.

After Reconstruction, Zoe had moved on to other ventures—witchcraft and divination, it was said. The brothel had been managed ineptly by a series of halfhearted managers, finally falling into the hands of a watery-eyed white landlord who maintained that he merely rented rooms. That his tenants were all errant ladies was no business or concern of his.

Vyda Rose had been attracted by this brothel's hands-off approach to management. Its professionals were encouraged to develop their own clientele, and left alone. She kept eighty-five percent of what she earned, the rest going to cover her share of room, board, and administrative costs. There was no pressure here to turn over customers quickly. Vyda Rose charged them more than the standard. Her services were long-lived and well worth it. Her clients paid by the evening, and were served only one per night by appointment. If the scheduled client did not arrive within a reasonable period after the appointed time, Vyda Rose took walk-ins on a first to arrive, first-served basis.

Her client list was limited if not exclusive. The extent of her talent as seductress was a secret. Her clients kept the secret because they wished to remain a small coterie, thereby eliminating competition for space in Vyda Rose's appointment book. Sometimes they found it open on the table next to her bed. Vyda Rose would catch them straining in the dim-lit room to discover their rivals. She would close it firmly and gently turn their faces toward hers.

Some girls did not kiss their clients. Vyda Rose valued the intimacy. Her customers tipped her well and never forgot her. She took her work seriously—art, not work, it was to her, requiring concentration and skill. She nurtured and indulged her clients. They provided her comfortable subsistence in return.

Vyda Rose loved sex. She had loved it since she was a child, and men sneaked into the kitchen at the Feels Good Inn to flirt with her mother and make eyes at Vyda Rose, luring her out behind the barroom to set her on a stool, her legs held wide apart or slung over their shoulders. They gave her nickels or dimes. When she was twelve and growing breasts, three young men seduced her in a wood cart attached to a buggy, taking turns until they were exhausted. The next time, she charged them each a dollar.

Later, she dated students from St. Augustine's and Shaw, making their eyes wide with shock when she tackled them to the ground, or matter-of-factly removed her brassiere, earning for herself a reputation as a spirited and fun-loving evening companion. She did not ask them for money. They brought her fudge or flowers, or read to her from books of poetry. Occasionally, they paid for her visits with the local abortionist, clandestine trips across Shocco Creek where the large yellow woman with slanted eyes had been driven by popular disdain and suspicion.

The woman gave her bottles of death that brought about spasms of her womb, and caused it to eject whatever lay therein. She returned from these trips feeling empty and exhausted, overwhelmed by the enormity of the destruction she had wrought with the assistance of the yellow woman. She always vomited for days thereafter, sickened by thoughts of lost bloodlines and life and potential; and dreams of her own babies, transparent and barely human, rising from puddles on the floor of the yellow woman's shack to scream at her in terror and indictment, making her cringe with pain and horror at her own evil.

So by the time anyone told her that she had been rendered impure by her countless lovers, it was too late for amends, and if there was a God who sat in righteousness and judgment, as she supposed there was, she felt herself far beyond his redemptive powers. She had chosen her god, and it was sex, powerful and bewitching and possessive.

Sometimes, on mornings like this one, bright and warm, she went to the creek where she had been baptized as a child, to swim naked or float among the lily pads, her arms spread out in front of her, her breasts half-submerged. Young boys would come sometimes to see if the naked lady was there, floating peaceful and still, her eyes closed and her head thrown back. Ordinarily, they were ignored. She had come for solitude and reflection, and she would not be disappointed.

Today, as usual, she hoped they would not come. She needed the quiet. Slowly, painfully, she unbuttoned her dress, letting it drop to the ground at the bank of the creek. Last night's client had been rambunctious, leaving her fatigued this morning, longing for the quiet and peace. Her muscles ached from the contortions she had performed. She needed the water massaging her back and calves, the throbbing of her temples silenced by the calm.

The adolescent laughter interrupted her thoughts just as she had begun to relax. She tried, at first, to ignore them. But they began to throw pebbles that shattered the tranquil surface of the creek. She opened her

eyes, annoyed but unwilling to indulge them in the satisfaction of knowing this. It was not until a small rock fell with a loud *kerplunk* just shy of
her that she jumped to her feet. The water touched her chin as she spun
around to see several boys of perhaps twelve years disappear into the
shrubbery surrounding the creek.

"Who dat?" she screamed, her eyes wild, struggling to maintain her
balance on the slippery floor of the creek. "Who dat out dere? Why
don'tcha get yo' scrawny black bee-hinds out here, you wanna get man-
nish wit' me! I'll snap yo' skinny black necks! Come on!" She waded toward the edge of the water, her henna-dyed hair wild and dripping. Her
challenge was answered with silence. "Come on, ya skeerdy-cats! Scared
of a *woman*? Come *on*! Be a *man*! You so big and—"

He appeared suddenly, startling her into silence. His steps were tentative, and his head was bowed respectfully. She shrank into the water, his
decorum making her aware of her nakedness. She could hear the shrieks
and laughter of his fleeing companions. The boy licked his lips nervously,
shifting a little, and uncertain.

"Ma'am," he began, and looked away from her, embarrassed. "We
sorry, Ma'am. We ain' mean to d'sturb you." He looked at her again, his
eyes indeed disturbing. "We jes be goin' now, Ma'am. We sorry." And he
disappeared into the shrubbery.

Vyda Rose stood frozen in the water for a long time after he had gone.
When she came to herself, she realized that she was cold, terribly cold,
and more alone than she had ever felt. In one moment, she had found and
lost; exactly what, she was not certain. But the loss was certain, as certain
as lost innocence, or a lost child. Vyda Rose waded toward the bank of the
creek. She was sickened with loss.

INEZ, NORTH CAROLINA

SEPTEMBER, 1900

The Feels Good Inn was closed on Mondays. Vyda Rose knew this. She only came on Mondays, and then only when she could not avoid it. Today, she had to talk to her mother.

She had put it off for weeks, but when the boys never came back to meet her at the creek, she had realized that she had no choice.

Fields was there, behind the long bar, sharing a bottle of corn liquor with several of his suppliers, who leered at her, their eyes like dirty hands on her body, making her feel nasty in her loose-fitting dress.

"Evenin', Vyda Rose," Fields greeted her, coming around the side of the bar. "How you dis evenin'?"

"Oh, I'm jes fine, thank you," she replied. "My mama here?"

"She back dere. You can come on 'roun'," he replied, jerking his head toward the swinging doors behind the bar.

She held her hips carefully still as she moved past the men seated at the bar. Steam assailed her carefully combed hair as she opened the swinging doors.

Queen Marie had grown fat. The flesh on her upper arms shook vigorously as she washed glasses and plates in a sink full of steaming water, stacking them on a clean towel. It took her a moment to notice Vyda Rose standing just inside the doors, and even then she did not speak. She examined her daughter with the discriminating eye of a mother, confirming that Vyda Rose looked well, prosperous, and in good health, no marks or bruises evidencing a bad customer or jealous would-be suitor. Queen Marie waited for Vyda Rose to speak, and when she did not, opened her arms. "Hi-ya doin', baby?"

Vyda Rose fell into her mother's arms, grateful, once again, for acceptance and acquittal. Any other mother in this town would disown her. Vyda Rose knew this, and it shamed her, making these visits both rare and brief.

Queen Marie never came to the clapboard attachment to the redbrick house. She knew that her only child lived and practiced her profession there, but it broke her heart and filled her with guilt to visit. Vyda Rose had been sixteen when Queen Marie had been informed, by reliable sources, of her daughter's adventurousness. Inside herself, when Queen Marie was in bed at night, with Fields sleeping soundly beside her, she knew that it was her fault. She had been preoccupied, and had failed to adequately supervise her child. Queen Marie had cried many nights because of this, while Fields held her, helpless to assuage her guilt. She had since then given up crying, and resolved to make it up to Vyda Rose, somehow.

She took her daughter's hands and led her to a table and tottering chairs.

"Mama," Vyda Rose began, as she always did. "I want you to know that I'm happy. My life is good. I make good money . . ." She studied her shoes. Her mother, she realized, would never believe this. Vyda Rose swallowed and decided it would be best to be direct—undemanding, unaccusing, but straightforward. "Mama, I saw a boy, a good lil' while ago now, an' he look like me. I saw it, Ma. I know you say my daddy ain' had no people 'roun' here, but he look like me. An' I was jes thinkin' maybe—" she glanced up at her mother's impassive face. "Maybe he some kin to me. Maybe some o' his people know my daddy." Vyda Rose stopped to stare at her mother. Queen Marie was not sharing her excitement. "Mama? D'ya hear? He might be my daddy people."

Queen Marie stared back at her daughter, her expression stoic. Then she sighed. All her muscles seemed to slacken. "Dis boy. 'Bout how old you reckon he is?"

"Oh, I don't know. 'Roun' twelve or thirteen, I guess. He real han'some, Ma. He got light eyes like me. An' he tall, jes like you say my daddy was." Her mother did not respond. "Mama, you *sho'* he ain't got no people 'roun' here? 'Cause if he do, I mean if he might, it sho' would be nice if I could jes, ya know like, talk to somebody, somebody who knew my daddy, and might know some o' his kin 'roun' here." Vyda Rose could not interpret her mother's expression. Queen Marie seemed suddenly to have grown old, sad, and terribly, terribly tired. "Please, Mama. I gotta know who dis boy is. Think hard who might know some kin to my daddy."

Queen Marie had tried hard to maintain the secret of Vyda Rose's paternity.

That boy of Prince's would be grown now, probably with children, and very possibly a boy of about twelve.

There was nothing to be gained by bringing Prince Junior into unpleasant enlightenment now.

But Vyda Rose was so hopeful. Queen Marie had not seen her so excited since she was a child. She owed her daughter this. If she could not give her daughter the relationship with her father that had been lost, she could at *least* give her the knowledge of her flesh and blood. Queen Marie thought hard while Vyda Rose watched. Not Sister. She would not trouble Sister. But the girl—Lilly. She was married now, and living in Henderson.

Lilly would see her father in Vyda Rose's hooded hazel eyes. No doubt, she would assume that Vyda Rose was her own sister. Queen Marie sighed again. This was probably best. Prince was dead. His son, no doubt, had a family. *No use in stirring up the pot,* Queen Marie thought.

She stood wearily and carried her bulk across the small steamy room. Finding a pen and paper, she wrote a name and approximate address.

"This lady might he'p." Queen Marie held out the piece of paper but moved no further. Vyda Rose stood and crossed the room to accept it. It was a familiar address—an old Henderson neighborhood where no one was new in town. Vyda Rose looked at her mother, who seemed to be shrinking into herself as Vyda Rose realized they had been there all along. Vyda Rose's family, or someone who knew of her family, had been there, right there in town, all the time.

HENDERSON, NORTH CAROLINA
SEPTEMBER, 1900

The house, it turned out, was just what Vyda Rose had expected: large but unimposing, with a dignity worthy of its inhabitants. All of the houses along this road were sturdy and well-kept, set back some distance from the road, with carefully tended gardens beside or behind them. Lilly Cheeks' house was the one at the end, just east of William Street, closest to the white folks. It was a flat board structure painted white, with a bed of geraniums on either side of the door. Real gingham curtains, not flour sacks, graced Lilly's windows which, Vyda Rose noted, were real glass windows, not wooden-shuttered crude holes.

A well-behaved child sat quietly on the short steps that led to the front door. He stood as Vyda Rose approached, a boy of about ten, built as sturdily as the house, and equally as well-maintained. His hair was neatly cropped, and enormous ears stood out on each side of his well-scrubbed face. He was meticulously dressed in short pants and an open-necked shirt, and he regarded Vyda Rose solemnly.

"Evenin', Ma'am," he said, his voice startlingly mature.

"Evenin'," Vyda Rose replied. "My name is Miss Vyda Rose. I'm lookin' for Miz Lilly Cheeks. I reckon 'at would be yo' mama."

"Yes, Ma'am," the boy answered, turning and opening the door wide. "Mama!" he called as he led Vyda Rose inside. "Miss Vi'let Rose here to see you!"

Vyda Rose, hesitating just inside the door, surveyed the spotless room. A combination living, dining, and bedroom, it was slightly over-decorated with dried flowers in pastel painted vases, photographs in wood frames, and pillar candles decorated with lace. But everything, Vyda Rose observed, was coordinated and immaculate. In fact, she noted as Lilly entered the room, this place fairly glowed. One could easily have eaten from the gleaming wood floors.

"Miss Vi'let Rose—" Lilly was saying, wiping her hands on her apron. Vyda Rose turned to face her. Lilly's eyes grew wide with surprise and—fear? Vyda Rose peered at Lilly questioningly. Lilly was a tall woman, like Vyda Rose, with long hair neatly braided and piled high at the top of her head. She was wearing a brown dress—a day dress, but fancy by Negro standards—and shoes on her oiled feet, even though she was indoors and had not been expecting company. Vyda Rose glanced behind Lilly to the kitchen, which shined as Vyda Rose had suspected. Her eyes next fell upon a portrait on the wall just above Lilly's head, a handsome portrait of a handsome man and woman, poised and unsmiling. Lilly sat erect in a high-necked dress, neutral-toned and otherwise nondescript. The man stood just behind her, his manner reserved, his enormous ears lending a certain ridiculousness to his otherwise dignified appearance. They did not touch.

Lilly was, Vyda Rose decided, frighteningly, perhaps obsessively, sanitary and *neat*, the kind of woman who bade her guests remove their shoes before walking on her rug, and scooped up cups and plates to wash them almost before you were through; the kind whose children could not play in the mud, or talk to children who did; who could not stand nappy or ashy or musty or sweat.

Vyda Rose wondered if Lilly enjoyed sex.

Lilly, meanwhile, was taken aback, cut short in midgreeting by this woman whose hooded hazel eyes and long lithe body were much like her aunts', too much like her daddy's sisters for Lilly to ignore. And the *spirit* of this woman—daring and stubborn and free, strong and nonconforming, like the women who had nurtured, taught, and helped to raise Lilly, women whose proud necks and strong backs made others bristle with outrage and fear. Lilly wrinkled her brow, trying hard to remember: Had there been the mention, during the raucous extended family gatherings of her childhood, of a long lost and errant baby sister; or a daughter or auntie shamed and disowned, recalled with regret or in wistful tones, whose lineage may lately have produced this woman-girl? Nothing came to mind. Lilly remembered her manners.

"Miss Vi'let Rose?" she began again tentatively, disturbed by this woman so haunting, sensuous, and familiar.

"Vyda. Vyda Rose." Lilly seemed confused, but Vyda Rose could not guess why. "I'm sorry to just stop in like this—"

"Oh naw. Naw. Please. Have you some siddown." Lilly motioned toward two arm chairs arranged on either side of a small ornate table at one end of the oblong room. Vyda Rose sat on one of them, resting her purse on the table. "*Harvey?* Git Miss Vyda Rose some tea, won't you honey? I'm pleased to meet you, Miss Vyda Rose. I'm Miz Lilly Cheeks. You must be new 'roun' here. *Harvey!*"

"Oh, no! I'm from 'roun' Inez. I stay out near Warrenton now." Vyda Rose flushed, then added quickly, "My mama, she name Queen Marie Fields," she disclosed. Lilly was nodding, smiling. Her smile froze. Her eyes widened again. Queen Marie—the brazen young whore who with fire in her eyes had stood proud and defiant in a roadhouse beside her daddy years ago, her fingers curled around his arm, her touch intimate. *Daddy's girlfriend.* A lump rose in Lilly's throat. Again she challenged her memory, trying to recall having heard that Queen Marie had had a child, or her father mentioning that she, Lilly, had a sister. Surely such a tale could not have eluded the rumor mill in Warren County. Yet the girl's mysterious eyes and level stare were all Yarborough and Alston, all Daddy and Queen Marie. Lilly felt a wave of sickness threaten to overcome her.

Oh, Daddy. Why you wanna do this . . .

Lilly could only stare at Vyda Rose, who stared back.

"Miz Lilly Cheeks, I b'lee you know my daddy people," Vyda Rose whispered. She had not intended to shock or upset Lilly with her revelation. She had had no idea that her disclosure would engender such consternation; for Lilly was in fact more than merely surprised. She was troubled, staring absently toward the kitchen now, as if Vyda Rose was not present with her in her pristine home. Anxious and impatient to know what Lilly knew about her father, about *her,* Vyda Rose fidgeted on the edge of her seat, fighting the urge to scream at Lilly, to reach across the table and *shake* her until her teeth chattered and she spilled the secrets that her composure, regained now with effort, concealed.

Finally, Lilly sighed, a deeply tired sigh. "Girl," she said quietly. "I b'lee I *is* yo' daddy people."

WARRENTON, NORTH CAROLINA

MARCH, 1901

His first visits were sporadic and, ostensibly, fortunately timed: He was just passing through, he explained that first night, his hat in his hand; dropped in and no one was in the waiting room, so he had just come on upstairs. Yes, he understood that she worked by appointment, but there was no one down there—she could check for herself. He had been told that she took walk-ins, and he would be much obliged if Vyda Rose would take him as a walk-in, Ma'am, as she was looking mighty pretty over there on that bed in her baby-doll pajama top and bloomers, with her lips and cheeks rouged a deep red, and her eyes just a little angry and annoyed and suggestive of a passion he could surely satiate if she would allow him the opportunity. She asked him flat out if he had any money. *Why yes Ma'am I do* he replied, pulling a roll of bills from the pocket of his overalls and identifying himself as a railroad man, gainfully employed and staying over for the night en route to Charlotte from Brooklyn. And long as he was staying, he might just as well enjoy the company of a refined and well-reputed lady such as herself—this proposal delivered with a broad and confident smile of gleaming white teeth and round, glimmering eyes. He was a black, black man, the way Vyda Rose liked them, tall and stocky and powerfully built. He had the speech and self-assured manner of a city

Negro, from The North—she supposed that Brooklyn was up North somewhere. And his hungry-eyed, libidinous appraisal of her told her it had been some time since his no doubt considerable appetites had been attended to. While she paused demurely, a prelude to a clever response Vyda Rose was preparing to deliver, she felt, suddenly, a lightness and breathlessness and was surprised to realize after the fact that she had been lifted bodily from her position upon the bed and was resting comfortably in his able arms, her legs wrapped around his torso, and he was kissing her, so gently that this, too, took a moment to sink in. She forgot to explain her rules and negotiate her fee, and soon forgot her surroundings and her name and all other distractions as the taste of expensive scotch mingled with the smell and feel of his smooth skin the color of strong coffee and isolated her in this place with this man/god who was erasing her equanimity and the practiced aloofness with which she usually won her captives' hearts before fixing their loyalty with open attentiveness and esteem. And then, he lifted her dexterously to his stalwart shoulders, sucking her greedily and noisily and making her shudder with surprise and delight before she felt herself this time flying with grace and surety as he swooped her with one fluid downward motion of his arms and his body and hers; moving together onto the bed and onto and into each other. And she felt that they had been here before and had done this together and he belonged here fitting her perfectly and touching all at once all those places that needed to be touched but seldom were. And even when their coition came to an unhurried end he held her still counting her heartbeats and measuring others of her internal rhythms as they lay still, surprised and even frightened, afraid to move and afraid to break their solemn silence with the sacrilege of mortal speech.

And so they neither moved nor spoke until the indigo sky had given way to gray, and the sun peeked over the eastern horizon before it began its ascent. He kissed her once, their mouths open only slightly, both urgently and languorously before he stood to walk into his overalls and don his hat and look back once before closing the door softly behind himself.

He had not paid. She knew he would be back and he was, when nearly a month had passed, pressing a bundle of bills into her hand and calling her his baby he had come back to take care of. And again and again he came, always on Saturday nights. She was aware by now of his habit of scaring away her scheduled clients with his bellowing and barrel chest. She did not mind. They always returned on their next-scheduled date, and he never failed to make those nights well worth the cancellation. And even at the midpoint between her menses she allowed him to delight and enrapture her, thinking that nothing unintended could result from their union.

And for many months, nothing remarkable, other than his visits themselves, occurred. Vyda Rose thought, on those rare occasions with him when she thought at all, that perhaps those unhappy trips across the creek had wrought some damage to her inward parts. She had suspected this, not without some sadness, for some time now. But Vyda Rose had never had much time, or much use, for regrets. Life rolled on. She could not go back and undo. And even if she could, the wisdom of this would not be clear. She had made her choices, for reasons that seemed good at the time that they were made.

And she was making a choice now: to brave the uncertainty and unfamiliarity of love, much ballyhooed love, heretofore unexplored by Vyda Rose. She had, until now, preferred the certainty of uncertainty, the comfort of multiple and occasionally new faces and bodies, each of with whom she shared a lukewarm intimacy for as long as the arrangement suited both parties involved. These intimacies were neither uninterrupted nor everlasting—she knew this, and it was the knowing that made these trysts not only bearable but comfortable. They stayed at her will and for as long as it pleased them. Things never became nasty or boring.

But this—this longing and need that stretched from the mornings of his departures until the evenings of their reunions—was made worse by the near-certainty of The End, that period of nastiness or boredom between man and woman, preceding those relieved and mutual fare-wells, often heard of at houses of pigs' feet and blues; or that period of mourning and loss and regret sung of at rites of eternal homegoing. She began to dread The End. Visions of herself in black soon marred his bit-tersweet early morning departures, and she fought the urge to fling her-self to the floor and beg him to stay. The weeks or months of worrying that he would not return had begun to wear on Vyda Rose, and she was often irritated when he arrived, all smiles and cheer, bearing chocolates or nighties or fur-trimmed suits from New York, entertaining her with stories that he swore were gospel truth—stories of gang warfare in the streets, of union disputes, of white ladies from the South sent North to bear colored babies before returning to Dixie all innocence and up-rightness.

The folks in town were all a-prattle over Vyda Rose and her new man. Much was left to speculation, for Vyda Rose—

sho' kep' him to herse'f, locked up in that upstairs room wit' de head-board jes a-knockin'. And Queen Marie all happy and smug that her baby done caught herself a fine man from New York wit' plenty money . . .

"Long as my baby is happy," was all Queen Marie would say when pressed for details of the affair. In truth, it was all that she knew to say, other than his name: Julius. Vyda Rose had not been around the Feels Good Inn to speak with Queen Marie since she had learned of the longtime proximity of her family. Whether her absence was related to this discovery, Queen Marie could not tell. Vyda Rose had never been much for visiting.

But tongues had wagged when the townsfolks' speculation as to Vyda Rose's paternity had at long last been confirmed. Vyda Rose had been seen, and had admitted to visiting, with her *sister* Lilly, shooting the breeze with her *brother* Prince Junior. And couldn't anybody just *see* Prince all over that child anyway? Just look at those eyes. Hm hm hm!

But Vyda Rose, oblivious to the murmuring touched off by her newfound paramour and kin, moved about in a confused state of fear and excitement, her moods controlled by his comings and goings and the length of his absences; his gifts and his mere presence bringing luster to her otherwise bleak days. Once he was there with her, she dared not attempt to extract from him dubious promises of faithfulness and soon returns. In her profession, she had learned that men are often quick to abandon their allegiances. She did not wish to demand or coerce. She wanted his visits to be unconstrained, not obligatory, and any commitments on his part must be of his own volition, and not of her urging. So she kept her fondness for him concealed and prayed against the day when he would confirm her fears of the impending End.

A year had passed since he had first appeared at the doorway to her room, so charming and beseeching, when he disappeared without warning. It took Vyda Rose some time to realize this. He was gone. She felt the finality of this after a time, and it filled her with sadness. This was The End.

She resolved to let him go in his own way—wordlessly and without ceremony. She would not seek after him. He had kissed her softly before leaving that last morning, as he had on many other mornings, mornings that had looked and felt no different, no less tragic, than this one. He had saved her the memory of a painful, lingering good-bye. She appreciated this. She preferred to grieve in solitude.

For a while, she struggled against hoping that he would return, laughing deep within his barrel chest, to sweep her from her bed again. Vyda Rose knew that it was best not to hope, not to love if this could be avoided. She could cherish her memories—she allowed herself this—but she could not allow herself to love, or hope.

Yet hope insisted, urging itself into the cycle of her body's menses, into the sway of her back as she walked with Lilly to the creek.

"Yo' skin so clea' and purtty." Lilly stopped, her arm stopping Vyda Rose, to examine her face closely. "Yo' eyes so sad, but you's jes a-glowin' like a gal in love." Vyda Rose did not answer Lilly, only began to walk again, her eyes now worried, Lilly noted. "You know," Lilly began quietly, catching up to her, "I ain' judgin' you none, Vyda Rose. You's a fine gal and a good person, an' I's glad to know you." She ventured a peek at Vyda Rose from the corner of her eye. "An' if you need any he'p, I'm yo' *sista*." Still, Vyda Rose did not respond, would not even look at Lilly. "You hear me, Vyda Rose?"

Vyda Rose sighed. "What kin'a he'p you talkin' 'bout, Lilly?"

"I mean whatev'a kin' you need. You need money? Or the name of somebody who can 'fix' thangs . . . ?"

Vyda Rose rubbed one eye with two fingers, and stopped in the middle of the road. "You think I don't want my baby?" She had not, until now, acknowledged her pregnancy to anyone other than herself. She had never mentioned her abortions directly to anyone; not her lovers, to whom she had communicated her condition with opaque references to the moon or the rag or to buns in unspecified ovens; not to the woman who lived in the creek, who had simply looked at her and known, as Lilly had known. It hurt her that Lilly thought her capable of what she had done on several occasions in a past unmentioned to Lilly; that Lilly, while acknowledging her good, had sensed also Vyda Rose's terrible and shameful evil.

But Vyda Rose wanted to have this baby. She wanted this child for her own sake and for the sakes of all the others she had destroyed. She needed to make it up to them, her dear dead babies, to redeem herself and show that she *was* good, that she *did* deserve this gift. And she needed something—someone—permanent in her life; just one somebody to hold on to with the ferocity that she had felt when she had held him in her room in their world inaccessible by others. Vyda Rose had never thought so before, but she knew now that she needed, more than anything, this child to love free of charge, at whatever cost to Vyda Rose, and whether or not she was loved in return. And she needed to give this child the best possible chance at as charmed a life as a whore from the backwoods of Warren County could give her. Suddenly—

"I know what you can do to he'p," Vyda Rose told Lilly, excitement in her expressive eyes. "I got to go to Brooklyn, Lilly," Vyda Rose said earnestly, clasping Lilly's hands in her own. "He'p me get to Brooklyn."

WARRENTON, NORTH CAROLINA

JULY, 1902

Lilly had begged her husband, borrowed, and considered stealing to buy Vyda Rose's train ticket to Brooklyn, while Vyda Rose, working steadily and saving every penny she could, spent hours at the St. Augustine's library learning what she could about Brooklyn. It seemed a modern-day Sodom and Gomorrah to Vyda Rose, who had never been farther than to Charlotte by wagon cart as a child, and even then, had sat frightened by her surroundings as Fields had negotiated the prices of whiskey and cigars. She would be a stranger in a paradise of sorts in that vast city, and an angel in the utmost depths of hell.

She had gone to visit Queen Marie, to make peace with her for years of deception; to tell her that she understood, and what she had to do for her own child. Queen Marie had cried and kissed her, and told her that she was brave. But Vyda Rose felt no pride in what she was doing, only the urgency and necessity of doing it.

So it was without misgiving that she canceled her standing appointments indefinitely, knowing that she risked losing loyal clients by abandoning them to her competitors, but also knowing that she needed to take as much time as was called for. Brooklyn was a great big town, and hers was a mammoth mission.

As she boarded the great black train that would begin her journey to Brooklyn, a tearful Lilly wishing her well, Vyda Rose did not look back. She would be back. No point in getting teary and sentimental. She would be back.

chapter 7

brooklyn

bustled. It danced. It leapt and spun in a whirlwind of perpetual activity, and Vyda Rose was both frightened and mesmerized by its vibrance. She sat on a bench at the train station for several minutes, her bags arranged around her feet, gathering the nerve to ask someone, any one of the people rushing past her in all directions to point her toward the nearest lodgings. She noted that the ladies wore hats—most of them. She would buy one at her earliest opportunity. It was important that she look presentable while carrying out her difficult task.

A young man in an elegant suit watched her from a distance. He saw a young woman in her early twenties, sitting on a bench, watching her surroundings with increasing dismay. She was very tired—and hot. Her shoulders slumped, and she fanned herself with her hand. He noted the bags arranged around her feet. She had no doubt traveled very far, and was probably here to stay. The young man had seen many young ladies come from the South, alone and easily daunted, easy game for predators like himself. He began walking toward her, noting her slender arms and upstanding breasts as she raised a hand to lift her hair, damp from humidity and perspiration, from the back of her neck. She surprised him by turning suddenly to face him. Her eyes—sleepy, seductive eyes—widened when she saw him. He felt caught, as if he had been sneaking upon his prey. He thought he discerned a slight upturning of the corners of her lips before she caught herself and fixed a cool stare upon him.

It was a practiced, confident stare. This was no guileless country hick. This was a woman aware of her own allure, and accustomed to using it to her advantage. She stood, as if she had been waiting for him, nearly his height, and poised as if balancing a pitcher of ice water on her head. But the stance was clearly natural to her. She was a proud woman, the young man thought, and streetwise, perhaps even cunning.

Vyda Rose had been warned of city men on the prowl for ladies traveling alone. This one had the look of a gigolo. She noted the handsome suit and gold watch, and wondered how many women took care of him.

She needed help at the moment—from anyone. But she wanted him to know from the start that she was no dupe, but a woman neither cheap nor easy.

"So . . . you new in town?" he asked. Vyda Rose glanced downward at the luggage surrounding her. He blushed. "Can I—can I help you get somewheres?" he stammered. Vyda Rose arched an eyebrow and smiled teasingly. She was having the effect on him that she had hoped for.

"Yessir," she replied. "I'd shore 'preciate your tellin' me how to get myself to the nearest hotel."

He eyed her several bags as he noted the Southern accent—not the twang of Georgia or Alabama, but the flat, less melodic speech of Negroes from North Carolina or Virginia. But she had traveled far, as he had suspected, and not for naught. "How long you stayin'? If you don't mind me askin'."

Vyda Rose hesitated. "I really don't know," she replied. He waited. She did not explain.

His eyes fell upon her bags again. "Well. Look to me like you'll be around for a while. You oughta try to get in a boardin'house. Cost you a lot less money, Miss—"

"Vyda Rose. Vyda Rose Alston. An' a boardin'house will do jes fine. Anywhere outa dis heat." She fanned herself again, looking around the station, emptying now as passengers found their loved ones and drivers.

He knew of several places, but had no idea of this lady's means. Lacking the daring to ask, he lifted two of her bags without further comment.

On the street, Vyda Rose saw more white people in one place than she had seen in all her life. Colored men in tasseled uniforms tipped their hats and greeted her respectfully as she passed with her companion. They nodded to him their appreciation of Vyda Rose's comeliness and grace. She felt the eyes of these men on her back as she passed them.

"Did you say your name?" she asked.

"Hiram," he answered as he touched her elbow, steering her to an automobile parked in front of the canopied entrance to a limestone building much like the others they had passed. "Hiram Stokes." He opened the door. Vyda Rose hesitated. She had never seen an automobile before, much less ridden in one.

"Is this yo's?" she asked, her naïveté showing for the first time.

"No, Ma'am," he told her honestly, though he did not know why. "This belong to Mister Gresham Hayes. I am his chauffeur." He bowed ceremoniously, extending his arm toward the open door. Vyda Rose climbed in, her long legs awkward. Hiram climbed in on the other side, sweeping a cap the color of his suit from the seat onto his head. With exaggerated gestures, he steered the car into the mixed traffic of buggies, horses, and occasional automobiles. He could see that she was impressed.

They were quiet for a time as she stared out the window, taking in the buildings and diversity of people. She wondered where she should begin, in a city so vast, so fast-moving, and so crowded, her search for the man she had traveled so far to find. They crossed a bridge—Vyda Rose had never seen a bridge so large and majestic—and she began to worry about where this stranger was taking her. She noticed that he kept glancing at his watch. "Are we still in Brooklyn? I hope I'm not takin' you too far out de way . . ."

"Brooklyn?" he turned to look at her. "No, Ma'am. We bound for Hun' Seventeenth Street. I thought you wanted to stay near some colored folks. Ain't too much happenin' in Brooklyn. Unless you—" He realized that he had assumed too much. "You ain't say nothin' 'bout stayin' in Brooklyn."

Vyda Rose did not know what to say. Was there something *wrong* with Brooklyn? Were colored people not welcome there? What else did she *not* know that she *should?* Vyda Rose sighed. It was time to confess complete ignorance, as she should have at the train station.

"I need to find a place to stay in Brooklyn. I'm lookin' for my cou'in, an' it's real important that I find him. I have no idea where to start. All I know is he in Brooklyn, an' dass where I need to be."

Hiram removed his cap and scratched his head. She hoped he did not think her stupid. "You mean you come all this way, to find somebody you don't know where in Brooklyn?"

Vyda Rose flushed. "It's very, very important," she repeated, her eyes downcast. He ventured a glance at her, dejected and humbled and as cute as a button, and he thought for a moment.

"I don't know no colored people in Brooklyn." Hiram glanced at his watch. "But if you got a little time, I might be able to find somebody who does." He turned the car around. "Right now, if you don't mind, I got to get back to the train station and get Miss Virginia home. We might need to get your bags out the back, too, so I can put hers in there. I'll be back to get you after I take her home."

Vyda Rose blinked. "You be *back where* to get me?"

"Back to the train station. I'm supposed to get Miss Virginia around three. She comin' back this afternoon. Won't take me long."

"You mean you takin' me all the way *back* to the train station, and I got to wait there while you take somebody home?"

Hiram blushed deeply. "Won't nobody bother you. I'll just be a little while."

Vyda Rose was speechless. Exhausted, lost, and confused, in a city whose vastness and strangeness she had not been prepared for, she felt, to her horror, tears of frustration welling in her eyes. She leaned back in her seat and closed her eyes as the tears began to fall. She wanted to go home.

Horrified and embarrassed, Hiram sputtered. "I'm sorry," he pleaded. "I didn't know you wanted to stay in Brooklyn. I just thought you—" He glanced again at Vyda Rose, and a thought occurred to him. He turned the car around again. "Tell you what. I'll take you to Connie's now. You can stay with her 'til I come back, and we'll see 'bout gittin' you to Brooklyn."

"I don' wanna be no trouble," Vyda Rose managed to sob. "You can jes let me out here." She could not, Vyda Rose reasoned, become any more lost.

"Aw, shucks," he waved his hand. "I can't put you out here. Now I said I would get you to a boardin'house, and I'm gonna get you to a boardin'house—in Brooklyn." He might, Hiram thought, even find her a nice family to stay with, so he would always know that she was safe, and where to find her.

Vyda Rose continued to sob. Awkwardly, Hiram tried to console her. "Aw, don't cry now. Here, take my handkerchief." Finally, not knowing what else to do, he grasped her hand in one of his. She stopped sobbing abruptly, and looked up at him in surprise, her nose red, her eyes wet. Hiram blushed again, but stopped the car and closed both of his hands around hers.

"Miss Vyda Rose," he said, looking at her squarely. "Now you hush up. Everything is gonna be just fine. Hiram will see to it. Okay?"

Vyda Rose nodded and straightened in her seat, staring straight ahead as Hiram maneuvered the car along the crowded street.

BROOKLYN, NEW YORK

SEPTEMBER, 1902

Winter was going to be difficult for Vyda Rose. "I seen snow before," she had said, defensively and with a touch of indignation, each time someone advised that she should go back home before winter. But Vyda Rose had not expected the chill that sneaked beneath the door and around the windows of her room on the seventh floor of a Brooklyn boardinghouse. She bought extra blankets and flannel gowns, and as her pregnancy progressed, neighbors offered warm clothing and baby things.

Vyda Rose did not like accepting charity. But she had no choice. Advised by a doctor to rest as much as possible, she was barely working a part-time schedule, doing hair at Connie's Beauty Parlor on Sixteenth Street in Manhattan. Hiram did what he could, helping her with groceries, rent, and other necessities. A blessing to Vyda Rose of the sort that could not be attributed to luck, Hiram also continued to ask around Brooklyn and lower Manhattan. But it seemed no one recognized the name of Vyda Rose's "cousin," a stocky colored railroad worker from Brooklyn.

At first, Vyda Rose had wandered the streets of Brooklyn alone, stopping at businesses and subway stations, dressed like the finest of ladies in the city—so people would *want* to talk to her. Before long, she had discarded her fashionable shoes for comfortable flats, visiting churches and bars, restaurants and theaters. When she decided to venture outside the colored community, Hiram had insisted upon accompanying her, driving her across the boroughs in his borrowed automobile, between his duties as the colored chauffeur of Mister Gresham Hayes.

Always in good spirits, he made Vyda Rose laugh, and at times, forget the futility of her search, a futility becoming clearer each day. And he did not make her feel foolish by asking of a link between her advancing pregnancy and her "cousin." They became good friends, but theirs was a friendship predicated upon boundaries—he did not make certain inquiries. Vyda Rose did not offer details of her past.

She wrote letters to her mother, and to Lilly, whose letters kept Vyda Rose entertained with stories of her slightly offbeat mother, Sister, and of Prince Junior and Suzanne, and their growing family.

Sister, whom Vyda Rose had never met, had a boyfriend—a preacher, no less—trying to save her soul. And Sister was giving him a run for his money! And Suzanne had just lost a baby—gone into labor at least three months early and lost that child in the tobacco fields.

But Vyda Rose could not care less about Suzanne, who had snubbed her because of her status as both fallen woman and bastard child. Suzanne was due a miscarriage, as far as Vyda Rose was concerned. But she did feel badly for Prince Junior, who had accepted her, if not with open arms, at least in his own reserved manner, as his sister. Vyda Rose made mental note to send him a note of sympathy. As far as the rest of Warren County—well, Lilly reported, things were still the same.

Lilly was tactful enough not to ask Vyda Rose if she had found him. She knew that Vyda Rose would have said so if she had. But by September, Lilly was asking, at the end of each letter, when Vyda Rose was coming home; and didn't she want to have her baby among her family; and whether Vyda Rose had anyone "up there in New York to take care of" her.

Vyda Rose was not offended by these not-so-subtle inquiries into her intimacies, or more accurately, these references to her lack thereof; but Vyda Rose had not completed her mission, and she fully intended to—if she could. And then she had begun to grow large, and to feel vulnerable. A train ride to North Carolina sounded unbearable. By all appearances, she wrote Lilly, she would be having her baby in New York.

She was getting around a bit, learning the city and its people as Hiram shepherded her from Brooklyn to lower Manhattan to Harlem. Unashamed to be gallivanting about town with a pregnant woman, a grotesquely pregnant woman, in Vyda Rose's opinion, he offered no explanations and no answers to the unasked questions, communicated through raised eyebrows and open-mouthed stares.

Vyda Rose had become conscious of her Southern speech and manners, discovering quickly that she could not hide them. But these people were themselves, for all their feigned city sophistication, only one generation removed from sharecroppers' shanties, and Vyda Rose was quick to remind them of this. She earned a reputation for having a sharp tongue; and when people asked her of her past or of whereabouts she was from, she gave them curt responses and changed the subject.

No one asked her directly who her baby's father was. They asked Hiram, and he laughed and said, "I don't ask no questions. I'm just helpin' out a friend." Sometimes he added: "It's the Christian thing to do," and threw back his head in laughter; for everyone understood that Hiram Stokes was no Christian. Son of an evangelist mother and an apathetic father, he had departed the church at as early an age as he could, in search of adventure. He was, of course, harmless, "except to pretty women," he would cackle with his infectious laugh. But his relationship to Vyda Rose and, of greater interest, Vyda Rose's child, remained a mystery to all but himself and Vyda Rose.

Hiram found her a midwife when she could no longer afford the ser-

vices of a doctor; and in December, her baby was born, brown and already
stocky like her father, strong and insistent with an earsplitting cry. She
would bring her Jewell home, Vyda Rose wrote Lilly, in the spring.

But by winter's end, Vyda Rose had a good job, as a hostess at the
Turkish baths in Harlem. Soon, its clients became her personal clients,
and she began inviting them home to the Brooklyn boardinghouse.

At first, the building supervisor, or super, as he was called, would look
the other way, allowing the slow trickle of men in and out of the vestibule
and up and down the stairs to escape his attention. Tenants paid their
rent. He attended to his own affairs. That was the arrangement.

But soon, he noticed that the tall Negro girl no longer rose in the
mornings to walk to the train. He had assumed that she worked in
Harlem, perhaps cooking or doing hair. She had begun to develop the polished appearance and manner of a cosmopolitan girl, and Harlem, he had
been told, was becoming the fashionable venue for sophisticated Negroes.

The young man in the handsome suit still came some evenings to
whisk her away in his borrowed car. But most weekends she entertained
men at home, and sometimes, well into the morning, he could hear them
whispering, or her laughing indulgently, as he passed the insubstantial
door of her room, and he imagined her lying naked on her back, the
heavy-lidded eyes closed in contentment, the sound of her laughter drifting upward like smoke from a chimney, suggestive of a warmth and comfort within.

She did not look at him as she passed him in the hall, or when she
came to his apartment to pay her rent. In deference—or indifference, he
finally decided—her eyes slid past him, around him, and over his head,
then downward as he counted the bills on the massive oak table that

dominated his living room, a room where not much living was accomplished, he thought ruefully, recalling the sounds of living that regularly emanated from the tall girl's room.

He wanted her to look at him. He wanted to ask her the source of her income now that she no longer went to work in the mornings. That, he considered, might startle her into a direct glance, perhaps of trepidation—she was either the kept woman of the young man in the handsome suit, or the lover of many for a price. Perhaps she was both. In any event, she would realize, her errant doings had not gone undetected. Perhaps, he thought, she would feel no fear or shame, but stare at him defiantly before turning on her heels to stalk from the room. Or perhaps she would smile slyly, and raise her thick, kohled lashes slowly to meet his eyes above the oak table, then turn to saunter away, her hips swaying an invitation as she turned to close the door behind herself and cast upon him one last meaningful look. She would not answer his question. He would not care. He only wanted her to look at him.

"Cop-per came by," he surprised himself by saying one day as he counted bills on the oak table. Conscious of his Irish brogue, he did not talk much to anyone. In particular, he minimized his conversation with the fully Negro occupancy of this boardinghouse that he had "supervised" loosely since the Negroes had converged upon this part of town. He needed to maintain, he felt, a certain authority, and this goal would not be advanced by opening his mouth to reveal himself but one step removed from their own status.

But the locale of authority could be a lonely place to inhabit, he had discovered. He needed, at least, an acknowledgment of human kinship, a recognition of his *being*.

He needed her to look at him.

He glanced up at her as he spoke, surprised at hearing his own voice, and hoping to catch the girl's reaction. She was standing in front of him, across the table and staring at it as he sat counting and placing each bill face downward as he counted. She did not look up or react. He wondered if she had heard or understood.

Then, she raised her eyes to look at his face.

Her own face was motionless. She simply looked at him, making him swallow with discomfort. He lost count, gathered up the bills, and began counting again. The girl continued to stare at him, her face unreadable, and he wondered what she saw: a middle-aged immigrant, unattractive and unskilled, hiding his inadequacy behind a mask of superiority and power? A lonely man, and minor despot of a makeshift domain, desperate for validation from his subjects? A longing man, longing for veneration but finding none, aspiring instead to mastery, pathetic prisoner of his own arrogance?

He stacked the bills, finally, at the corner of the table, uncounted. "They was askin' 'bout your, er, visitors, *and how you was payin' your rent.*" He paused. She did not respond. "They said they would be a-watchin'," he continued, his words slow and measured. Still, the girl did not answer or move. He wondered again if she understood the implications of his words. He sighed.

"Prostitution is 'gainst the law. If you are caught, you could be fined or sent to jail." Her eyes seemed to widen slightly, he thought. He had her attention. He licked his lips. His eyes traveled down to the hollow at the base of her throat. "Of course, I may be able to, er, *protect* you. That is, if yer *nice.*"

The girl's eyes narrowed perceptibly, and her mouth seemed to take on a sardonic set. She shifted her weight to one foot, staring at him thoughtfully now. He noted the slight bulk of her hips, barely discernible beneath her loose cotton dress. Finally—"Thank you—" she said in a near-whisper, her voice sweetly husky and sultry. "But I can do 'thout yo' *protection.*" And her eyes slid past him, around him, and over his head, then down to the pile of bills on the table. He felt insignificant, belittled, dismissed. Without another word, she turned and left the lonely man in the lifeless room.

When he saw her next, she was coming into the house, arm in arm with the young man in the handsome suit. Neither of them seemed to see him, much less acknowledge him, even though they had to step around him to pass through the vestibule; even though he bowed his head and uttered a grudging greeting, barely audible, as they passed. Their laughter drifted down the stairs as they ascended to her room, mocking and reducing him to nothingness.

She would scramble across the room on hands and knees, he imagined, when he slapped her and made her bleed, knocking her to the floor. She would crawl toward the door, and rise with effort to her knees to open it. But he would slam it shut and kick her in her mirthful mouth, no longer laughing. It would widen in pain as the somnolent eyes swelled with tears; and he, moved with compassion, would stand before her, allowing her to kiss his boots, to wash them with her tears and with her hair.

And then he would have her, gently but assertively; and she would submit herself to him, offering oblation for having mocked and disregarded him. From then on, she would be his servant. He consoled himself now, each time the Negro girl passed his open door en route with some new stranger to her room on the seventh floor, with this figment of his mind's concoction; each time she laughed at him behind her firmly shut but ineffectual door. She would pay for this. He would make her pay, reduce her to the humble status nature had conferred upon her kind.

HARLEM, NEW YORK CITY

APRIL, 1903

It was dusk when she arrived at the brownstone on 139th Street, carrying her baby wrapped in blankets and a man's coat. As usual, the door had been left ajar, despite the early spring chill. Vyda Rose pushed it open further with her toe.

MUZZLE NOT THE OX THAT TREADETH OUT THE CORN, a large handwritten sign warned in the semidark vestibule.

THE WORKWOMAN IS WORTHY OF HER HIRE, proclaimed another on the door that led into the first-floor apartment. M. STOKES, a small label announced quietly beneath it, just above the buzzer, which Vyda Rose ignored.

"Magnolia!" Vyda Rose cried, annoyed that the door was shut. There was no response. Vyda Rose shifted the baby's weight and kicked the door softly. "Magnolia! Come an' get the do'!"

It opened suddenly, startling Vyda Rose. A squat woman stood on the

other side of it, her hands on her wide hips, and expression of feigned annoyance on her heavily made-up face. She had once been voluptuous, in a
long ago past that she rarely discussed. Once, Vyda Rose had been told,
Magnolia had been a looker, a gifted prophetess and healer of question-
able virtue. Magnolia, of course, had always dismissed such slander as the
affliction of the righteous, and its proponents as conspirators to blacken
the name of the Lord. But Vyda Rose liked to think that there was a kinship between herself and Magnolia, who had accepted her without judgment or recrimination, nodding conspiratorially, and without asking
questions, when Vyda Rose had indicated that she "worked nights" and
needed an able surrogate to look after her child; even hinting, now and
then, her approval of Vyda Rose's association with Hiram, and her hope
that Vyda Rose would take greater interest in her son.

But Hiram remained Vyda Rose's friend, and only occasional lover.
Vyda Rose had no wish for emotional entanglement. She cared for her
child. Her lovers could care for her, if they wished, at their own risk. In
Hiram, she had found friendship without obligation. In his mother, she
had found a ready familiarity and mutual esteem.

Magnolia regarded Vyda Rose with mock disapproval, her heavy eyebrows knit. "Girl, must be you done lost your mind, kicking on doors and
carrying on. This a civilized house. You better mind your behavior."

"I ain't stutt'in you," Vyda Rose laughed, pushing past Magnolia into
the crowded, gaudy room. Everything in it was brown: brown velvet curtains, couches, and upholstered chairs; mahogany tables and desk;
bearskin rugs on a brown-tiled floor; and rich coffee-colored walls. The
walls were covered with gilt-framed pictures of brown people: Magnolia's
mother and father, her brothers and cousins and friends.

Jewell seemed to love this brown room and the woman who was this apartment's sole resident. She always seemed content here, nestling against Magnolia's bosom as Vyda Rose left her here on Fridays and returned to retrieve her each Monday.

Vyda Rose served her clients only on weekends in New York, and rested during the week as much as Jewell would allow. She had wearied of her fruitless searches for Julius, finally placing adds in local newspapers, and was waiting for a response. In six weeks, no respondent had appeared. But as her daughter grew more and more like him, reminding Vyda Rose each day of her mission, she began to lose hope of ever finding Julius. This worried her.

Magnolia was of no encouragement. She smiled sadly when Vyda Rose spoke of Julius, and occasionally told her what she ought to do. Today, she offered this advice unsolicited and unprovoked: "Get you a man, a good one, and have you some more babies. I know you got needs in that direction. Now, *Hiram*, he's a good man. Little on the wild side, but once he get settled, he'll make you a good husband—"

"Magnolia," Vyda Rose sighed, lowering the baby onto a couch and unfolding the man's coat. "Now why would I want a husband, good or bad? I'm too free for that. I jes wanna keep doin' what I'm doin' and make good for my baby." She unbuttoned her coat and sat next to her child, unwrapping the layers of blankets.

"But what you gonna do when she ain't no more baby? What kinda mother you gonna be living like you is now? And what's gonna happen when you old and ain't got no more zip in your dip?"

Vyda Rose frowned. "I got my whole life to think like a old woman. Now, I jes wanna do what pleases me, and find my baby's daddy. One day at a time, dass all I can take. Dass all I want to right now." And her mouth took on the stubborn set of a child who had raised herself and was supremely confident in her own wisdom. Magnolia knew this meant that as far as Vyda Rose was concerned, the subject was closed, or ought to be. Yet she could not stop herself from persisting.

"But Vyda Rose, life ain't long like you think it is. It don't stop goin' 'cause it's more than you want to take, and it don't wait 'til you ready to make plans. It just keeps on goin', with or without you. You wake up one day and you saggin' in places you hadn't noticed. Your hair is turnin' colors, you all by yourself, and don't nobody want you. It's a fright'nin' thing, and an end nobody deserves."

Vyda Rose opened her mouth to point out what a lot of good Magnolia's marrying had done her, but thought better of it. "The end," she said evenly, "is jes the end, dass all. Don't make no difference how you live— we all leavin' here by ourself. In the meantime, I'm jes livin' the best I can, doin' what I like doin' and do the best. I don't bother nobody, long as they don't bother me. And I'm gon' do better for my baby than somebody did for me. Don't you worry." She handed Magnolia the fretting child. "Here," she said. "You mind my baby, not my business." And she gave the older woman a brief hug. Fear knifed through Magnolia's body, making her stiffen in Vyda Rose's arms. She watched uneasily as Vyda Rose buttoned her coat.

" 'Bye now, Baby," Magnolia mumbled. "You look after yourself, you hear?"

Sometimes, Vyda Rose passed his room at night, and as she climbed the stairs, alone or with a client, he would open the door slightly and peek out at her, like a child spying on his parents, or hoping for a glimpse of Santa at Christmas. Later, he began swinging the door open wide, staring obnoxiously, with scorn and, yes, *judgment*—the thing she hated most—on his pasty face, leering and derisive and condescending. She found his implicit criticism of her ironic in light of his earlier proposition; and at least *she* was not closeted, as he clearly was, living vicariously and only occasionally in those brief glimpses outside his room and into the lives of others.

She became more adept at ignoring him; more consciously and obviously incognizant of him. He became smaller, progressively more transparent to her. She instructed her friends to ignore him—the voyeur pretending to live, with his hypocritical smugness—ignore him, she would say. And they would oblige, not seeing him, not hearing his door creak as it opened; their eyes fixed on Vyda Rose, fascinated and entranced by her; and the super would follow them with his eyes and then with his mind's eyes, up the stairs and into her iniquitous room, in his mind sharing in their frantic carnal indulgence, hating himself for this, and hating her, for making him want and hate her in spite of himself.

Lickskillet, North Carolina
June, 1903

Sister awoke, summoned by the urgent pleading of a young woman she did not know—a young woman in a place she had never been, her heart pounding, struggling for breath, in desperation and fury kicking and thrashing with every limb. The young woman begged—demanded—strength and survival, her inheritance and just claim.

She demanded her legacy of faith.

But Sister turned her back on the woman, whose fight for survival seemed a threat to Sister's own; crawling, clawing at the burlap sheets that entangled Sister's arms and legs as the cornhusk mattress, now turned to violent waves that pulled and sucked at Sister, betrayed and delivered her into the clutches of this depraved young woman, whose face appeared to Sister both alien and familiar, twisted in an agonized grimace, distorted by the blue-green waters and floating detritus of a distant bay.

It was the face of a woman she had not wished to know; the face of betrayal and hope; the face of Sapphire's daughters fallen from grace and indifferent to their state, struggling against a hateful and contemptuous tide, clinging for dear life to Sister's feet, at the end of their mortal reserves.

The young woman relaxed her grip, surrendered to the tide.

And Sister awoke in her, surmounting the blue-green waters, carrying her daughters to their dwelling place, transcending the tide.

BROOKLYN, NEW YORK
JUNE, 1903

At night, Vyda Rose missed the stars. She missed the counsel of her mother, Lilly's friendship and candor; even her grandmother's forbearing and disapproval. She missed the lovers she had left in Warrenton; the neighbors and girlfriends she had rarely ever seen. She missed them, as she missed the rural homeliness of home, the sweet and simple cloudless, starry sky.

Her window opened into an alley. The building next door was much like the one in which she lived. If she leaned outside the window, twisting her neck to just the right angle, she could see a sliver of unfriendly, starless Brooklyn sky. She could hear, too, with her neck strained outside the window and her ear inclined, the sobbing of a woman, the mumbling of inebriates, the tantrum of a child. *Living sounds,* Vyda Rose thought, and evidence of a dread and frightening side of life, a deep despair she wished to avoid but felt, always, one step behind her, too narrowly outdistanced for Vyda Rose's comfort, but avoidable if she maintained her focus on her lovers and her child.

The clouds parted suddenly, revealing a bright and beckoning full moon that filled Vyda Rose's room with a rectangle of light so startling that it woke the baby as she rested on the bed.

Jewell stretched her arms and gurgled good-naturedly.

Vyda Rose scooped her up, following the lure of moonlight onto the living street.

It was late when Vyda Rose returned to the boardinghouse that night, invigorated by the long walk with Jewell. She supposed that her neighbors were soundly asleep.

The windows of the super's apartment were dark. She was relieved that he was not at home to witness her arrival, and to follow her with eyes filled with ugliness to her room.

As she climbed the stairs, the baby began to cry. Vyda Rose hastened her steps, making the clucking sounds that seemed to calm her child. Carefully balancing the baby on her hip as she fished through her purse, she found the key to her room, and as she unlocked the door, she was shoved mightily from behind and nearly crashed into the footboard of her bed.

Spinning around, clutching her baby to her chest, she faced the super, his face twisted in a cruel mask of anger and insanity. He lunged at her, grasping her hair in his fists and tugging viciously. Tears stung Vyda Rose's eyes, and she twisted away from him, intensifying the pain but enabling herself to toss her baby onto the bed and turn to face him again, her hands barbarous claws scratching and tearing at him. The baby began to wail in earnest. The super leapt upon Vyda Rose, knocking her to the floor and beating her with all of his might, months of frustration and humiliation in each blow, years of impotence and failure, losing himself in the rhythm of his blows as his fists fell brutal against her flesh.

Crouching helplessly against the wall, Vyda Rose bowed her head defensively, her arms covering her head, hoping, waiting for this torrent of injury and rancor to stop; not mindful of the pain, of her own inability to defend herself; conscious only of her weeping child, enduring only to survive this hellish episode, to comfort her daughter at its end.

She managed, once, to glance up at his eyes. They were vacant. He was mad, she realized, mad with hatred and fury having nothing to do with herself. And all at once she understood that she must bring to an end this depraved assault; that neither surrender nor endurance would accomplish this; for in his madness the super was not assaulting a woman, a worthy woman and fellow human being; a feeling, thinking, living woman with a mother, and a child, and a life filled with people who loved her. In his devastated mind, the super was assailing a thing; not a thing that Vyda Rose was, but a thing that she represented.

And although she could not discern exactly what this thing was that she embodied in the super's mad mind, this thing so loathsome, perhaps in himself, that it drove him to slaughter a woman in the presence of her anguished child, she knew that she would always be It; would not cease to be It when his arms surrendered to weariness and refused to respond to his will. In a moment, she understood that surrender or endurance would not save her, that it could not counter hate; that in the face of his infernal madness, she must at once decamp, or stand and fight.

She stood, catching several blows to her ribs and stomach, and doubled over, reaching out toward a chest of drawers to regain her balance.

But she fell against it violently, its edge stabbing her stomach. A mirror crashed to the floor. And still, he pummeled her back as she stood braced against the chest. A cutting internal sensation, as if a scissor was gnawing its way through her viscera, sliced through her consciousness and made her aware that she was still alive, could still feel; but if she did not end this assault on her body and on her spirit, if she did not defend her right to feel and to be, she would most assuredly die. She knew this, and in that moment of cognizance Vyda Rose dove toward the floor, cutting her hand deeply as her fingers closed around a shard of glass twice the length of her hand. Without allowing herself a moment to think, she twisted her body around and stabbed upward at him. The glass sank into his belly.

His eyes widened, almost imploringly.

He toppled toward her.

Her baby was crying. The super had slumped half on top of her and she was aware that he needed help but her baby was crying. She scrambled out from beneath him and went to comfort the infant, and as she sat on the bed, lifting her baby to her lap, she met the eyes of a stranger—one of the many neighbors, she supposed, that she had never met. He was standing just outside the open door, wearing a striped nightgown, and his mouth was opened. No sound emanated. He glanced down at the super who lay bleeding on the floor, and he covered his open mouth with his hand. Vyda Rose comforted her child. The stranger hurried away.

She began to hum—a tune she could not recall learning, or associate with a person or place or experience. But the baby seemed to understand. She gurgled contentedly and succumbed to peaceful sleep. And still, Vyda Rose continued her humming, murmuring, rocking the child restively. Moments passed. At some point it occurred to Vyda Rose that she could be in danger of some sort. Gathering her purse and a few of her baby's belongings, she tiptoed down the stairs and took to the calm, deserted street.

It was cool and humid outside. Vyda Rose stood on the sidewalk for several minutes, shivering beneath the glow of a streetlamp, holding her baby tightly. She felt as if there was something she should be thinking about. A large house just down the street caught her eye—the only house lit from within at this hour. She began walking toward it, uncertain of why, oblivious to her surroundings.

LOWER MANHATTAN, NEW YORK

JUNE 1903

Hiram Stokes was not a man carried away by his emotions. He had never loved a woman, other than his mother, and had certainly never been in love. But Vyda Rose Alston had found a crevice in his heart that he had not known was there, and had crawled right in and filled it. She evoked in him a tenderness that surprised and troubled him, and he had always known that if the time ever came and the need arose, he would be there for her, asking nothing but that she trust him. And need him.

It was dark and the buggy was a block away from his stoop on South Street; but he could see that she was disheveled in appearance, an unusual condition for Vyda Rose, and clutching her baby stiffly. The driver of the buggy, a woman called Carrie, was visibly upset, her lined face conveying the urgency of their visit. He glanced at his watch. It was nearly 3 A.M.

He noted with alarm the deep red stains on Vyda Rose's dress, and her bleeding hands, as the buggy stopped in front of his stoop and Carrie alighted. She was a sensible woman, Hiram had always thought, and demonstrated more levelheadedness than most prostitutes were willing to make apparent. Her tone was almost businesslike as she related the facts as she had been able to ascertain them: The building supervisor had attacked Vyda Rose in her room; she had fought back, finally stabbing him with a piece of glass. There had been quite a ruckus, and at least one eyewitness. The police were surely involved by now.

Hiram received this news with dread and a deepening sensation of nausea. He recalled the super's glaring resentment on those occasions when he and Vyda Rose had passed his room, his hostility unclear in its direction—toward Vyda Rose? Perhaps she had rebuffed his advances. Or toward Hiram, for being with her in the super's stead? He had never been sure until now. He desperately regretted having not cared.

Hiram rushed to Vyda Rose's side and took one of her hands, looking into her face. She did not appear particularly upset now, but her face was swollen and streaked with dried blood. He noticed that her hands trembled. Hiram looked at them, those hands that had traversed his body on those rare and cherished occasions when she had allowed him to make love to her, then returned to him the favor, matching his skill as well as his ardor—each time resurrecting in Hiram the hope that she felt what he felt when her long, dexterous fingers kneaded his flesh in long, languorous strokes that made promises Vyda Rose never seemed to recall thereafter. But he would relive for weeks the gentle, healing impact of her touch, the taste and texture, sweet and smooth, of her skin, the warmth and liquidity of her center. He would experience again her stirring scent, and the soft bushiness of her hair. And a void would replace the space in his heart that Vyda Rose had inhabited—not merely an absence of flesh and voracity, but of kindness and caring; generosity and warmth; determined strength and courage that were Vyda Rose.

Even now, an ironic dignity surrounded her, as she reached around her child to clasp their joined hands at her baby's back.

He knew that she must go, and this filled him with sorrow. He began to miss her, then hung his head ashamed of his own selfishness. This was her moment—she needed him, and he would come through for her. He must get her to some place safe. But where was safety for a colored girl who had killed a white man, of humble circumstances, but a white man nonetheless? Vyda Rose's hands trembled more violently, and she began to sob. Carrie took the baby from her arms, and Hiram helped her out of the buggy and into his home.

It was small, only one room, and bare, its only comfort the sleigh bed that he had occasionally shared with Vyda Rose. Carrie sat beside her on it now, holding her tightly and speaking to her in a comforting tone. Hiram glanced at them as he moved about the apartment, searching through boxes and drawers. He was surprised by their intimacy. He had not known that they were close.

The baby slept soundly in the center of the bed. Piece by piece, Hiram assembled an outfit—brown trousers hemmed too short for him by an inept tailor; a shirt and tie; an inconspicuous tan jacket that would be too large for Vyda Rose but would have to do; and shoes that might nearly fit—thanks to her large feet. As he searched for a hat to cover Vyda Rose's long, unruly hair, Carrie glanced at him, then abandoned her embrace of Vyda Rose to turn fully toward him.

"Watchoo doin'?" she inquired.

"I'm gettin' her things to wear. She gotta get out the city, and she can't do it like that," he gestured toward the two women with his hand. "I'll take her to New Jersey in the morning, and from there we'll get a train and go."

"Go where?" Carrie demanded, her eyes narrowed.

"Wherever we can get to," Hiram replied. "First train leavin', we on it." He extracted a wad of bills from a shoe on the floor of a closet and stuffed it into his pocket. Vyda Rose and Carrie glanced at each other, Carrie's expression doubtful, Vyda Rose's eyes immense with fear.

But she recalled the train ride from North Carolina to Staten Island, and the ferry from there to Brooklyn. Her shoulders straightened. She could do this, especially in disguise.

"But what about my baby?"—her baby just six months old, her new life's purpose. She could not escape with Jewell. She could not leave her behind.

Hiram thought for a moment. The look of panic on Vyda Rose's face was not lost on him, the only child of a mother who had lived only for him. "Carrie will take her to Mama's. Won't you, Carrie?"

Carrie looked from Hiram to Vyda Rose. Her expression softened. Resignedly, she let out a sigh and nodded. Hiram gathered the clothing in his arms and held it out to Vyda Rose, who took it gratefully, her face wet with tears.

HUDSON RIVER

JUNE, 1903

Watching her had been agony. Standing on the stoop as they left Hiram's building, she had held the infant tightly to her breast, tears streaming down her face, her eyes closed meditatively; and Jewell had giggled naïvely, her fingers laced in her mother's hair. Time was escaping, but neither Hiram nor Carrie had had the heart to tear mother from child. Finally:

"Vyda Rose," Hiram had nudged. Vyda Rose had not seemed to hear.

"Vyda Rose," Carrie had offered gently. She and Hiram had looked at each other helplessly. "Honey, we got to go. You'll see her when this is over." But Vyda Rose had kissed the child and tickled her ribs, eliciting more giggles. "See?" Carrie had pointed out. "*She* knows that."

Vyda Rose had smiled sadly. "She don't know nothin'," she had said, drawing Jewell close and planting several kisses on her small face. Finally, Vyda Rose had allowed Carrie to lift the child gently from her arms.

A fitful night's sleep and an early morning subway ride later, Hiram and Vyda Rose had boarded a ferry for New Jersey. She stood near the railing now, her thin shoulders and slim hips drowning in the oversized men's clothing, something fragile and unmanly in her stance. Hiram wondered if it had been wise to try to disguise her. She might have attracted less attention in a plain dress. He could have asked Carrie to provide this. But in the panic and despair of last night's events, he had been unable to think clearly. Now, there was nothing they could do but hope that the authorities would be uninterested, or at least less than diligent, in searching for the super's killer.

He stood beside her, resisting the urge to hold her tightly, and remembered fallen women who had graced his mother's home with their presence during his childhood; beautiful women, wearing more makeup and less clothing than the church ladies with whom his mother also prayed in her home, less passionately, on other nights. These women— the fallen women—wore bright colors and voluptuous perfume, their arms bare and their breasts spilling from the tops of their dresses. They cried prettily sometimes as they prayed, and smiled at him, embarrassed, as he stole glimpses of them from the doorway to his room. These were women "with concerns," his mother had said. The church ladies had called them sinful, fallen, shameful. But Hiram had thought them beautiful; their sadness, which no one had explained to Hiram but which he felt he understood, mysterious and passionate and beautiful. These were women who needed something, and their need was beautiful, beckoning. It beckoned as he grew to maturity. It beckoned still.

One of these needy women would unearth in him the ghost of passion resurrected in boys becoming men, the ghost that lay dead in his own flesh, waiting for the kiss of enlightenment, awakened to a self-defeating quest for yet more and different and greater indulgence, and in the groggy confusion and excitement of awakening, Hiram would learn to crave this need in women with a bloodthirst that rode him, forever enslaving him to his own need. And he would hate the source of that need, and the source at which it was satisfied; the various sources to whom he believed he made love, but with a gentle horror; apologizing as he extracted himself, delicately, from the webs of disillusionment and disappointment he had not intended to create. His own need gratified for the moment, he lacked the wherewithal to meet theirs; and it was their need that hurt them, and hurt him as well.

Later, he was to learn that those fallen women knew what others needed, and knew how to provide it, a knowledge that grew out of their understanding of themselves.

Vyda Rose, too, knew what others needed, but she did not understand, Hiram felt, the source of this knowledge: her own need, the gasping collective need of women given the illusion of love, only to have even that snatched away; women trained in soliciting the love of others, but never learning to adore themselves.

But Hiram understood. The passion of these women for their paramours, and of his mother toward her God, were one and the same; and what the church ladies resented in those women was the love greed that they recognized as their own; and Vyda Rose, heiress to this estate, differed only in her comfort with her own passions.

A breeze caught a tendril of Vyda Rose's hair. Hiram moved to hide it beneath her hat, but stopped himself. "Tuck your hair." He motioned toward the straying strands. She stuffed them hastily beneath her hat, and peered up at him sadly, breaking something within Hiram. He wanted badly to touch her, reassuringly, as Carrie had touched her, as his mother and the fallen women had touched one another, and tell her that he understood and needed her.

But he could not. Not until they were safely ashore; perhaps not until the train had taken them to some faraway place where he could rescue her from what he only presumed, with passion and conviction, was her need.

People ambled past them—colored people nearby, and whites at a comfortable distance—stopping to look over the railing at the waves as they crashed against the ferry; nodding at one another, and at Hiram. Vyda Rose kept her head bowed, watching the waves and the New Jersey shore that loomed ahead, willing the ferry to make haste in getting there. She tried in vain to keep her mind still and silent, to keep her hands steady. At times, her entire body trembled and she could hardly stand. She ached for her daughter, her mother, and her grandmother; for Lilly, and others she might never see again. She had fought back tears all morning. The effort was exhausting her. Were it not for Hiram's comforting presence, she knew that she would have crumbled.

She feared that she did not make a convincing man. Men stared at her, inclining their heads to look at her face beneath the brim of her hat. She tried to appear nonchalant, but she knew that they knew. Men could detect pussy through some sixth sense intrinsic to them and passed to their sons through their genes, Vyda Rose thought. Hiram had assured her that it did not matter—another dead immigrant would hardly merit a police report, much less a dragnet. But then, Vyda Rose thought, they were running, were they not? Only for the sake of caution, he had reasoned aloud, discerning her thoughts.

A white man approached her, breaching the boundary between white and colored, staring, openly curious, at her face. She tried to meet his stare, then looked at Hiram, her eyes wild. Hiram did not look at her, but rocked on his heels, whistling as he had all morning. The man passed on. Vyda Rose grabbed Hiram's arm.

"You think he was the po-lice? Oh, God. Help me—"

"Vyda Rose," Hiram said coolly. "He ain't no police just happen to be on this ferry."

"But if they lookin' for me—"

"Vyda Rose," he said again, evenly, the effort to sound rational in spite of his fear making him seem annoyed. "You killed a low-down white man who was nothing but trash. Police ain't goin' out of their way, unless you get in theirs. Okay?"

But Vyda Rose ducked around a corner where no one was standing, fighting to control her tears. Hiram followed her.

"Okay?" he demanded. But Vyda Rose was irreparably shaken. He held her in the shadow created by the ferry's great awning, and she cried profusely and as silently as she could. Several passersby stared at the unusual pair—colored passersby. They would not tell even if they suspected Vyda Rose's crime.

The white man had disappeared.

Hiram thought, again, that he should tell her. Her shoulders shook pitifully, and she took in great gasps of air between sobs. He felt that he should tell her that he cared for her, and would always be there for her. But she knew this, he rationalized. Wasn't he here for her now?

By the time they emerged from the shadow, the ferry was approaching the shore, perhaps two hundred feet away. Vyda Rose's face lit up with relief and anticipation as she stared across the bay; but she glanced behind herself nervously. "Let's go, Hiram," she begged. "Let's be the first ones off." And she turned toward the gang plank.

The white man stood a short distance away, this time with two others. They were staring at the colored woman dressed like a man. Their expressions might have conveyed curiosity, humor, or triumph, and Vyda Rose would not have known the difference. A look of horror replaced the excitement on her face. Reaching to steady her, Hiram opened his mouth to say, "Calm down. Just don't panic."

But Vyda Rose had turned to run, pushing past the astonished crowd. Too stunned at first to react, Hiram gathered himself and ran after her, reaching the front end of the ferry just in time to hear her splash into the bay. Without hesitating, Hiram leapt after her, trying to recall if Vyda Rose had ever mentioned that she could swim. He tried to see and to think as he adjusted to the initial shock of the cold, deep water. He wondered if the white men had been cops or merely fascinated passengers. He thought he saw her, far, far away, the legs of his too-short pants flapping in the blue-green water, moving away from the shore. He was confused. He began to tread water, his head jerking in one direction and then another, frantic and unable to see or breathe. And then an overwhelming sense of failure and despair began to engulf him as he felt himself being dragged heavily down, down, into the murky waters of the bay, recalling all the things his pride had not allowed him to show her, the things that he had nearly said.

He imagined, as he often had, the girl he thought she must have been:

pigtailed, stubborn, and proud; perhaps flamboyant, with dreams of glamour and distinction, but a nature lover at heart; that girl, enjoying the sensation of the water as it pressed itself against her belly and back, squeezed between her toes, forced itself behind the lids of her tightly closed eyes. He imagined an expression of surrender and of rapture on her face, and the beauty of this struck him as boundless and enchanting. He imagined that she did not fight the undertow, no flailing arms losing a hopeless battle with nature's inevitable will. She moved instead in concert with it, her legs flagellar, fluid, moving *with* the water as it eddied around them, propelling her upward, her body straight and rigid; an arrow piercing the water, clearing a path through its depths; a rocket soaring through the hydrosphere, bursting through its surface. He wondered that she did not proceed, in projectile manner, to penetrate the canopy of the sky. And as sunlight, harsh bright sunlight, struck his own shuttered eyes, shocking them open wide, and air filled his lungs, he thought he saw that girl, her hair a hennaed halo around her head, as she emerged naked from the rocks around the pier, not looking back, but moving with the grace and desperation of a gazelle chosen through some mischance for prey, moving with fear and an instinct for survival across terrain unfamiliar and hostile; moving as across a native plain, in a native country across the sea, the winds of a God and an ocean at her back.

chapter 8

RALEIGH, NORTH CAROLINA

SEPTEMBER, 1903

queen Marie had not been inside the library of St. Augustine's College for many years. Much had changed, she noted. The students, for example, were less reverent, the atmosphere less sacred in this once-hallowed hall that smelled, as it had smelled from its beginning, of old books, of dust, and of mold. These students, some of them second-generation students of St. Augustine's, had a greater sense of worthiness, of belonging here; a confidence born of breeding and privilege. Queen Marie allowed herself a few minutes of wistfulness, then took a deep breath and marched up to the reference desk.

"May I be of assistance?" A woman looked up at Queen Marie over the rims of her glasses, then removed them to stare solemnly at Queen Marie, as if pondering already the response to a query not yet voiced. She was young, Queen Marie saw once the glasses were removed, as she had herself once been, in what seemed a short time, but was in fact a lifetime, ago.

"Yes," Queen Marie replied. "Do you have any, um, newspapers from, um, Brooklyn, I reckon. Yeah. Brooklyn."

The young woman's frown deepened. "Brooklyn. Hmmm. We do have a fine Negro publication from New York . . ." She paused for Queen Marie to respond. Then, "I don't know that it will contain the information you are looking for . . ." And when this elicited no response: "What, exactly, are you looking for?"

Queen Marie felt foolish. Her question had not been specific enough. "Um, jes news." She lowered her head. Tears stung the backs of her eyes, and she could feel her nose reddening. "My—my daughter is there. I—I haven't heard nothin' from her here lately, and I just wondered if . . . you know . . ."

The young woman's features softened. She knew; but she would not say "obituary," or even "news," as that would imply *bad* news. She rose and led Queen Marie to a stairway that led down to the depths of the building, to a yet dustier, book-filled room; and another, and another. Finally, Queen Marie and the young woman faced rows and rows of stacks of paper. One such row bore the designation: "*Contender* (New York)."

The young librarian heaved a pile of newspapers into Queen Marie's arms, and lifting another for herself, she led Queen Marie to an apparently unfrequented area where dust-covered tables and empty chairs were arranged. Here, they unloaded their burdens onto a table. Queen Marie was grateful for the solitude. She had felt frumpy and incongruous among the youthful, smartly dressed students. The librarian offered her further assistance should it be needed. Queen Marie thanked her departing back.

She sat staring at the formidable piles for what seemed a long, long time, her heart filled with dread. Finally, she began thumbing through pages, starting with the most recent issue. Headline after futile, meaningless headline presented itself, bold in brazen black type, and full of self-importance. Queen Marie decided to begin her search just over three months back— when Vyda Rose's letters, usually biweekly or so, had ceased to arrive with regularity; had in fact ceased to arrive at all, she had realized over the passing weeks. Slowly, painfully, Queen Marie began scanning headlines, reading death notices, society news, even, desperately, editorials and fashion articles. And a world unknown to her but inhabited by her child began to unfold to Queen Marie; a world of gaiety and violence, of irony and change; a world where colored people could sport the most recent trends from French and Italian couturiers, live in spacious apartments, and create their own newspaper, by, for, and about themselves; a world that had swallowed her baby whole to contribute barely, if at all, to the girth of that great city.

She slept for a time, her head resting uncomfortably in the space on the table between editions read and editions untouched. She dreamed, at moments recalling Vyda Rose the infant, stubborn and ill-tempered; Vyda Rose the child, playing content and nearly docile, alone with her imagined friends. Queen Marie had missed almost entirely Vyda Rose's early teens, a period during which Queen Marie had herself been in the throes of maturation. But she dreamed of the woman Vyda Rose, proud, uncertain and hiding her uncertainty behind her self-assured gaze, always respectful, but never apologizing; and she dreamed of herself, Queen Marie, as judgmental and unforgiving of herself as her own mother.

She thought, too, of Sister, her nemesis in a past existence, the grandmother of her daughter; Sister strong, haunted and harrowed, but lately come into her own, minister to others of a newfound peace that Queen Marie envied; Sister whose lined face held a beauty born of an unenchanted youth and the knowledge of God, the knowledge of her own power; Sister who knew things, and for whom the knowing was enough, sometimes far too much; and the two princes, Sister's princes, who had given Queen Marie the most enduring joys of her life.

Including her Vyda Rose, of whose presence in her life Queen Marie had not been worthy.

Awakening, standing to stretch her arms and legs, she looked at the stack of editions unread, and thought again of Sister.

> *may I discern between the lines*
> *of ancient truth that adorn*
> *your face*
> *the secrets that our daughters will discover*
> *in distant ages when we have forgotten*
> *the hiding places*
> *of old*
>
> *for we are their dwelling place*
> *and our God is etched into your*
> *face*

She sat and picked up the newspaper at the top of the unread pile—
the one dated just before the letters no longer arrived. She read voraciously of a school for colored children; the slaying of a white man by an
unnamed colored girl in Brooklyn; an upcoming vaudeville show; a wedding on the Harlem River; and in the next edition, finally:

WOMAN BELIEVED DROWNED

Police report that a woman who jumped from a ferry near the
New Jersey shore is believed to have drowned in the bay early on
Saturday morning. The incident is being treated as a suicide.

The woman, identified as Vyda Rose Alston, was a resident of
Warrenton, North Carolina, visiting with friends at the time of
the incident. Passengers on the ferry who witnessed the suicide
say that the woman was clearly distraught. Police would not confirm reports that Alston was wearing trousers and a man's coat.

Tears had been waiting for their cue, which they had known would
come. Nodding at each other, they stepped out from behind Queen
Marie's eyes. Now was the time for grief to spill—again.

After a time, she noted again the date on which the short article had
been printed, recalling that her news of Fields' death had been returned
to its sender, postmarked just after the date of this *Contender*. UNABLE TO
DELIVER, the envelope had read, sending the fear of the worst down
Queen Marie's spine to the place in her stomach where her heart had then
begun to reside. BELIEVED DROWNED. Had no one bothered to know
for certain? Had the bay, the river, the ocean into which it flowed, been
drained and their bottoms combed to confirm to Queen Marie and to the

world their loss, the appropriateness of mourning, the necessity for burial of Vyda Rose's memory, someplace safe, known of, and accessible? Had the waters been commanded to yield their dead for inspection, lines and rows of them, standing erect and shoulder to shoulder, colored and white, woman and man, in various states of decomposition, their clothing tattered by the merciless sea, their shins scraped to the bone; some of them only bone and teeth, perhaps hair; some missing body parts severed by sharks or moving vessels, torn apart by winds that tossed the waves directionless and witless?

But the Africans would have endured, Queen Marie felt. The ones who had sank themselves unanchored with their children had endured, and Vyda Rose would be among them, erect in men's clothing, perhaps with her baby, if the seas gave up their dead. She preferred to think of it this way. Fields would urge her to think of it this way: her baby, and her baby, yielding themselves to the awful sea, rather than be taken by a world so fierce as to swallow them, involuntary and whole. How she wished she had been there when that beast, whatever the beast, had opened its hideous mouth, its noxious breath threatening the breath of her daughter. She would have set fire to its nostrils, and died in a flame of her own setting, to rescue her own blood from the beast, whatever the beast, that Vyda Rose had found more awful to face than the death of the sea. But if she could not have been there, she preferred to think of it this way: her baby, chin lifted, eyes expectant, yielding herself to the sea.

INEZ, NORTH CAROLINA

OCTOBER, 1903

"I am a *widow*," her mother had often said, lifting her chin in that haughty way intended to put moral distance between herself and others, and to distinguish herself from the scores of women, indecent or unde-sired, left manless at the close of an era of frank concubinage; when for the first time, Negro women were free, ostensibly, to love a man of their own choosing. But he had better be a Negro man—not the enslaver, the perpetrator of shame upon a race and its women; but a fine, Negro man, no matter how humble his circumstance, and no matter how ill-matched the union. A *widow*, Queen Marie had understood, was a validated woman, a step or two above the partnerless strumpets; more dignified, even, than a wife.

Now, at forty-six, Queen Marie found herself counted among them: the widows, survivors, outlasters; enduring after death's partition.

Others had gone on: Prince; and Dottie, who had died during child-birth; the father she had never known. Fields' departure, attributed too hastily, in Queen Marie's opinion, to a heart attack by confounded doc-tors, had left her stunned and pondering, while others saw to the burying of her husband's remains. And now her daughter, her baby, had gone on. She felt this in her spirit. But then, her spirit had been wrong before.

She had taken to drinking—it eased the pain of uncertainty, making her days sufferable. She had strange, vivid dreams. Sometimes, as she drank alone in her house at night, she saw Dottie, pigtailed and large-breasted, giggling with Queen Marie over some adolescent conspiracy; or Prince, silent, his face closed, or his broad back to her. She did not mind his silence. It comforted her to have someone, anyone, near; even her mother, with whom Queen Marie visited infrequently, and whose silent judgment Queen Marie had borne since the beginning of her involvement with Prince. She wanted only to have someone, anyone, near.

Queen Marie ran the Feels Good Inn now—competently, to her own surprise, through an alcoholic haze. She knew that Fields would restrain her, if he were here, gently taking the bottle from her eager hands, and holding her until the pain subsided. She missed him horribly, and needed him more than ever before.

Queen Marie watched the wind a lot; or rather watched the evidence of wind. It was not seen or heard from her stool before the window of her house, now great and empty, colossally lonesome. But leaves drifting toward the ground from nearly empty branches were disrupted in their downward path, caught up by the unseen, soundless wind. And Vyda Rose emerged—from behind a tree, Queen Marie later supposed—wavering in her mother's drink-impaired vision and delirium, and dressed oddly in the oversized clothing of a man. She did not speak at first, but waited, as she often had, for Queen Marie to greet her, her hooded eyes direct in their stare, even though she was, Queen Marie knew, ashamed and uncertain.

It took a moment for Queen Marie to find her voice. Her heart was beating rapidly, and her palms began to sweat. "Hi'ya doin', Baby?" she slurred. Vyda Rose sighed; in relief, Queen Marie thought, and tears welled in her daughter's eyes.

"Mama?" Vyda Rose whispered, and her fingers rose to her mouth in a gesture Queen Marie had never seen her affect. She stepped closer to the window as Queen Marie rose unsteadily to her feet. They stared at each other, knowing that this was their last meeting, and Vyda Rose wiped a tear from her cheek. "Mama. I want you to know that I'm all right. My life is good . . ." Her voice trailed off, as it always had; and she looked down at her bare feet for a long moment. Then—"Got me a little girl, Mama." She giggled, and her fingers moved back to her mouth. Another tear escaped her eye, and her hand moved to wipe it away. "She so precious—" And her voice caught in her throat. The two women stared fondly at each other for a long moment. Vyda Rose swallowed. "Mama, I need you to do one thing for me. You let my daddy raise my baby, okay?" She met her mother's eyes with understanding and forgiveness. Queen Marie stared back relieved and freed from reprehension. " 'Cause she got her mama spirit," Vyda Rose continued, "and she need him to nurture her soul." Her language did not strike Queen Marie as odd or incomprehensible. She understood completely, and nodded her acquiescence.

Prince Junior would recognize in his grandchild the spirit of the daughter he would never know was his: the spirit of his mother and his aunts; the spirit of his furtive lover, whose name he had not known; and he would nurture it in ways that Queen Marie, in her present state, could not.

Later, and more lucid, Queen Marie would recall her words: "My life is good," Vyda Rose had said. And her heart would lift with the hope that Vyda Rose was alive and, more importantly, well. But now, she reached toward her daughter, her hand grazing the glass of the window; touching her face, she felt, though a glass pane separated her from her only child. Vyda Rose smiled once more, reassuringly, almost happily, and vanished as suddenly as she had appeared.

INEZ, NORTH CAROLINA

APRIL, 1904

Queen Marie was not surprised to see a man as he approached her house, a tall man with a reckless appearance and a swaggering carriage. He held a woman by her elbow as they made their way through the soft red mud, the high, narrow heels of her shoes making the trip difficult and perilous. Several times, she nearly fell, and the young man caught her, bearing her considerable weight, and that of the child she carried, in his long, strong arms. Her hat was askew, and she was breathing with effort by the time they reached Queen Marie's house.

She watched them from her chair on the porch, thinking of other cool spring evenings spent on this porch, waiting for someone to come, as she had believed they would. She waited as they climbed the three short steps to her porch.

The woman was short and stout, with an air of dignity that reminded Queen Marie of her mother. She held the child in a manner suggesting a fierceness of attachment, as if no manner of arm-twisting or pulling of teeth could induce her to yield the child. Yet that was the reason for which she had come.

The young man had loved Vyda Rose, probably more than he had ever told her. He lowered his eyes just as Queen Marie noticed that they were damp. He was in pain, and his pride could not conceal this.

The woman spoke first, her voice pacific and intense, like quiet thunder. "Queen Marie Fields?" she asked.

Queen Marie nodded. She had assumed, correctly, that the pair knew whom they sought. "Evenin', Ma'am," she replied.

"Good evening," the woman smiled grimly. For a moment they were silent. The baby whimpered, and the woman bounced her gently. Finally, Queen Marie grasped the arms on either side of her chair and struggled to her feet.

"Come on in. Come on in," she said, in that way that Southern colored people have of repeating themselves. She opened the door of her house, and her visitors followed her inside.

Queen Marie motioned toward a settee, and the two strangers sat uncomfortably. "I am Magnolia Stokes, and this is my son, Hiram. We are friends of Vyda Rose."

There was a long silence. Hiram stared absently out the open door. Queen Marie watched him with interest. The baby gurgled happily. Magnolia continued. "We wanted to keep her." She pointed her chin at the baby, holding the child away from her own body. "But we couldn't. Vyda Rose had family down here somewhere. We thought it wouldn't be right." Magnolia's eyes were serious, troubled. Queen Marie almost asked her if she had seen Vyda Rose in the months since her passing, but decided against this. "We knew she had relatives around here," Magnolia repeated. "We seen the letters she got sometimes . . ." She glanced at Hiram, who stirred uneasily. "We thought you wouldn't be hard to find."

Queen Marie wondered what they knew of her daughter. Did they know that Vyda Rose had made love for a living, and was happiest giving and receiving love? Had they known that she had been courageous in her wantonness, heedless to models of purity, attuned to her own needs, and the needs of those who met them? Did they know that Vyda Rose had acquired—no, inherited—defenses to ignominy from her mother, and her grandmother?

Vyda Rose had chosen a vocation that few mothers could be proud of. Queen Marie would never stop regretting her role in this. But Vyda Rose had come from a lineage of women struggling to balance their own longing with the expectations of others, and had determined to live on her own terms. Queen Marie was proud of her.

Magnolia was standing with the child. "Well, it was nice to meet you, Mrs. Fields." She held the child toward Queen Marie, who stood and took the baby, surprised by the child's heft. She was nothing like Vyda Rose— it was hard to believe that this was Vyda Rose's child. Brown and round and dimpled, the baby gurgled cheerfully. Queen Marie bent her head downward to kiss the tender cheek. Her heart swelled with love for the motherless infant, then sorrow as she envisioned what must lie ahead for this child.

> *hush hush*
> *somebody's callin' our*
> *mama*
> *sister*
> *somebody's*
> *discovered our blackened*
> *name*

"We gonna be goin' now. We'll let you know if we hear from her."

Queen Marie's head snapped upward, her eyes wild with both surprise and relief: These friends of Vyda Rose were keeping her alive. Her startled reaction seemed to surprise Magnolia. Queen Marie looked at Hiram, whose rigid jaw declared his own determined hope. He had loved Vyda Rose, and in his heart she had survived.

She was, after all, from a lineage of survivors.

WISE, NORTH CAROLINA

JUNE, 1904

As she turned down the grassy incline and approached the rambling house, Queen Marie was reminded of the awkward building in Warrenton where Vyda Rose had lived and worked. The multiple and obvious additions to this house gave it an irregular appearance, like a mangled octopus, Queen Marie thought, its arms reduced to nubs, immobile, powerless except to offend the aesthetic senses.

Several children ran into the house when they saw her approaching. A tall, sun-bronzed woman opened the door and came out, holding a child on her hip. She raised a slender hand to shield her eyes from the noonday sun. Queen Marie raised a hand to wave at the statuesque woman in bare feet and a faded dress. The woman waved back, reluctantly, Queen Marie thought, and motioned her restless children back into the house.

It was a warm day, even for June, and Queen Marie felt sweaty and frumpy beneath the gaze of this subtle beauty, whose not so subtle appraisal of Queen Marie and the plump brown child she carried on her hip had found them both wanting. The woman's stare turned wary and took on a slight frost.

"Evenin', Ma'am," Queen Marie offered breathlessly. The woman assessed Queen Marie's tight-fitting dress and the dark, wet rings at her armpits. She nodded slightly. "I'm Miz Queen Marie Fields, and this is my grandbaby."

The woman arched an eyebrow and regarded Queen Marie with open curiosity. She was the kind of woman Queen Marie had once expected to be, before Prince and the rearrangement of her priorities: a decent, respectably married woman, though her literary talent would surely have taken her beyond Warren County, Queen Marie thought with some superiority. *She* would not have been the wife of a laborer.

"How you doin'?" the woman finally responded, her voice low and surprisingly husky. "I'm Miz Suzanne Yarborough." There was an awkward silence. Queen Marie shifted the child to her other hip. "Come on in," Suzanne said, almost grudgingly, opening the door and stepping inside the dark house.

The windows were covered with heavy brocade drapes that blocked out the sunlight completely. Queen Marie squinted at the pattern that laced the dark, emerald green fabric, then scanned the room briefly in the light that glowed faintly from a hallway behind the room. It was sparsely furnished. A wood burning stove crackled in a corner. A couch dominated one wall, and a large bed with a headboard of thick iron bars languished across the room from it, draped in a light green bedspread of soft, nubbled fabric. Queen Marie's eyes fell again upon the curtains with their curious, raised pattern.

"Have some siddown." Suzanne motioned toward the couch. "I got those from my mama when she died," Suzanne volunteered, nodding toward the curtains. Then, she added proudly, "She was an undertaker's wife—" whose husband, Queen Marie had heard, had lost his business in a gambling loss, at least two decades before his death. She had heard of the family and its misfortune, long before she had heard of Prince Junior's marriage to the only daughter, the widow of a traveling evangelist. What a disappointment, Queen Marie thought, to have sank to being the wife of a common tobacco hand!

"And this is my husband, Prince Junior."

Queen Marie started as a tall dignified man entered the room, looking for all the world like the best in Queen Marie, and all that she had
worshiped, adored.

You look like a world
to me
like the mountains of Abarim
my sorrow
like John the beloved's
sea of glass like crystal
my tears
you look like the Venus
of a cloudless heaven
radiant as rubies
my passion
my joy

"Dis here Miz Queen Marie Fields, an' dass her lil' grandbaby."

Prince Junior smiled with recognition—of the name, not the woman.
"Well, look here!" he exclaimed, smiling broadly at Queen Marie and offering a large, work-toughened hand that reminded her of cured tobacco.
"Dis here Vyda Rose mama," he revealed to his wife, who nodded,
mouthing a silent and thoughtful "Oh!" and turning to regard Queen
Marie with a knowing look, an evil, judging look, Queen Marie thought,
as if Prince Junior's revelation had clarified something about Queen
Marie that Suzanne had been struggling to discern, something nasty and
shameful, cause for nausea and distaste.

"Hah you?" Queen Marie inquired politely of Prince Junior, ignoring his wife, recalling a supply shed at the edge of the woods, and a night long ago; tempted to smile coquettishly—but she was not a girl anymore. She was a tired woman, heavy and haggard, her heart filled with regrets.

Prince Junior laughed suddenly as the baby caught his attention. "I reckon dass Vyda Rose lil' gal, ain't it? She a cute lil' thang. Ain' she a cute lil' thang?" he asked his wife, who did not respond, only regarded the child without interest, her mouth set in a thin line. But Prince Junior had not looked at her. His face became solemn. "We was so sorry to get the news 'bout Vyda Rose. We all loved her. She was a sister to us."

Queen Marie looked down at her feet. There was a long silence. Prince Junior sank into the uncomfortable couch beside Queen Marie. Suzanne stood near the beloved curtains. Prince Junior's forehead puckered as if in concentration, and Queen Marie took his hands in hers, not stopping to consider the appropriateness of her action. Suzanne glared at them, unnoticed by the pair as they shared in their common grief for several moments. "She wanted you to have this chile," Queen Marie finally blurted. It was not the explanation she had prepared. This meeting was not what Queen Marie had envisioned. But Prince Junior nodded, almost absently, certainly not alarmed. Suzanne remained mute, watchful from her place near the window.

It had taken Queen Marie some time to collect herself, and her granddaughter, and to give the child away; this child who was all that remained of Vyda Rose, the only legacy that Queen Marie could claim. She looked up at Suzanne, whose eyes had softened somewhat, thinking, Queen Marie felt, that the child was, after all, a child, and innocent, in need of training in uprightness—if she was to be the kind of woman, Queen Marie thought dolefully, that she had herself expected to be.

Queen Marie hugged the child tightly, until she began to squirm, then wiped a tear from her eye as Suzanne took the baby without a word. One of the children, or perhaps a breeze from the hallway behind the room, closed a door gently. No one spoke in the darkened room for a long time. Then, Suzanne spoke softly.

"You come on by and see 'bout us sometime—" A signal to Queen Marie that she should go, and leave the baby, becoming a caller, an occasionally passing shadow, in the little girl's life.

INEZ, NORTH CAROLINA

JULY, 1904

Lately, Queen Marie's vision seemed to be failing. She was thirsty a lot, and given to frequent urination. A yellowish cast tinged her skin, and an acrid, metallic odor settled on her breath. She slept a lot, and woke to strange noises. The house seemed to rock and sway, with a life and will of its own.

She began to attend church, not out of an interest in finding God, but to fill the lonely spaces in her heart created by the absences: of Fields, of Vyda Rose. Uncomfortable with silence, Queen Marie had never learned to be with herself.

Sometimes, she visited her grandchild, telling her stories of her mother's life, not hoping that the child understood, but hoping that this repetition of history would keep Vyda Rose alive. But the ever watchful Suzanne always lingered in the doorway or behind the chair where Queen Marie sat with her grandchild on her knee, making Queen Marie feel like an unwelcome guest, an intrusion upon the proper rearing of a child who was to become a lady.

Most days, Queen Marie felt as though she might as well die, of use to no one, not even herself. She drank incessantly, until she had to drink, and her days became less than a blur, her life an ongoing stupor, punctuated with periods of sleep and hallucination. She visited the witch, telling herself that she had come to effect a blessing upon her grandchild, a shield for her against Suzanne's cunning and arrogance, protection from the venom of her contempt.

But when she arrived at the clapboard house, the sorceress chastised her with a penetrating yellow stare, until Queen Marie was shamed to tears. Falling into a straight-backed chair, she sobbed and muttered incoherently. The sorceress watched from her own chair across the small battered table, patient but uncaring.

The sun set. It rose again. Queen Marie could not recall sleeping. But she awoke with her head resting on the table, to find the sorceress still sitting, still and silent. Queen Marie noticed that the sorceress did not blink, had never blinked in Queen Marie's presence, the yellow eyes phosphorescent and hard as marbles.

It was rumored that the sorceress had lived since the beginning of time. Queen Marie shifted nervously in the hard wooden chair. Others said she had come to be two centuries ago, the product of a white man and a conjure woman from dark Africa. It was said that she had run a brothel, where devil-children were schooled into magical whores, their services phenomenal and costly.

It was said that she knew all things. This, Queen Marie believed with all her heart.

"You brought it on yourself, you know," the sorceress told her without speaking. "You and your helplessness, your selfish greed."

Queen Marie felt defenseless. "But nobody told me—"

"Your mama told you. You shoulda heard her actions, not just her words. Sister showed you. All you ever needed to know, you knew. And you still ain't come yet to faith. You never will."

Queen Marie closed her eyes. They ached, as if heavy weights were pressed against them. She saw Vyda Rose, a teenager. Vyda Rose had been here several times, desperate and afraid, her face the face of an ancient woman. Queen Marie shook her head; but she saw Vyda Rose's babies, rudely ejected, unequipped for survival, into a world that did not want them, a world they did not want. She saw their bodies lifted from the hard, wooden floor of this room—

"I fault you for that," the sorceress said.

—and buried in the soil of Queen Marie's heart. She had not known that Death was there. She had not known of the babies. Her heart bled. She felt her tears becoming a sea. She felt a tugging, as if she was drowning, the sea opening up to swallow her.

She wished that it had been her.

But it had not been her. And now it was too late.

"Help me," she begged, as the waves began to lap at her chin. Couldn't the sorceress see that she was drowning in tears and the blood of her granddaughters?

"I can't help you," the sorceress answered, her face stone. "You will have to help yourself."

And the sorceress left the room. Her body remained upright in the straight-backed chair, her eyes fixed upon her guest. But Queen Marie knew that she was gone, as surely as she knew that she had just conversed with the devil, without once opening her mouth.

"You selfish ol' hag!" Queen Marie screamed aloud. "You took my Prince from me! You took him! You killed my Fields and my baby, and you took my grandbabies away! You hateful ol' woman! I know where you come from! I know you come from hell!" Her throat felt constricted, aching and raw. The waters receded. She got up to stumble blindly out the door, past the church where the voices of young women much like herself had urged her to grace, but she had not heard; past the home of her mother, and the woods where she and Prince had first made love, changing irrevocably the course of her life, setting her feet upon a quest to find her calling in another, her affections upon a false and wooden god, the gifts of her heart, her spirit, and of her hands hidden, unknown to her daughter, and to *her* daughter.

Queen Marie began to run. She would share the gift. The child would not understand, but Queen Marie would share it now, while there was breath in her body, and inspiration in her soul. She turned abruptly to cross the road. She never saw the truck coming. She heard the horn, her calling to another plane.

A blue-gray transparence enveloped and absorbed her. She was aware that she was lying down, aware of a light weight resting upon her body. She was aware of her neck, that she could not move it. She wanted her granddaughter. She wanted to die.

There were people—somewhere. She heard hushed voices in conver-.

sation. She wanted to move. She wanted to die—though not in any tragic way. She wished no ill upon herself. She simply wished her life to end, quietly here, in this blue-gray transparence, where no one would notice and hushed voices would continue in conversation. She wanted the world to end, the tragedy of living erased, having never been. What was the point, anyway? She wanted the curtain called, her life a mere satire on something meaningful and real.

She thought that she was dozing. Her mother appeared, shaking her head sadly. Queen Marie reached for her grandchild, who did not recognize her. Suzanne was there, a serpent spewing venom; and Prince Junior, without judgment. She felt profoundly the absence of Prince; but Sister, who had neither needed nor wanted him, was there to testify to this. Queen Marie understood her now, and understood her own error. She wished, now, to die peacefully.

But the child would live, and Queen Marie would live within her. Queen Marie saw her, a toddler, a precocious child, a confident teenager, a woman unafraid of fear, unafraid of her Self. Queen Marie would live within her, all her genius dormant, preserved for posterity.

chapter 9

> *Because he hath set his love upon me . . . because he hath known my name.*
> —*Psalm 91:14*

it was December, and cold. Jewell hesitated for a moment before raising the knocker on the great Gothic door and letting it fall with a single, clamorous *clack.*

She seemed apprehensive, the man was later to tell her, holding her buttonless coat closed around her ample figure. He noted the slender, tarnished ring that encircled the fourth finger of her left hand, before his eyes moved back to the woolen coat, and down to her large feet clad in army-issue boots.

"Do come in," he said. "You must be freezing. May I take your coat? Please have some tea." He motioned toward the cherry buffet which held a silver teapot and silver-edged cups. Her eyes widened and he realized she was actually quite young, perhaps not yet twenty-five.

"Please," he said. "Sit down."

"Yessir," she barely whispered, and lowered her thick black lashes in a manner no doubt intended as deferential, but unintentionally coquettish. She offered him a brief nervous smile, revealing a deep dimple in one plump cheek, and moved hesitantly toward a stiff chair that stood before a blazing fireplace. Perched primly on the edge of her seat, she glanced up at him expectantly as he filled a silver-edged teacup from the pot.

"Cream or sugar?" He turned to face her and found her staring at him, her mouth agape. She really was lovely, he noted, in that way some Negro girls are lovely, her skin brown and clear as maple syrup and her eyes as large and luminous as twin full moons. There was about her an innocence, though a Negro girl of twenty-five, he thought, must certainly be far from chaste; an amazement—perhaps with the opulence of her surroundings, he realized, envisioning the shanties in which the Negroes lived.

"Sugar," she said abruptly when she realized she had been staring.

He was aware that his actions, in treating her as his guest, were causing her some discomfort. "Sugar," he repeated. What a fitting name that would have been for his new employee had their relationship been less formal, more . . . personal. It certainly suited her, he thought, better than—what was her name again?

She smiled suddenly and disarmingly, a smile as broad as a cane field and as blissful as a honey bee; sweet and lingering, like molasses from the icebox in a warm kitchen on a cold, cold day. His own aristocratic, clean-shaven face came within an arm's length of hers as he carefully presented the steaming hot teacup to her. She accepted gratefully, holding the teacup tightly with all ten of her cold, pudgy fingers; and puckering her full lips softly, she leaned forward and kissed the hot tea gently with her breath, her blackened eyelashes resting on her cheeks, her breasts falling, then rising as she took in another breath and opened her eyes. She did not seem surprised to find him still standing, leaning toward her with his arm extended. She smiled again, and he drew away from her with an exaggerated clearing of his throat.

Still standing, he began to babble. Duties. Wages. Working hours. She lowered her head, turned her incandescent eyes up toward him, nodding her comprehension. She assumed that there was no wife, and that she would answer only to him. She recalled stories, whispered around outhouses and kitchens, of lonely white men venting their passions on Negro women, and quickly dismissed the thought. She was a married woman, respectably immune to the hackneyed image that had plagued Negro women since the tobacco-filled days of chattel bondage and sexual servitude.

He was done, at last, with his litany of details they had spoken of the week before, when her predecessor, an ancient Negro woman called Mae, had announced her retirement from his service and gone to live with nieces in New Jersey. She knew that the old woman had kept a clean kitchen, but asked to inspect it and her room. He obliged with ceremony, pointing out where Mae had kept her cast-iron pots and large iron tub; how to operate the wood-burning stove; the time at which he took breakfast and tea. Her room was a tiny alcove beneath the sloping eaves of the attic. He was apologetic in explaining Mae's wish to remain in the attic even after the boys were grown and had moved away, and suggested that perhaps she would like to sleep in one of the larger better-insulated rooms. No, really, the boys were long married and off on their own, and it really would be no trouble if she chose one of their rooms. In fact, he insisted. "Just choose one."

She chose the smallest room, farthest from the master bedroom with a door that led out onto a balcony. She had dreamed of a room like this but never hoped to have one.

Not even as a servant in borrowed quarters.

Henderson, North Carolina

June, 1931

The early days of Jewell's tenure as maidservant passed without incident. He was kind to her, and gentle when his eggs were slightly overcooked or his collar was not pressed just so. He would talk to her in the evenings, making awkward conversation across the great chasms of race, caste, gender, and power that separated them, as she dusted, polished, and attempted, tactfully, to discourage conversation. Oblivious to her lack of interest, or perhaps mistaking her curt "yessirs" and "nosirs" for respectful restraint, he would ask her opinion on matters that she supposed were of concern to white people. She rarely had an opinion, or knew what to say, or how to say it diplomatically.

Occasionally, he would make her have lemonade or tea with him when she served him on the porch. These interviews were agony for her. Had she possessed the vocabulary and dared to be impertinent, she might have pointed out to him, as he seemed to forget, that she was a Negro, and far too much about the business of her own survival, and that of her children, to trouble herself with philosophical abstractions; that she only wanted to be left alone in the evenings to rest her weary feet and that, by the way, another night or two off to be at home with her children would be nice. That was her opinion. But then, she would look at his long, equine face, so intense as he droned on and on in his clipped, Yankee locution, and feel badly for him and for her unkind thoughts. He paid her generously for working all day and attending to his comfort into the night, drawing his bath and serving him warm milk, and listening to the prattle of a lonely man too far removed, in distance and in time, from the company of a family he loved and longed to share these evenings with.

And he was *gentle* toward her, she reasoned one early evening in late winter as she polished the mammoth piano that dominated the dining room. It had belonged to his late wife, and he cherished it. Sometimes, his eyes became glassy as he gazed at the piano, recounting to her some story of his wife's adventures as a concert pianist. These open displays of emotion, coupled with his genuine concern for her, were a distant departure from the gruff and hardened dispositions of the men in her life: her father, loving when she was a child, but stubborn and, as she reached adulthood, withdrawn; her adolescent boyfriends, groping and insensitive; her husband, unkind, unloving, and uncaring, unreachable and immovable despite her efforts to please him. It had been a long time since someone had been *gentle* toward her. Lord knows, she admitted to herself with a sigh, sometimes her children's shrieks and the crude demands of her husband made her want to run; run far away and be *free*. Sometimes she wanted to be a girl again. She paused, held the dust cloth over the gleaming grand piano, and studied her reflection in the rich, polished wood. She wanted desperately, sometimes, to be a girl again, protected and diminutive in her father's arms; to believe that no peril could befall her in his arms.

She wanted to be held, as she had been as a girl, beneath the lattice church steps in a blackberry patch, where a thrill had coursed through her small body, carrying with it the promise of something else: something richly delicious and satisfying, like bowls and bowls of chocolate tapioca, or soft, ripe melon eaten with abandon, its sweet, sweet juices dripping down her chin. She wanted someone to soothe her with soft sweet words and make her feel . . .

Precious. Dear. She stared for a moment at her callused hands, her belly, round and sagging from too many babies and too little attention to herself. Her eyes came to rest again on the reflection of her face, worried, beleaguered by the strain of being giver, caretaker, provider—too many things, and to too many others. She had never been tended to, had never received the promise, made beneath the church steps, of sweetness and *life*.

She sank heavily onto the piano seat. An early evening breeze, slight but insistent, stirred the branches of the oak tree outside the dining room window. She thought she felt it around her ankles. In the living room, the fire chuckled softly in the fireplace. It made her think of the wood-burning stove in the old church near the creek where she had been baptized. Her fingers found the ivory keys. They picked out a tune.

Take me to the wa-a-ter . . .

Absently, she began to hum the second line:

Take me to the wa-a-ter . . .

Tears came to her eyes, startling her. Why in heaven's name was she crying? And with so much work to do! She meant to jump to her feet and resume her chores; but her body would not obey her mind's command. A lump formed in her throat. She swallowed with difficulty. Without rising, she clutched the dust cloth and began polishing, *scrubbing* the shining wood, her teeth clenched, her knuckles nearly white. Youth and innocence had toyed with her, hinting at a glimmering kingdom come, and saddling her instead with a sorrow and bitterness so intense that she could taste it. Tears began to trickle down her cheeks. "Do you play?" he asked.

She jumped up from the piano seat and turned to face him. He was standing in the shadow of the doorway that led to the living room. Hastily, she wiped the tears from her eyes, but it was too late. Boyish elation turned to concern as he saw that she was crying.

"Sugar? Is something wrong?" He moved a step toward her, and the sloping, horselike planes of his face caught the light from the lamp across the room. In them, she saw tenderness, caring. It was almost as if, she thought for a second, he felt the pain and disappointment that she felt but could not explain; but in truth, even if she could explain, he could never understand.

None but the ri-ighteous . . .

Baptized in privileged, patriarchal whiteness, he did not know the bitter gall of toiling thanklessly, each moment fighting for one's very survival and that of others. He did not know the sting of discovering the loss of one's innocence, unjoyously, and long after it has passed, finding all your expectations disappointed, the promise unfulfilled. He did not know the heavy burden of needing, the futile *wanting* of things unreachable and unknown. He did not know that he had called her Sugar. The planes seemed to soften before her eyes. She sniffed, rubbed her nose with the back of her hand, a gesture he found puerile and endearing. "Not really," she replied, in answer to both of his questions. It moved her that he thought of her that way: sweetly. He did not even know that he had called her Sugar.

Henderson, North Carolina

December, 1931

Today she came bearing her usual large purse, filled with he could not imagine what, and a child of perhaps six years, the small head resting on her shoulder, wrapped in a woolen scarf. Plump arms and legs seemed to stick out in all directions, awkward and restless from the nearly two-mile walk that brought her mother to the house on Chestnut Street each Monday morning. Watching her from the window of his parlor, he shook his head in disbelief. It was a pleasant morning, warm for December. Still, he worried about her predawn treks to work, and had offered more than once to drive her.

He rose from his chair in the parlor and hurried out to meet her. Jessie, she announced as he took the child in his arms, was under the weather. He looked at her questioningly and was startled when the child's forehead, burning with fever, brushed his neck. She had had no choice but to bring the feverish Jessie with her to work. She hoped that he did not mind if Jessie slept quietly upstairs this week while she went about her chores. "She a good chile. She won't give no trouble."

"Of course not," he said. "But shouldn't she see a doctor?"

"Oh, naw," she replied with a wave of her hand. "It's just a touch of the fever. She gits that sometimes."

Supposing that she knew about these things, he carried the child inside and placed her gently across the bed in the upstairs room with the balcony. The child stirred and muttered incoherently. Watching her remove Jessie's coat and calm the fretting child, he was moved, as he often was, by the efficiency and grace of her capable hands. Feeling awkward and unhelpful, he asked if there was something he could do.

"Why, yes," she replied, glancing upward to smile at him. "You can bring up some ice water and a couple of glasses." He nodded obediently and started toward the door. "And some aspirin," she added. "I'm almost out."

"What does your husband do?" He rocked slightly in the old, creaking rocker, trying to appear indifferent to her response, as if making polite and obligatory conversation. In truth he was concerned. Jewell was wary. Jessie had been asleep in the room with the balcony for most of the day. His casual *what does your husband do* had really been a worried *is there enough money to see a doctor?* She did not care to discuss with her employer any aspect of her life other than her employment. But she appreciated his concern. She smiled at him from her seat on the porch swing and did not answer immediately. She had come to regard him with genuine affection in the months since he had found her crying and called her Sugar.

"Jessie will be jes fine," she said, glancing away from her mending to give him a knowing and reassuring look, "and she don't need no doctor." He responded with a brief sheepish grin. They returned to the comfortable silence that had replaced his earlier attempts at conversation. He rocked. She mended. They listened to the crickets.

Jessie tossed restlessly in her borrowed bed.

Night had fallen, and moonlight spilled through the knotted limbs of the oak tree outside the window, casting shadows like long, dark fingers across the bed in the upstairs room and Jessie's ravaged face. *Jessie?* he had asked her. *Not Jessica?* She had looked at him in surprise. She had never noted before the care that white folks took to give their children lengthy, pretentious names, only to shorten them later in the interest of brevity and practicality. Always Joseph, William, or Patricia Ann. Never Joe, Billy, or Pattie Mae. *Jessica,* she realized, had never occurred to her. *No,* she had answered him. *Just Jessie.* He inclined his angular head and parted his lips in that way that she had come to recognize as inquiring. *Jessie,* she explained, *was named after my husband's mama,* who had died, she was convinced, of exhaustion; overworked, used up, and begging, if not for love, for sympathy at least. This child, she thought now as she rocked her precious Jessie, she would rescue from that fate. Somehow.

A light sweat had broken out on the child's forehead. Her condition seemed to have worsened since yesterday when, running a slight fever and too sick to go to Sunday evening worship, Jessie had vomited just before bedtime, and fallen into a fitful sleep, interrupted by periods of wakeful restlessness and confusion. She reached again, as she had done at six-hour intervals yesterday and today, for the bottle of aspirin that stood on the night table and, breaking the small white tablet in half, she parted the weary child's lips gently with her finger and deposited the half-tablet on her tongue. The child recovered from her grogginess long enough to accept, almost desperately, a glass of water; then another. Finally, Jessie fell back in her mother's arms, exhausted and relieved.

It broke her heart to see her child so tortured. Perhaps, she thought as she placed the child in the center of the bed, she should take Jessie to a doctor after all. Tomorrow, she resolved as she turned off the light and settled into the large overstuffed armchair to sleep. Tomorrow morning she would take Jessie to the doctor.

The red-gold sun nudged her, gently, out of a restive, uncomfortable sleep. Her neck ached. Her Jessie lay peaceful and content in the center of the bed. Happy that the child seemed rested and not wishing to wake her, she stood and tiptoed to the door, closed it softly behind her, and hurried down the stairway to begin the morning's chores. The child looked better, but still, she couldn't be too safe, she thought as she recalled Jessie's fretful state on the evening before.

When he came down for breakfast, his face was lined with the concern that was causing her, slowly and with near-reluctance, to *see* him: past the blue-green veins that drew a cobweb pattern beneath his transparent skin; past his peculiarities of speech and manner, the myriad eccentricities of whiteness and privilege. And a kinship, at once unfathomable and inevitable, born of kindness, familiarity, and shared humanity, was coming to be. As she studied him, a look of open curiosity on her face, a blood vessel jumped at his temple. It made him appear, in some way, vulnerable, accessible. Slowly, she extended her hand, nearly rising to her toes to touch, gently, the paper-thin, delicate white skin of his temple. For an instant, neither of them moved, her fingertips warm and dry on his moist skin. His hand clasped her outstretched hand, his fingers thin and strong, his grasp firm. She loved this man, she realized without surprise. She wriggled her fingers. The brilliance of her smile startled him, as it always did, and he realized that she could not disengage her hand.

Embarrassed, he released her fingers and watched her turn and move toward the stairs. "Me and Jessie are goin' to the doctor," she announced without turning or breaking her stride. "Would you take us, after breakfast?"

A moment passed before he realized she had spoken. He was noticing her purposeful stride, the determined wiggle of her hips when she walked, the proficiency with which she always went about her tasks, the unconscious passion and, yes, sensuality, that pervaded everything she did. Her words penetrated this reverie, taking several moments for their meaning to register. His throat was dry. He went to the sink and filled a glass of water, swallowing it in several great gulps. *Yes,* he whispered, as her footsteps traversed the floor above. *Yes,* he repeated, although she could not hear his pledge. *I will do for Jessie whatever you need me to do, because she is yours and therefore mine.* The enormity and certainty of this realization filled him with hope and dread, and he reached again for the spigot.

An awful scream, tormented and hoarse, emanated from the upstairs room. The drinking glass shattered in the sink. His heart raced as he hurried up the stairs and down the hallway, then tore in two as he flung open the door to find his domestic and the object of his newfound devotion doubled over on her knees, vigorously and desperately rocking the lifeless Jessie in her arms.

chapter 10

> *For the Lord hath called thee as a woman*
> *forsaken and grieved in spirit, and a wife of youth,*
> *when thou wast refused, saith thy God.*
> —*Isaiah 54:6*

her clients rarely came before dusk, and were even more rarely hesitant or apologetic. Hers was the port of last resort, she often chuckled to herself, a final, desperate hope when human effort proved ineffective and nothing else had worked. So this woman, clad in the modest attire of a domestic, and appearing at lunch time, captured the interest of the sorceress long before she approached the clapboard house surrounded by rye. She had seen, with her spirit's eye, the woman leaving the great Gothic house and slamming the door behind, pondering and vacillating as she walked. The nervous apprehension, the tortuous guilt, recalled another young woman, in another time years before.

This woman was plump, with worried red-rimmed eyes and a dimple in one cheek; a girl with good manners, from a spartan Christian home. Oh, the trivial dilemmas of the moral, the unholy longings of the holier-than-all. The sorceress had known this girl, as she knew most of her clients, and the nature of her dilemma, without asking. But it was such an entertainment to watch the upright squirm on their respectable rear ends at the home of a witch as they whispered confessions of desire, consummated at last. They never meant to, you see. These were not the kind of girls who were *prepared* for these encounters, much less for their consequences.

So she had allowed the plump brown woman to sit down at her table and explain, beginning in a tentative near-whisper that seemed to gain vehemence as her story rushed to a pinnacle and spilled onto the little table in all its garish wickedness. He had been white, this woman's paramour, and apparently a man of some social stature. A caring man, the sorceress sensed, for the girl softened as she spoke of him. Her manner became unaffected, natural, and she answered the sorceress' questions with an unexpected candor.

The woman recounted the story of the tender coupling that had brought her, ultimately, to this place. Her brown eyes pleaded for understanding, as her hands clasped her rotund belly, an unselfconscious gesture, and her eyes filled with tears as she spoke of her Jessie—her dear sweet six-year-old treasure; and of the gentle comfort of his cheek against her tear-dampened cheek, his hands resting on her weary hips.

She had not rested, she recalled, since the day of her loss. Friends had kept a vigil, offering food and bible verses and feeble words of comfort, mumbled uneasily but sincerely.

The Lawd knows how much, jes how much, we can bear.
He works in mysterious ways.
We'll understand it better by and by.

Some sat with her through the night, her grief so weighty, the pain so obstinate, a great mountainous grief here, in her chest, that would not be moved, too stubborn even to allow the tears to fall. Finally, when the last of the sympathies had been expressed, and her Jessie was alone in a cold, dark cavern six feet below the ground, she went to the house with the upstairs room, and sat there for days, staring at nothing in particular, her loss too great for words. As night began to fall, he would stand helpless outside the door, his hands at his sides, his mouth open, saying things, she was vaguely aware. *There was nothing you could do. You do know that. Don't you. Oh, Dear. Don't do this. You do have to grieve, you know. Let yourself. Please. I can't bear to see you . . .*

Some days he held her. She could not recall when this had begun. She had become aware, all at once, that he was holding her, as she expected him to; that he had held her before, had done this, perhaps, for some time. He rocked her gently, reacquainting her paralyzed mind with other times; cherished times of her youth, of tender looks and kindness. Slowly, something inside her had begun to open, like wood lily petals in the noonday sun; like floodgates opening slowly on rusted hinges. He rocked her, until something broke loose and rushed out of her; something soft and warm and flowing as she had always imagined milk and honey flowing.

Their tears flowed freely that night in the upstairs room, his cheek next to hers, his sinewy hands strong, reassuring, holding her firmly as she flowed and flowed beneath him, their bodies, their souls a river, a rhythm flowing into morning and evening and again into night; that great mountain of grief molten like lava, and flowing out of her each night. Jessie, her baby, becoming an angel of light in the memory that he was giving back to her each day in the house on Chestnut Street; her chores, his routine domestic needs forgotten, these moments in the upstairs room bringing her back her Jessie and the promise of blackberry passion, the secret of unbridled joy heretofore unknown to her, but disclosed in all of its unfolding mystery there in the upstairs room where she had lost her child.

And suddenly she knew in the unkempt room of the sorceress that she wanted this baby, wanted badly and at the cost of propriety this tawny child of auburn locks and easy smile and dewy eyes. She clasped her belly. She wanted this child. The brown woman's eyes fell upon the yellow woman and the proffered unmarked bottle of death on the table before her. Suddenly, the spirit of this woman and of death in this room became unbearable to her, and without another word she stood and left the room, closing the door resolutely behind her.

SANDY CREEK, VANCE COUNTY, NORTH CAROLINA

MARCH, 1932

The frost melted and springtime came, bringing with it the hope of warmth, life, and gaiety. And as she went about her chores at the small home she shared with her husband, and at the house on Chestnut Street, performing for both men such services as she felt bound by duty or love to perform, Jewell frequently dropped a basket of dirty linen to rush to the door and spot a hummingbird before it sneaked into a tree hole; or allowed a flatiron to overheat as she rushed to capture two lungsful of cool, rain-drenched air; and a smile of peace and satisfaction would spread across her round face.

It was on such a cool and rain-drenched morning that Eugene first noticed the life that had swelled within his wife. She stood barefoot on her toes in the yard, her round chin raised and her eyes closed, leaning forward slightly. She seemed oblivious to the heavy raindrops splashing red mud around her ankles. For weeks now, he had been sure that Jewell was going mad. And of late, he had noted the dwindling of his usually ample supply of blackberry wine. He had never actually *seen* her pilfer it, or smelled it on her breath. But this exuberance, this newfound love of *life*, was raising new suspicions of his wife.

She had always hummed as she worked, her scrub brush moving across the wooden floor to the cadence of soon-ah-will-be-done-ah-with-the-troubles-of-this-world. Now she sang aloud, sometimes even whistled or leaned a broom against a wall so she could dance a brief jig alone. He felt, at times like this, that she was unreachable, filled with a life force that undermined his tenuous hold on her, and he resented this.

Yet he loved her, in his way. Today, he watched her leaning into the rain and thought of Easter picnics when she had been a girl, cheerful and eager. He was moved with affection for and fear of that girl. Later, Jewell sat silent and unsmiling in a straw-bottomed chair, her dress draped primly over her wide-open knees, towel-drying her woolly hair before the open, pot-bellied stove. Her hands worked deftly and expertly in quick, jerky motions of the towel. He felt compelled to, and so he asked her:

"Do you have a lover?"

Her hands stopped in midmotion for a moment, then resumed their task as she eyed him from beneath the mass of wildly tangled hair. "Do you," she asked, her knowing eyes reminding him of late-night returns to their bed bearing the scent of whiskey and strange women encountered in juke joints and bordellos; silent women, and never mentioned; strangers meeting needs he could not articulate to his wife. He looked away.

"I have many lovers," she answered superfluously, still gazing at him with the knowledge of ages and he thought of the rain kissing her face, the wind running its fingers through her woolly hair; her toes embracing red mud and the look of rapture upon her face as she danced with or without the broom; and he wondered what other lovers his wife had found to replace what they had lost, the dying embers of a passion he had promised and failed, he knew, to deliver, in the face of her righteousness and domesticity and what he presumed to be her contempt toward him and his manifold shortcomings. She laughed, a pleasant, mocking laugh that made him smile with guilt and slink out the back door, her laughter following him into town and haunting him there, relentless and cruel.

HENDERSON, NORTH CAROLINA

APRIL, 1932

She amused him with colored folk mythology of men who could heal and women who could fly. He taught her to make liverwurst and call it pâté, feeding it to him on water biscuits from behind the rocking chair where he sat speaking passionately of the world war; interrupting his frequent discursions by passing glasses of champagne in front of his nose and spilling it playfully down his chest, his soft stomach. He laughed the first time it was blackberry wine that stained his white starched shirt; pâté and blackberry wine on her tongue as she hovered over him, one plump brown leg slung over each arm of his rocking chair. He began, over time, to feel a *merging* with her, even as he wondered when this fellowship would end, and she would leave him to return to her own mysterious world, the one she inhabited with family and friends beyond his Gothic door.

She would someday be lost to him, he knew. This kinship would not, could not last. He loved her profoundly and with desperation, fearful that each sun-filled day with his Sugar would be the last. Each Monday morning he waited anxiously in bed for her to arrive, climb the stairs, and wake him before she made breakfast. Often he caught her as she turned to leave the room, and held her ferociously, breathing deeply the aroma of coconut oil or Dixie Peach®, and holding it deeply, lovingly in his lungs, willing it to enter his veins and fill his heart so that she, some part of her, would always be there with him, even after she was gone. He wanted to *savor* her, preserve the taste of liverwurst and blackberry wine; feel forever the tremor of her voice as she sang spirituals in his ear until he slept, peaceful and content, only to awaken on Saturday morning and find her gone—to that other world that she inhabited and of which he could never be a part.

He asked her of her aspirations. He wanted to imagine in his dotage what she might be doing, and with whom. He wanted a glimpse of the future he felt certain he could not share; needed to know she would be happy and at peace with herself in some industry that gratified her, for he felt certain that this wonder of innocence and discernment was both capable and anointed. He felt certain, as he watched her listen to the moonlight or commune with the magpies, that indeed she would someday fly. It was only a matter of time.

"I think," she told him cautiously and with an embarrassed smile as they lay on their backs in the yard, "I think that if I had my rathers, I would study the clouds." She lowered her lashes and blushed profusely but rushed on. "I would study the clouds, and showers and hurricanes. I would study the mercy and anger of God." She ventured a peek at him from the corners of her eyes. "I know that sounds silly."

"But of course it doesn't," he told her gently. "There are people who do that, you know. They are called meteorologists."

She grinned at him suspiciously and giggled. "No there ain't."

"Yes there are. Meteorologists."

"Me-de-or-ol-o-gist." She repeated the word twice, and tilted her head thoughtfully, meditatively to one side, her expression sober, then grim. "Well. I don't reckon a colored girl like me—well. You know. They wouldn't let me . . ." Her voice trailed off, and for a moment her eyes lost their usual gleam. His heart broke for her, and for the loss of human potential that she represented. "But it's okay," she finally said slowly and evenly, as if to comfort him, or to convince herself that indeed it was okay. "I'll be a me-de-or-ol-o-gist in my heart." She smiled brightly and stood, smoothing her skirt. "And I'll start dinner," she tossed over her shoulder as she started toward the house.

"You really don't have to," he reminded her, as he often did.

But she wanted to. She wanted to make him pot roast with turnips and candied carrots. She wanted to serve him iced tea and sundaes because he had taught her to love and forgive herself, and to appreciate her surroundings. She was not sure how, or what was the relationship between these two lessons, but he had done this: made her recognize her worth and see the beauty of the earth. She had needed him. She no longer did. She desired him the way one desires watermelon and fly swatters in summer. He made her existence *nicer*. She wished him happiness and comfort. She wished to give him these things, even at her own cost.

So when he began to make oblique references to the swelling of her ankles and the occasional morning dyspepsia that drove her to chew mint leaves and drink honeyed vinegar, she needed only to know that he wanted this, that it made him feel pleasure and pride. She knew without basis for this knowledge that this was the outcome of their doing, and she hoped that he would understand this too; but he never asked. As The Day approached he often propped her feet on his lap and leaned over her to massage her belly with olive oil. One night he found the scent of cloves beneath her belly, and paused to investigate this with his tongue.

But the baby came, that night and half the next morning, bringing with her gifts to her father that indebted him forever to her mother: a heightened anticipation of life; a decreased sense of his own mortality; and a shared purpose—their precious baby girl.

The sun did not shine that day, but hid behind a thick and barren cloud, upstaged, the new-again mother was sure, by the light of her new gift of love; for this child's pale narrow face confirmed her mother's knowledge that she had been conceived of love and not of duty. A veil of yellow downy hairs dusted the tiny precious crown. She called the child Amber because she had upstaged the sun. But he called her Clovey, his sweet clove, with a sprinkle of cinnamon embellishing her small round nose, and a sensuous nutmeg mouth so like her mother's. He owed them both. He would never let them go.

SANDY CREEK, NORTH CAROLINA

NOVEMBER, 1932

In the darkness of evening, Eugene watched her as she struggled out of the car. Their children ran barefoot to meet her and to help her unload the squash and bread pudding and yeast rolls she had brought from that house. She handed each child a covered dish or pan and graced each braided head with a kiss. She would keep the children nearby her all evening, he knew, feeding and fussing over them, helping them with homework and the urgencies that childhood imposed upon a mother. She would carefully avoid his eyes until she had put the children to bed with a hug and another kiss. And all the while the baby would sleep soundly, to wake again during the night, giving her the much-needed excuse to leave him alone in their bed while she nursed the weeping child.

He watched her now, as he had every day for over a month, leaning into the gleaming car and carefully removing a bundle of blankets. His hatred toward her boiled. He had assumed that she was his alone to love; indeed, that her dusky skin, thick thighs, and wiry hair were unlovable by anyone other than himself. This child, a foreign thing to him and unlike himself and his wife in more ways than he could ignore, was a mockery and a humiliation to him, as was the gleaming car and the jaunty step with which she approached the house, smiling at the children, stopping on the step to rest the bundle on her knee for a second, and sigh. She looked past him into the house for a moment and he had a fleeting understanding of the enormous will that supported her love for her two families; two lives so carefully and separately maintained, until this child who had failed to darken in the passing weeks; two husbands dutifully attended to. And he had not credited his wife with such indomitability of spirit, had never understood her capacity to love. And even though he knew in his heart that he had failed her in some way, he had assumed that she would endure this in silence, as had his mother, and her mother and, he was sure, her mother and hers.

But he had been fooled. As she brushed past him into their house, he imagined her thighs wrapped around a thick white torso and a bitter taste filled his mouth. *White man's whore,* he hissed. She seemed to freeze, but for only a second, and he was not certain that she had heard. But she looked directly at him that night, for the first time in over a month, as she served him his pigs' feet from a pot, and her eyes narrowed fiercely before they moved again toward the children.

"*White* man's whore?" she muttered later that night as they prepared for bed. "*White* man's whore?" she repeated, her voice rising, then falling as she glanced toward the children's room. "As opposed to being what? A *cullud* man's whore? What good *that* ever done a cullud woman." It was a statement, not a question. They faced each other half-dressed, half-crazed with hate. "You dishonored me when you made me your wife. You near 'bout killed me. Made me think I was nothin' but your slave. You promised to love me," she accused, "and when you couldn't love me, you let me think it was my fault, when all the time you knowed you had nothin' to give me." Her voice caught in her throat. Her anger seemed to subside as she regarded him, *appraised* him, he realized with horror. "You miserable, *miserable* excuse for a man," she said without malice. "*You* had nothing to give." Shaking her head in genuine pity and disgust, she turned away from him and he knew, as he had thought before, that she loathed him. He understood, for the first time, the nature of his failing, and his loss.

He recalled again the girl she had been when he first became aware of her on a Sunday, the Lord's day, she dimpled and vivacious, not yet ten, he, dapper in a hand-me-down suit, holding the door open as she drew near the church, dusting her shabby but carefully polished shoes without breaking her stride as she hurried up the steps, a feat he admired and made mental note to emulate. She had smiled at him, an uncertain smile, genuine and spontaneous. And Eugene's ten-year-old heart had blushed at the tentative beauty of this ordinary brown girl. He had perceived, in a moment of poignancy that was to prove rare, a near-hopeless wish for his approval, to which he imagined she did not feel entitled. She had passed through the church door and slinked shame-faced down the side aisle before he recovered from this comprehension and allowed the door to close, but she turned as she settled into her seat in the deacons' row next to her father, and glanced at him once more. Hopefully? he wondered. He had never been quite sure.

But in that moment at the church door he had seen his mama and his grandmas and his aunts. He had recognized, he believed, in the smile of a girl not yet ten, their hopeful and hopeless look of expectation and defeat, their eyebrows arched as they made quilts and corn pudding, small gifts of love and devotion offered silently and accepted without gratitude by fathers and grandpas and uncles who had offered nothing in return.

He would come to accept, without acknowledging, this love-greed, and to expect it from his wife. And indeed, Eugene had often looked up to find her staring at him expectantly; and he had begun to look away from her, to shrink from her dark and deadened eyes, from the defeat that had become her life with him, appalled at himself.

The furtive glances and silent waiting for thank-yous, for some sign of love or appreciation—when had they ceased? When had his wife stopped begging for his love? She was humming now, tunelessly; unaware, it seemed, and indifferent to his presence. Her mouth curved up in a small self-possessed smile as she climbed into bed, turning her broad back to him, conclusive and dismissive. He hated her, helplessly and diminutively, and derived no satisfaction from his hatred: It was not the contemptuous hate that he had always felt toward women, even those that he loved; it was the sullen, resentful hate of a child powerless to avenge himself against his father, a man against his God. Silently, he turned off the light and, careful not to brush against his wife, lay down to sleep.

On summer days when she was a child, her father had held Jewell high upon his wide, bony shoulders, his hands the color and consistency of cured tobacco leaves. The tobacco fields seemed, back then, to stretch an eternity in all directions. *Their* land, he had said; or at least, *rightfully* theirs. For years his father's family, and his fathers' fathers' families, had worked these fields sun-up to sundown with nary a dime for their labor. By the time she was born, he received a dollar a day for picking and wrapping tobacco, and for hanging it to dry. He seethed as the four coins were placed in his palm, knowing that he and his had earned for their masters the value of this land many times over, unable to throw the meager change at the smug faces of the white trash who "oversaw" these fields and demand what was due him for centuries of labor. Even then, her fat legs dangling over his shoulders, she understood his pride in the land.

And as she grew older she came to understand that this vast field that was theirs was really not, that the dignity in her father's broad shoulders was a dignity born of hard work and an abiding faith in the realness of his birthright: He and his had labored tirelessly and honestly, and these fields, as far as the eye could see, would always belong to him, and he to them.

Pay no mind to what they say, he had often told her as he lifted her from his shoulders to rest her on his hip. *Know who you are, and whose you are, and what is rightly yours.* His eyes would become glossy for a moment as they gazed at the fields. Then he would smile his dimpled smile, the color of tobacco, and tickle her ribs. And Jewell would understand the truth of pride and self-love, and a worth not measured, much less granted, by others.

It was not until she was married, tired, and depleted that she would forget this—her father's legacy to her.

She developed an affinity for dimpled smiles the color of cured tobacco; and large hardworking hands that brushed her calves and tickled her ribs. She had a near-lover when she was almost ten; an awkward and surreptitious encounter beneath the church steps with a skinny yellow boy of fourteen, bashful and adorable, whose shoulders and hands and feet had outgrown him. A stranger to the ardor of a fourteen-year-old boy, she had stood on her toes to kiss his cheek, catching him by pleasant surprise. His eyes surveyed her comely calves and burgeoning breasts and, beside himself, he had pulled her beneath the steps to further explore this, his newfound atlas of the feminine geography. There, he held her tightly until her heart raced and she felt that it would burst at the pleasure of him, the strength of his arms—the arms of a man much like her father—the taste of his sweat, the warm softness of his mouth. The sobering memory of gravely delivered lessons on the lust of the flesh bade her to stop as *something* urged her to surrender and explore this *somethingness*, compelling and forbidden. Breathless, she pushed him away with a force that landed him on his rump. He stared wild-eyed and bewildered as his unwitting teacher turned and rushed away.

It was years before she reminded herself of their adventure beneath the steps—years during which he had courted the pastor's daughter up those very steps and down the off-center aisle to the makeshift altar in modesty and yellowing lace; years during which she had learned: The *thing* that had happened beneath the steps was unspeakable and unthinkable, a cause for shame and secrecy. She kept her head lowered throughout the drawn-out ceremony and did not attempt to catch the bouquet. Throughout her own courtships and until her own wedding night, she dared not try to recapture the *thing* reserved to euphemism and restraint. And then she was married and maternal, and the *thing* had not yet reappeared, leaving her wondering and hopeful and disappointed, a field unripened, harvested before its time.

By the time he told her she was beautiful, she had known this for years. Hers was not the embellished, assertive beauty of moving picture stars, or even the delicate, enchanting loveliness of her mother and sisters. Hers was an earthy, elemental beauty that had caught her father's heart and held it captive—she, not her saccharine sisters, was his favorite, his matrilineal and kindred spirit, familiar and ancient and beautiful.

Daddy's brown baby, he had called her, even when her legs became long and voluptuous, and when young men came to call. *Daddy's brown baby,* in those silent moments as they walked through the fields, their arms loaded with wide green leaves, sweat beading their brows and soaking the bandannas they wore around their heads. *Daddy's brown baby,* as he shook his head in mock pity at her pathetic pile of tobacco leaves— Daddy could pick tobacco like three men—and smiled his infectious smile. And she would grin like the small child he could make her become with the smile and embrace of his words.

So she had learned, by the time she reached sixteen, to accept praise with quiet confidence, and with none of the hunger that Eugene had come to expect, had thought he had detected, for only a moment, in a shy girl nearly ten. A bridled passion lay behind her clear-eyed, direct stare, unsubtle and unabashed, and she acknowledged his compliments with a nod. She did not say thank you, only nodded slightly and lowered her lashes, but not in modesty. In thought, perhaps? Thinking, he understood, was something she did often, deeply, and well. She knew that she was beautiful and, he suspected, her thoughts were beautiful, too. *Talk to me,* he begged her, and smiled. She smiled, too, and talked to him, staring out across the tobacco fields, twirling a dandelion stem absently as she spoke, and ideas seemed to flow from her like water from the rock of Meribah, like prophecy in an unknown tongue: the insight of ages spoken in the cadence of a country girl of scant education and humble circumstance, in the simple speech and unaffected manner of a Negro girl unaware of her own genius. She spoke of the earth and its gifts, the accessibility and communality of nature, the prevailing concept of personal property as synthetic and, possibly, wrong. The earth was owned, she reasoned, only by those willing to be owned by it. *Doesn't that make sense,* she queried, casting at him a sidelong glance. *The 'bacca fields are ours,* she continued without waiting for his response. *They belong to us, all of us who have worked and sweat and bled in them.*

And made love and gave birth in them, she dared not say aloud. She picked a new dandelion and gently stroked its delicate head with her forefinger. He did not speak. She continued. *White folks don't understand, do they?* She did not look up at him. He shook his head. She had not asked if *he* understood. She assumed that he did. He appreciated her confidence in him, although it was misplaced; and he held her, wanting to absorb and consume her, to engage in and share her in a way that he could not put into words.

So he asked her to marry him instead. And she said yes because she understood him to be offering her *somethingness,* and because in her world this was all there was, and yes was the thing to say: yes to belonging to and with. They were to marry next spring at the small white church, but she changed her mind and asked him to meet her in the tobacco fields on Valentine's Day. And the preacher married them there in the presence of their families, in the fields that she and the ancestors loved.

She thought he understood her, and for a while he behaved as though he did. So she settled into his home and waited for something to happen. She waited through planting and harvests as babies and more babies sucked her breasts and took parts of her away, their greed and neediness draining and straining her, causing lines to appear on her once hopeful face as spirit and vigor and curiosity left her, leaving in their place a dulled precocity and absence of will.

He took, too, giving, but taking and taking. No one had ever taught Jewell to be selfish, so she kept on giving, hardly noticing the selfishness of her family, barely missing her former joy, and finally, not missing it at all. She thought of Santa at Christmas, and the fairy when a child lost a tooth. She thought only rarely of the fantasy departed, the thing that she had missed; only when he rolled off of her and onto his side to smile at her; and she smiled back, damp and only slightly uncomfortable and thinking it would hurt his feelings if she got up to clean up and dust herself with starch. And she did not allow herself to miss it, that thing that she had once thought existed, but had since then come to disavow.

He had intended to leave. In fact, he had gone, briefly, on a three-day pilgrimage of self-pity and mental and moral sadomasochism. He had not been particularly missed. The children were accustomed to his absence, and his wife had been prepared for his inevitable departure. He had come back a changed man, chastised and full of self-realization. This was not apparent to his wife, who seemed to be holding her breath as they passed each other in the small house. He supposed that she expected a violent upbraiding, a volcanic and inebriated eruption of the rage he had presumably nurtured with bottles of corn whiskey for the past three days.

But Eugene had returned repentant, not enraged; and while he would never relish the small pink reminder of his wife's betrayal, he recognized his own role in bringing it to pass. He would maintain the peace in his home in penance for his own sin, and for the sake of the wife he had defrauded.

Her expression was one of surprise when she saw the peace offerings he had arranged on their bed: several yards of hunter green velvet from the piece goods store, and a bottle of lilac perfume he had purchased from a vendor on the road home. She did not smile or thank him for these things. Of the fabric, she fashioned for him a fine green robe that covered him to his shins. Herself, she doused in perfume. And life continued to live itself in their home.

HENDERSON, NORTH CAROLINA
OCTOBER, 1939

> *. . . The fathers have eaten a sour grape,*
> *and the children's teeth are set on edge.*
> *—Jeremiah 31:29*

Each year she was a pumpkin.

Her mother had made her an elaborate pink tutu the year that she was six. Her father had bought her tights and ballet shoes. Clovey was confused. Last year's ensemble had impressed itself upon her. She had thought herself a pumpkin. Her bottom lip trembled. Tears of confusion and loss filled her large brown eyes as she recalled the tent-like orange dress and black tights she had worn last year from house to house as patronizing white people filled her bag, and her sisters' and brothers' bags, with candy corn and butterscotch stick candy, fruit and nuts and an occasional silver coin; the half-pumpkin mask, fastened at first to her head with twine, then carried proudly in her arms as the evening progressed and the mask became uncomfortable; its squarish nose and half-moon eyes carved lovingly and perfectly, the mouth a painful smile that looked to Clovey like the mild unnamed discomfort she had lived with her whole short life; like the subtle nausea that no remedy had suppressed.

Trick or treat
smell my feet
give me something good to eat

She had thought herself a pumpkin.

Her parents decided to indulge her. The tutu was set aside for a time. It would come in handy later, when her father—her very own, special father—would insist that she take up ballet. Her mother would insist to him that her sisters do the same; even though they were not special girls like Clovey, whose special father had somehow bestowed upon her the specialness that Clovey loved and loathed. She had cherished and borne this specialness since she was four, and Aunt Suzanne had excluded Clovey from the family portrait. Images of that day would blur at the edges as Clovey grew older, but she would often see that portrait in the home of her Aunt Suzanne, and she would never forget that it had changed her life forever.

It had been Easter Sunday, and Clovey's mother, whose work with needle and thread had become renowned, had outdone herself this time: Clovey and her sisters were resplendent in outfits differing only in size; yellow gingham jumpers worn over crisp white cotton blouses, with yellow gingham ribbons decorating their pale straw hats. There had been an undercurrent of excitement as the girls were oiled and pressed that morning. A picture would be taken before dinner at Aunt Suzanne's, a portrait to include the entire Yarborough clan: Mama, and Papa—the Papa that Clovey shared with her siblings—dapper in a coat and tie; Clovey's sisters and brothers; her aunts and uncles and cousins; Great-Aunt Lilly and -Uncle Horace. Even the reclusive Great-Grandma Sister would be present for the occasion, the matriarch ancient and mysterious to Clovey, and almost never seen. To Clovey, this was just as well. Great-Grandma made her squirm, as many adults did; but Great-Grandma, in particular, with her fixed stare both void and full of a knowledge recognizable and frightening, even to a four-year-old.

And Aunt Suzanne. Clovey had noticed her, as she had noticed Clovey, that Sunday after church. Clovey had been standing with her three sisters, arranged in descending order of height, accepting compliments as bonneted heads bobbed their approval of Mama's handiwork. The yellow gingham jumpers in four varying sizes had stolen the show this Easter morning; and Clovey, the smallest and most darling, was the star of that show. Accustomed to, though still shy of, the attention of others, Clovey had smiled humbly and lowered her head, occasionally peeking from beneath the straw brim to appreciate the attention that she was receiving.

But once, she had glanced upward to meet the attention of her aunt, a look upon her face that Clovey could not interpret. The look passed, but Clovey had experienced, not for the first time, that vague feeling of discomfort in the pit of her stomach. She would feel it again as the day wore on.

There was a sprawling oak outside the house where Aunt Suzanne lived, where Mama had once lived, its branches expansive and glorious at the foot of a grassy incline toward the road. The family had gathered beneath it, children in front, boys kneeling, girls standing, their shoulders turned inward toward the center of the gathering. Clovey, the smallest child, had been positioned in the center, uneasy on Great-Grandma Sister's bony lap, when Aunt Suzanne had spoken:

"You know, she ought not to be there."

Clovey had looked up, twisting in her uncomfortable seat to see who had been spoken of. Her eyes had fallen first upon her mother, who had stiffened noticeably, her smile congealed. Then they had fallen upon her aunt, whose eyes were upon Clovey, staring hard and mean. To her horror, in fact, the entire gathering had stared at her, and a hush had fallen over the crowd. All motion had ceased.

"She really ought not to be sittin' there." Aunt Suzanne had repeated, and her jaw had taken on a stubborn set. Beside her, Aunt Lilly's face had registered horror and dread, and her eyes had shifted anxiously from Clovey to Mama.

Clovey would recall forever the look of pain and anger, the weariness and age on her mother's face as she had turned woodenly toward Aunt Suzanne.

"What did you say?" she had asked, as if the dreadful statement had not been made twice. Her voice was not the voice of Clovey's mother, the gentle, loving, scolding voice that Clovey had come to recognize as Mama's. It was a croaking, rasping voice; unpleasant and cold. It was a voice as hateful as a field rat frozen stiff and defiant in the privy one frigid winter, when Clovey had sought to use it in the middle of the night, its paws curled into weapons poised eternally for attack.

Aunt Suzanne had twitched nervously at this voice—it was one that she had never heard in all the years of mothering, adequately if not affectionately, this child adopted as a baby and now become a woman, spawned in iniquity, confirming the hereditary nature of wickedness. But Aunt Suzanne had stared back at her, defying Satan, daring her sometime daughter to attempt to defend her transgression.

"This is a *family* portrait," Aunt Suzanne had said, lifting her chin and squaring her shoulders. The two women had faced each other for a child's eternity, time suspended, and Clovey had stood teetering on the precipice of a short-lived simplicity, at four facing the great abysmal depth of enlightenment, guilt, and shame, driven from the Garden of Eden. Her mother's eyes had turned to slits, and her words had slithered out of her like venomous serpents freed from a snare.

"You evil ol' witch. You mis'able ol' bag o' self-righteousness one foot outa yo' grave—"

"Stop it!" cried Aunt Lilly, shocked. "Dass yo' *mama.*"

Great-Grandma Sister began to cackle inaudibly. Clovey could feel her laughter.

"She ain' none o' my mama." Clovey's mother turned on Aunt Lilly, then back to Aunt Suzanne. "You never could stand to see nobody happy, 'specially if happy didn' come like you think it ought. You think I ain' knowed you was judgin' my mama? Now you judgin' my chile. My *chile.*" She turned to face Clovey—bewildered, frightened Clovey—and tears suddenly filled her eyes. She rushed toward the child, the tears spilling onto her cheeks, and gathered Clovey in her arms, muttering all the while between clenched teeth. "Like you ain' got da res' o' yo' life to be dealin' wit' other folks' 'pinionatin' . . . she gotta start tearin' you down 'fo' you even big enough to understan'." She turned toward the speechless crowd. "Come on ya'll. We leavin' dis place—" and she started up the hill toward the wagon that had brought her here, her husband and children trailing behind her. "You is ev'ry bit much part o' dis family as anybody else, and don' let nobody tell you diff'rent . . ."

But the damage was done. The child's mind, already sharp and perceptive, had begun to assimilate facts and to draw unpleasant, if tentative, conclusions: She was different, hence her yellow-orange skin, red hair, "extra" father, and the vague discomfort that had persisted from her earliest recollection. She began to understand, on the most intuitive level, the source of that discomfort. Tossed furiously about in her mother's arms with each jolting step, she looked beyond her mother's shoulder, down the gentle slope toward her father—the one she shared with the others, the brown-skinned, round-faced, kinky-haired others. He regarded his feet as he walked, his hands in his pockets, and although she could not hear him, he appeared to Clovey to be whistling. She stared hard at him, tears stinging her eyes; but he did not look up, and she realized that he looked at her mother rarely, if ever, and never in all her recollection had he regarded Clovey directly at all. Her stomach began to churn. Her lip trembled. She hugged her mother's neck and began to hiccup and sob as she tried to express her confusion and shame; but all she could manage as they reached the wagon was:

"Mama why come . . . wh- wh- why—"

Clovey's mother placed one foot on the wagon, shifting Clovey from her shoulder to her knee, and looked into the pained, tear-streaked face for a long time. And as the others cleared the hill, she wiped that face and kissed it hurriedly. "You's *special*," she said earnestly, her eyes affirming the seriousness of her proclamation. "You hear me? Don' let nobody tell you diff'rent."

The pumpkin garb was large enough, and loose-fitting, to accommodate Clovey until she was nine, a thin child, and small for her age. The carving of the pumpkin mask became an annual ritual for Clovey, who demonstrated a level of skill and precision that raised eyebrows. "I carved it myself," she would tell people; and they would smile and say, "You did?" regarding the perfectly shaped symmetrical features so proficiently chiseled—surely not the work of a six-, seven-, eight-year-old child.

But her father—the Daddy uniquely hers—encouraged her. She began to work with wax, carving the shapeless lumps into donkeys and possums, trees and rivers and maps, Mama and Daddy and her teachers. Soon, hardened clay figures began to clutter the mantel above the fireplace at Daddy's house, to overflow from cardboard boxes salvaged to contain the increasingly well-crafted and imaginative figurines.

She finally outgrew the pumpkin gown; but still, she felt herself a pumpkin among the ghouls and witches and demons at Halloween. Pumpkins were benign, never confrontational. Their grimaces bespoke a determination to bear with a smile whatever anguish perturbed them. Always, they were silent; but always, their oddity brought them more attention than they expected, and they crouched behind curtains on windowsills, until someone noticed this and moved them to where they could be viewed from outside, reluctant stars on a stage opening onto the world for all to see.

Her mother made her another orange gown, this one accented with thin black stripes of felt that traversed its length; a longer gown, but not much longer. Clovey would always be short. She would always be slight like her father. As a preteen, she would hope that this would render her inconspicuous, but it would not.

Her two daddies, by this time, had become Daddy and Eugene. Generous, doting Daddy, who indulged and encouraged her to intellectual and artistic pursuits; and frosty, distant Eugene. She did not call him Eugene to his face. She did not call him anything. She established with him a kind of truce, of silent, mutual surrender. Each of them understood and accepted that the other *was*. Occasionally, and for the sake of her mother, she was later to understand, he would force himself to grunt a compliment at her carving or sculpture or sketch. He was never overtly hostile, but that fact, too, was owing to the delicacy of relationships in their home. There was a tension between her mother and Eugene. One false move or unkind word could topple the fragile structure of this tactfully maintained domestic tranquillity. Eugene and Mama shared a bed but lacked the warmth that passed between her mother and Daddy. And if Eugene demonstrated no affection toward his own children, he was yet more detached from Clovey.

Only the children—the other children—seemed oblivious to the suspenseful drama enacted daily in their home. Clovey was their baby sister, and although she did not resemble them, her uniqueness, to them, lay in her status as baby of their family. Yet Clovey remained lonely. Her siblings could not shield her from the taunting of her classmates at the public school for Negro children. So her mother moved them all to a private, Christian school. Later, Clovey had a tutor, who conducted classes daily at her father's house as her mother worked. A dreamy child whose thoughts meandered during science lessons, Clovey doodled at lunchtime and during "recess" while her work was checked for accuracy and comprehension. Once, she drew a girl, a friend, her mother as a child, and called her Jessie. Her father's jaw dropped. Her mother's eyes filled with tears. Even Eugene was moved when her mother showed him the portrait done in charcoal.

And Clovey became aware of the power of art to speak to the heart, to move things immovable. Neither science nor words seemed to hold this power for her, for Clovey could find no words to articulate the turmoil that stirred inside, the cauldron of unanswered questions and unresolved emotion that simmered beneath her mild-mannered facade. But these things radiated from her drawings and paintings, the conflict and irony and tragedy of her family's lives expressed in colors vibrant or subdued. She painted in browns and matte mauves the comfort of being sheltered in her mother's arms. She sculpted from a block of ice Eugene's distance and apprehension toward her. She painted the falsity of Aunt Suzanne's smile. Great-Grandma Sister's vision and intelligence were captured in a pair of finely fashioned disembodied earthen eyes. In clay, she rendered her own internal conflict, limbs and fists and outstretched hands reaching out from a formless, fiery base.

Her father smiled at her. Kindness fairly glowed from a page filled with the sunlight and favor of a gracious god. *Portrait of Daddy* won first prize in a local children's art competition. The judges had not known that the fledgling artist was a Negress. Hasty apology was made and the award withdrawn. They had understood the child to be a resident of Henderson, not merely a student there. *Let it go,* her mother admonished her father, whose face was reddened with embarrassment and seldom-seen anger. Clovey did not understand. She could not appreciate the significance of her loss, and at any rate had little interest in winning. *Portrait of Daddy* found a permanent home above the great fireplace in the master bedroom, replacing a gilded mirror that had been in the family for generations. Later, *Portrait of Daddy* would exceed the mirror in value and prestige.

And Clovey's value would increase in her own eyes, a valid basis for perceiving her own specialness discovered at last, lending credence to her mother's urgent insistence, recompense for her father's confidence in her, and refutation of Eugene's lovelessness, her aunt's muted disdain toward her.

Jessie began again to appear to Clovey, at first vague and nameless. Then with sound and fury, as if relieved from compression, she began to leap from Clovey's charcoal and paint and lead. These appearances were not intentional on the part of Jessie, or of Clovey, who had simply sought to reproduce her mother in a form more accessible to that part of Clovey that needed play without discipline, friendship without obedience. She felt that Jessie was her mother, her sister, her friend—her imaginary playmate, sprung from her pencil. She did not know that there had been another Jessie; that that Jessie was dead. The adults were hesitant to tell her. Her siblings assumed that she knew. And so Jessie grew alongside Clovey to adolescence, her legs stalwart, sturdy; her back straight and strong; in-fused with the strength of spirit that lived only barely within Clovey, weakened there by the presence of progenitors unacquainted with the af-fliction and anguish that demand audacity. Clovey was irresolute, of del-icate constitution. Jessie was her bulwark of strength and self-possession, native to another land, and generations old.

chapter 11

LICKSKILLET, NORTH CAROLINA

OCTOBER, 1946

> *Thus saith the Lord, Set thine house in order;*
> *for thou shalt die, and not live.*
> —*II Kings 20:1*

sister perceived a beckoning from that part of her that was divine; a calling to where her forebears had earlier come, to where her own spirit had yearned for years of Sister's desperate life. Vyda Rose, still stunned by her sudden redemption, was there, as were others like her, atoned for and at peace. Courage and Truth ministered to Sister. She relaxed her grip on something she had not known that she held, easing a tension to which she had grown accustomed. Hers had been a life of seeking, groping. Sister was surprised at how little it all mattered now. She chuckled as she thought of the un-happiness that had darkened much of her youth—and it was all youth, right up until this moment.

The beckoning became an urgency. Sister looked back—at her fam-ily, her life—then inward, to where faith and stillness resided. Her fam-ily would be fine, and her life, over. She would cross over with certainty and peace.

Meticulous preparation had preceded Sister's passing. She had emptied the great black trunks that held the most significant of her belongings, distributing their contents as she had felt led. She had insisted upon setting her own house in order, scrubbing, sweeping, and dusting, her hands stiff, her joints distressed. She had begun to babble, debating with herself issues resolved years before, recounting stories to herself— Lilly had arrived at the old log house more than once to find Sister cack-ling happily, her gray head thrown back, her mouth, still full of teeth, open wide.

She had talked of dying for weeks.

"Shush, Mama. You'll live forever. You know that," Lilly had chided, closing her hands around her mother's brittle fingers, covering the old woman's knees with a quilt as they sat in silence before a fire, or rubbing fatback gently on the parched lips. But Lilly had been con-cerned.

An eventual peace had settled upon her mother, a contentment, even satisfaction, beyond any that Lilly had seen in her before. Sister had dealt long ago with her demons, and reacquainted herself with her own spirit; but she had intimated that these last were the best few weeks of her life. And Lilly had braced herself against the inevitability of her mother's departure.

After all, Sister was a very old woman, Lilly thought as she stroked the slumbering hoary head. She had been blessed to have her mother's presence for so long. The time was nearing. She would have to let go.

The doctor pronounced Sister in good health. But Lilly still worried. Sister insisted that she was dying, willfully, happily. Prince Junior came by most evenings, and sat with Lilly and Sister outside the cabin. He talked desperately and incessantly, about everything and nothing at all, ignoring his sister's withering looks, afraid of the silence so like the grave.

"Let her sleep," Lilly would whisper. "Don't you see she sleepy?" But Prince Junior could see his mother's eyes folded only in eternal sleep, and he was not prepared to face this.

Once, during a short lull in Prince Junior's monologue, Sister began to speak. She cleared her throat, and began again.

"Let me go," she had murmured, startling both Lilly and Prince Junior with the urgency and difficulty of her utterance. It took a moment for the meaning of her words to settle upon them, and Sister reached out to take Prince Junior's hand, her eyes kind, her smile thin and labored. "Let me go. I'm ready. I been ready. I know you's been keepin' me here. But jes let me go."

Prince Junior's face seemed to pucker. There was a moment of silence. And then Prince Junior began to sob—great, heart-rending sobs that shook his body. Lilly rose to take his free hand. Sister placed his head upon her bony lap. And the three cried until the fire died in the hearth, and night overtook the small house, blanketing them all with a deep and merciful sleep.

⁂

The dying of Sister was the death of something else. People gazed at each other questioningly, and finding no answers in each others' faces, they shrugged their shoulders and walked away. Sister's death was the death of something, and the birth of something. They did not know what.

People came from near and far, to the homegoing of the ancient woman who had been a slave. Few of them knew her. Many knew of her. Others had not known of her until her death. But they came, bringing their children and their grandchildren, because they understood that her death was the death of something else, great in consequence and gravity.

The procession extended out the back door of the Bull Swamp Methodist Church. The newspapers arrived to snap her picture as she lay supine and somewhat haughty in a fine mahogany casket—Prince Junior's handiwork, carved from Sister's favorite wood, and polished by her grandsons. She would have balked at all the fuss, insisting that others not trouble themselves. After all, she was an ordinary woman who had lived a less than auspicious life, in a log cabin on someone else's property. She had tried to live quietly and had loved completely, for a time. Her children, as far as she could tell, had been her only offering to the world.

But others knew better. The girls from Shaw and Saint Aug's, their arms filled with flowers for the grave side, tears of awe and loss interrupting the powder on their faces as they leaned over the lustrous casket, knew better. They had not known her. They understood more of her than

Sister might have imagined. She was their mother, and the daughter of their mothers. The death of Sister was the death of all that they had been, the death of all that was honest and despised within them, neither the first nor the last of these deaths. They hoped she had lived well. They hoped that she had triumphed.

chapter 12

clovey struck a match in the near-darkness of the up-stairs room, and touched it to the wick of a beeswax candle. The flame flickered, then settled, as she extinguished the burning match with a flick of her wrist. And Jessie appeared, kneeling before the bed, as was her habit, her chin resting in the hammock created by the dark-skinned sides of her intertwined fingers. Clovey sat heavily on the overstuffed armchair, and the two girls sat in silence, each intent upon her own thoughts.

Clovey had often considered asking Jessie if she was real. They were fourteen now, past the acceptable age of childhood playmates, far ahead of senility. When she was not feeling foolish, Clovey felt blessed to have Jessie, whose silent presence provided Clovey the necessary backdrop for reflection, for facing her fears—fear of reproach, fear of insanity, fear of otherness; and for resolving the discord that still raged within Clovey at times—resolving it, at least, for a time.

She had begun to see herself as gifted and vital and approaching wholeness. Jessie smiled proudly at Clovey, as their mother often did, the energy of Jessie's smile filling and infusing Clovey. She had also begun to suspect that she had inherited a peculiar genius—from Great-Grandma Sister, whose knowing looks had frightened and fascinated her for as far back as she could recall, and whose death had left Clovey with a sense of loneliness for a woman whom Clovey had barely known. The torch had been passed. She had felt this at sunset on the day that Sister had died, also at sunset, sitting on a knoll near the wooded area outside the house in Henderson. Clovey and Jessie had been there since early afternoon, engaged in silent conversation, sharing with each other their feelings rather than their thoughts—Jessie calm and reasonable, Clovey confused and lonely, but less so as Jessie's presence began to soothe her.

Jessie had suddenly sat up and looked at Clovey from her position on the grass. "You feel that?" she had asked, her eyes wide and round.

And indeed, Clovey had felt it, a curious feeling of light and warmth and woe spreading from her stomach in radial waves throughout her body. She had flushed, and Jessie had regarded her knowingly without speaking.

Later, the news of Sister's death had not surprised Clovey. In her mind, she saw the old woman lying on her much-cherished cornhusk mattress, her frail shoulders, stiff, extending from beneath a white sheet that covered most of her body, her mouth open, as if death had sneaked upon her from behind, expected but not this instant, and startled her into surrender, the bright eyes closed in surrender.

The vision made Clovey shudder. A feeling of dread and responsibility made her want to run; but from what? Jessie offered no answers. Clovey began to feel occluded. She carved colored girls in invisible boxes, crouched in corners, standing with their backs against their confines, their hands pressed helpless on invisible ceilings and walls, their faces distorted with pain or fear. She began to run, short distances down the length of the gardens outside Aunt Suzanne's house, then longer stretches across the fields. She felt invigorated. Her legs grew muscular, strong. Jessie nodded approval. Clovey painted winds, ethereal, moving about and into each other confused, but free.

Her tutor began to notice the changes in Clovey's disposition. Less wistful than before, Clovey had become decidedly restless. Her compositions trailed off as their author gazed distracted out the window near the cherry buffet in her father's house. Beyond it, a calm sky stared back at Clovey. Neither spoke. Nothing stirred.

Are you challenged, Clovey? her father was later to ask her. She would be surprised by the question, thinking at first that he referred to the isolation that challenged Clovey daily, and in her father's austere study, Clovey would cry and bewail the confinement that was her "specialness." He would listen patiently and helplessly, as always, his hands hanging limp at his sides, his head bowed in that posture of surrender that seemed to Clovey to humanize him from omnipotent to man: white man, touched by the pain of his dark daughter, pain he could observe but could never understand or erase. Feeling wretched for him, Clovey would dry her eyes and lift her chin. This would comfort him—Clovey's pretense at composure always comforted him; and he would become again Clovey's almighty—advisor, problem solver—her benevolent father, letting there be light.

HIGH POINT SCHOOL FOR GIRLS
HIGH POINT, NORTH CAROLINA
NOVEMBER, 1947

Always a light sleeper, it was Clovey who rose, in the early morning darkness, when he rapped, softly, on the first-floor window, confident that she would hear, even through the din of high winds or clamorous rain, and rise to let him in. Always patient and long-suffering, Clovey lay breathless and still, pretending not to mind the sucking, kissing sounds from the narrow bed across the small room, the sounds of skin against skin, sometimes of giggles and later, moans; his occasional, low, and rumbling; hers more frequent, sultry, and gently coaxing. Clovey stared into the darkness, training her mind upon the downpour outside the window, or on the stillness of the autumn air.

But Shame crept over her, that vague discomfort that had found its name. Her cheeks burned. Her extremities tingled. She longed for her own room at the house on Chestnut Street, where she and Jessie had spent late afternoons, after the tutor had gone, imagining their freedom:

from that house, and the other house; from that town, and the other town; from the Shame of otherness that had plagued Clovey from her earliest recollection. She had wanted to get away. She had gone away, to this.

Sometimes, when they had finished, he would crouch over her on all fours, like an enormous, carnivorous cat, as he withdrew himself. And from her own narrow bed in the thin gray predawn light that had begun to filter through the curtains, Clovey would see his penis, shriveled and unimpressive. He would swing one leg, then the other, over the side of the bed as he stood to put on his trousers. A shock of hair would fall into his eyes as he buttoned his pants, and he would glance at Clovey briefly as he lifted a hand to push it behind his ear.

He would let himself out. Clovey would get up to lock the window.

In the mornings, Clovey would rise first to claim the porcelain bathtub. Otherwise, she had discovered, she would find long, pale hairs clogging the drain; thin hairs that clung to her skin when she tried to remove them; hair tenacious like cobwebs. And when she returned to their room, her skin damp in a long white bathrobe, she would not look at her roommate, whom she knew would be naked and shameless, her dough white back and buttocks facing Clovey as she rifled through her closet, pausing to consider one, then another nearly identical white blouse before selecting one to wear with the required blue skirt, often without bathing. Clovey could not imagine not bathing, especially on those mornings when he had come, with his strange fluids and peculiar smell, making Clovey feel dirty, debased, and ashamed.

She would dress, quickly and abashedly, and hurry to class, where she would sit distressed and unable to focus, fifteen, never kissed, and dreaming, as usual, of escape. She would marvel at the white girl's immodesty, reflecting on the absence of Shame at her nakedness, her trysts, and on Clovey's own complicity in an exploit she found discomfiting and embarrassing. As the day progressed and classes dragged on, she would wonder at the relationship between bridges and Shame, the latter of which she would render, perhaps, in oil or in relief; its absence in watercolors or airy mache, the freedom of it suspended from a limitless sky.

Clovey felt used up. She wanted to go home.

HENDERSON, NORTH CAROLINA

MAY, 1948

She had become aware, all at once, of the shame, or aware, at last, that it was Shame. Clovey had been stricken by her mother's, her sisters' persistent oiling and scrubbing and straightening; the cleansing and tucking and hiding; the opaque slips and confining brassieres; the silence and euphemisms and apologies for *being*—too this or that, not enough; the circumstances of her own origin, her mother's act of liberation and Shame; the obscurity of her ancestors, the absence of history, the seldom mentioned forebears of Shame: her mother's mother, and hers, posterity of whoring and filthiness, of meanness and madness, stretching so far backward into their descent that no one knew where the Shame had begun. No one recalled or understood how, much less why. Heiresses of contempt, they hid, powdered, covered the Shame, arranged themselves along church pews with lowered eyes, hems tugged self-consciously below the knees at intervals; covered heads—turbans, scarves, also tugged upon, concealing unkempt edges at the nape of the neck; thick stockings concealing hairy legs, large, shapely calves, sensuous, lewd, covered.

Chastity had been taught by solemn adults to nervously giggling schoolgirls in class rooms—purity classes. The biting of tongues and ingestion of bitterness had been taught as virtues, bitterness held carefully in check, unrationalized, unexplained. Clovey felt the burden, and the silence, of her co-conspirators against themselves, the great, gasping weight of Shame, borne on the backs of women already bowed down, their backs ostensibly strong, but breaking, slowly, the breaking to culminate finally, and with relief, but not for many generations; bridges breaking, crossed over with ingratitude by many and sundry others—husbands, brothers, sons, even daughters, mothers; bridges creaking, sagging; bridges spat upon, saddened, angry, hurt; groaning, but not speaking, silent; bridges of iron; bridges of clay; wood bridges with reinforcements of stone; straw bridges fortified only with mud; crumbling bridges; broken, the rifts filled in with mortar or sand; painted bridges peeling; covered bridges.

These adorned the walls, graced pedestals, and stretched across the floor of the Davis Gallery in Raleigh—Clovey's bridges. These had languished unborn within Clovey since her flight in horror from the nakedness of her roommate, the presumptuousness that had gone unpunished, the girl privileged, unmolested. Clovey had purchased oil and canvas. She had waited. Shame had not come. But the bridges had come, the first bridge insubstantial—as Clovey felt herself insubstantial—of plaster and paint; but vast, filling the backyard of the house on Chestnut Street, startling her parents, the neighbors, and the local reporters, on its surface bearing the imperceptible burden of Shame for which she had felt herself accountable, and by which she had felt herself indelibly marked.

The other bridges, mostly commissioned, had been inspired nonetheless. *Bridges,* her show was simply called, bearing many burdens, many secrets, many others. And the artist, modest and retiring, had been incessantly photographed, her image appearing above captions that read:

"... the budding young expressionist ..."

"... the mulatto sculptor ..."

"... beautiful newcomer to the arts community, Amber Hedgebeth, who prefers to be called Clovey ..."

She had never thought of herself as mulatto, or as beautiful. These designations fit her uncomfortably. She shrank even further into herself, dressing in baggy trousers and men's coats, a style intended as self-deprecating but interpreted by others as eccentric and chic. She avoided interviews and social affairs, working feverishly. Bridges began to appear in the homes of the local nobility, on bookshelves and mantels and walls. Her name sprang from the most revered tongues in the local art world.

The bridges stopped. The shame remained. And Clovey began again her search for escape.

NORTH CAROLINA COLLEGE AT DURHAM

DURHAM, NORTH CAROLINA

SEPTEMBER, 1952

You have the visage of a goddess, he had written, *the face of a cherub come to grace humanity with your presence. And I would be proud to be your escort, my Venus, my Minerva, my Juno ...*

She had thought no one would know her here—it had seemed the perfect hideout—no one except the professors of art, who had literally embraced her upon her arrival. And she had begged them for anonymity, no references, oblique or direct, to her work, please, during classes. She had needed a reprieve from stardom, asylum from the adulation of others that had dogged her ever since the bridges. Despite her parents' urging, college had not been in Clovey's plans. She had hoped to study, quietly, at the home of a noted multimedia artist, there to perfect and understand her crafts. But the cameras had followed her there, distracting and distressing her. Perhaps here, in this vast, yet undiscovered place, she would find the space she needed to invent and define herself, as woman and as artist.

She studied both art and science, writing and mathematics and dance. She attended football games and parties. She made new friends here, even joining a sorority. When the demands of a new environment, disappointing in its superficiality, began to tax her; when her peers bored or confounded her with their pretentiousness; when she could not concentrate or comprehend her courses, she doodled in ink.

And Shame sprung from her pen. It began to cover the walls of her room in the residence hall. She sold some of it—to classmates and neighbors who admired her work. Some of it remained in her windows, on her closet door, and on shelves and walls, dominating her small dormitory room, giving it an air of drama:

A small brown girl cried in a crowded train station, surrounded by white travelers rushing and indifferent, gripping with all her meager power a small, stuffed bear, its innards spilling from a vicious tear at its shoulder. A woman leaned toward her, smearing lotion from a bottle on the child's face . . .

A pregnant woman, naked, her face exhaustion, regret, and cowardice, arched her back, her palms spread out on her hips, her elbows bent outward and away from her back . . .

"Your subjects are always women," Aldridge pointed out to her one day as she sat doodling between classes beneath a stairwell, her knees drawn upward toward her chest. She had found she worked best in shadow. He had learned where she could be found, especially on gray and melancholy days full of a peculiar splendor, but without warmth.

She nodded. "Colored women," she added.

"Women with eyes that are luminous . . . knowing, and sad," he observed.

She looked up at him. "Colored women," she repeated. "With the eyes of my mother and my friends." His face registered no comprehension. She lowered her head and resumed her work. Aldridge sat beside her then, and watched her. He watched his mothers take shape with graceful black strokes of Clovey's pen. He did not recognize them.

"Who's that?" he asked.

"Isis," she replied. "The original Venus."

He laughed, a scornful snort. "A colored Venus?" he teased.

"Yes," she replied quickly. "Venus in black. Venus in shadow. Venus eclipsed." *Venus hidden and denied,* Clovey thought, *unrecognized by her own sons.* He stared at her without understanding. She looked away from him.

You have the visage of a goddess . . .

She had asked him to the dance at the urging of her roommate, and because he was dark, and quiet. They had often sat for hours, quietly, in the evening gloom of the library, sneaking peeks at each other from opposite ends of a long, polished table, while pretending to study. For two semesters, he had been unable to speak to the girl with the auburn hair and amber skin, dressed so oddly in oversized pants, a girl of the sort who did not speak, only cogitated and observed. He had stared, in awe of her, and she had doodled, for two semesters pretending not to notice him.

Finally, early last semester, she had ventured an open stare at him. And he had realized, when she looked at him—*toward* him, not directly into his face—that here was a girl of tender heart, fiercely guarded, and of seemingly aimless imaginings, unaware of her own beauty, or, he thought, of the discernment that flickered in her bottomless eyes. Her lip had trembled. She had not smiled or flirted. She had not known how. Clovey's mouth had parted slightly, her knuckles white as she gripped her pen.

Aldridge had smiled at her.

And she had resolved to ask him to the Sadie Hawkins Dance.

Aldridge had looked up when he heard the torn-off piece of heavy canvas slide across the table. Her writing had been small and earnest, the letters slanted anxiously, awaiting his response:

My friends are all going to the dance. Will you go with me?

He had glanced toward her, to find Clovey slouching in her chair, her face red, unnerved.

You have the visage of a goddess . . .

Clovey had learned not to expect much of others. She understood what they could not. A dark and buxom Venus was beyond Aldridge's mental and visceral grasp. Clovey pitied him, and she forgave him.

He stood over her now, his thighs muscular, filling his pants. She ignored him, as she often did when engrossed in her drawing. He had dated a white girl—she forgave him for this—a white girl free of shame, free to soil herself and yet retain the esteem of her paramour. Clovey did not have the luxury of this liberty. The thighs seemed to bulge. She squeezed her knees together and drew them more closely toward her chest.

"Why do you wear trousers?" he asked her.

She did not glance at him. "Because I can."

Because it is one of the few things that I can, is what she had intended to say. *Because they are warmer than dresses in winter, more comfortable in summer than stockings. Because they do not reveal my anatomy or draw attention to those aspects of me that cause others discomfort.*

"Because they are the one small liberty to which my artistry entitles me," she told him airily, and smiled at him.

He responded with the smile she had hoped to provoke. Next to his darkness, and his comfort with silence, she loved his smile most about him. It was neither a knowing, superior smile, nor an overly indulgent smile, neither patronizing nor ingratiating. It was the smile of an equal, of one who did not condescend or otherwise profess to know her, an honest smile, sincerely but not strongly felt; a smile she had not longed for or earned. His was a simple smile, uncalculated, uncontrived. She liked the stark white of his teeth against an outline of brown lips that stretched outward to each side and backward into his yet browner face; and the way his eyes sometimes danced with mischief and a secret that he would share with her, if she would allow him to.

He had not attempted to kiss her, and for this she was grateful to him. It was not that she found him unattractive. It was fear of the unknown that made Clovey's palms clammy. Clovey had never been kissed. She recognized the value of innocence, as did her sorors at this mecca of talented young colored men, eligible young men from decent families and with radiant futures.

And Clovey had something to live down. The Betas had known this.

"Clovey Hedgebeth . . . that name is so familiar. Are you a relative of . . . ?"

And they had smiled smugly as she acknowledged her mother, and implicitly her father, her origin, her Self. The Betas were local girls, daughters of the colored elite. They knew of her art. They knew of her family. They knew of her mother. And Clovey had refused to apologize or deny. Even when they wandered away from her, still smiling, to whisper among themselves.

"White man . . ."

"Whorehouse in Warrenton . . ."

"Vyda Rose . . ."

Vyda Rose. She had lived wantonly. She had died tragically, as some had thought appropriate. Clovey—and the Betas—knew little else of her. The details of her life had been shrouded in mystery, in rumor and innuendo. Vyda Rose was seldom mentioned—Clovey's mother had not known her, though her name appeared in the family bible, just below Queen Marie's and Prince Senior's; and because Vyda Rose had lived, joyously and irresponsibly; because Clovey's father was a white man and her mother had created a scandal, Clovey could never aspire to be a Beta.

But she could aspire to innocence.

And greatness. Not the greatness of title or high birth. But the greatness of wholeness and enlightenment, the greatness of exploring one's self, and of bringing vision to others. Clovey intended to create.

And to marry well. That Aldridge could be her salvation was not lost upon Clovey. That he might not be was equally apparent to her. This recognition, along with her absorption in her art and studies, allowed Clovey to pursue him passively and inconsistently, and to project an indifference to him, sometimes real, sometimes rehearsed.

He was intrigued by her. Clovey only partly understood why.

He had come from a family of blacksmiths, he had shared with her proudly, men who had worked for themselves for as far back as the family history was recalled. Their acumen as businessmen had led to a plethora of entrepreneurial ventures. His was a proud heritage—strong colored men who had withstood suppression and triumphed over it, achieving wealth and stature. He had grown up predestined, the progeny of men as outstanding in character as in skilled trades and business. He had grown up knowing he was called to great things.

Before long, he had discovered his mother's ugliness, the cruel yet pitiable ugliness of this woman who had borne him and nurtured him, and who would support him as he grew to adolescence and then a maturity of sorts, his contempt toward his mother rising with his ambition. He would be a great man. He was not yet certain how, but he would be as successful as his father.

He had often wondered why his father, Etheridge, had not acquired a more suitable woman—a beautiful woman, obligingly so, with smooth ivory skin and flowing hair; a quiet woman, and submissive. He did not know that his father, a man of independent tastes, self-esteem, and common sense, had loved his mother because she was himself—black, strong, and sweet like ripened plums; bitter as unprocessed cocoa, when this was called for; capable and courageous. Aldridge did not know that his mother was secure in a beauty internal, inherent, and indifferent to external standards. She had made Etheridge more of what he had already been, as Etheridge had known she would—a man of hard work and strong passions, of loud raucous laughter; a man given to excitability and shouting, argumentative, and temperamental.

Aldridge's mother could cut you with a stare, her head turned at a suspicious angle, her tone diminishing you, daring you to respond, knowing you could not. She had kept his father humble, human. But Aldridge felt her a hard woman. As he grew older, he did not recall the gentle, maternal care of his mother during his early childhood. He did not know of her softness.

Not until he was ten, and a look had passed from his father to his mother. She had been dressed for a wedding, ridiculous in a floral print dress that ruffled at the neck, squeezed her bosom into a funnellike bodice, and gathered at her thick waist before tumbling ungracefully downward over colossal hips. She had been standing before a full-length mirror, putting on the diamond and amethyst earrings that his father had bought her for no particular reason and on no particular occasion. A look had passed from his father to his mother, a look filled with an emotion he had not known his father capable of. And she, suddenly shy, had cast her eyes downward in modesty.

"But Baby, you sho' looks goooood to me," his father had bellowed.

His mother had waved her hand at him. "Pshaw!" she had responded, smiling, her eyes fixed upon her feet. It was then that he had noticed how hideous she was, how desperately, he supposed, she had needed reassurance. A dark, plump woman, she kept her mass of nappy hair braided and coiled around her head except on special occasions, when it was pulled into a severe bun at the top of her head or hidden beneath an ostentatious hat. Her nose was round, not large, but her nostrils sometimes flared, and her stubborn, full lips always seemed poised to say, "No." She, like Aldridge's father, had come from a proud family. She was known as a smart, industrious woman.

But not as a beautiful woman. Aldridge would have a beautiful woman. One, perhaps, with golden auburn hair, he thought as he stood staring down at Clovey's bowed head, and at her busy hand, scribbling furiously now, creating tightly coiled locks of hair that stuck out from a round, full-featured face.

"Ain't you got nothin' to do?" she teased, using the language he abhorred. "Ain't you got a class now?" And she glanced up again to smile at him.

"Ain't you?" he replied.

Clovey finished the unruly hair and took his outstretched hand, standing reluctantly with his assistance.

"I have Plato now," she said, referring to Greek philosophy, a course Clovey actually enjoyed. She had learned to be selective, avoiding ambiguously named and similarly described courses, accepting more readily the recommendations of upper-class students than the course descriptions in the college catalog. And this semester, a cadre of enthusiastic young associate professors was infusing her courses with a perspective to which she had never been exposed, remarking upon parallels to African folklore and alluding to the African origins of scholarly thought, linking Clovey to a lustrous past that had preceded all pasts and given birth to all cultures.

She began to talk increasingly, to babble in fact, about a greatness destroyed and buried, the wreckage of a people accomplished through sheer depravity and greed. And she began to reclaim that greatness, to claim the greatness of all cultures as her own, and the universality of that own-ness.

And so it did not surprise Aldridge when Clovey arrived at his residence hall in a togalike taffeta gown, her hair swept up in a Hellenic wrap, a crown of plastic olive leaves woven into her shining hair. Tonight was the night of the Sadie Hawkins Dance. Highlight of the spring semester, the Sadie Hawkins Dance was the only opportunity for well-raised young women to openly seek the attention of young men. Only once each year, proper young ladies wooed the young men of their own choosing. Young men waited to be chosen. And Clovey, by far the most classically beautiful girl at the dance, had chosen Aldridge to be her Zeus, her Jupiter, god and ruler of Olympus.

His chest swelled involuntarily when he and Clovey made their entrance, her loveliness and unusual gown attracting the attention of the entire party for a moment—the moment in which Aldridge decided to marry Clovey.

You have the visage of a goddess, and I would be proud to be your escort, my Venus.

chapter 13

PATERSON, NEW JERSEY
NOVEMBER, 1964

clovey had proven an asset of a sort that Aldridge could not have imagined when, at twenty-one, nearly prostrate with devotion and lust, he had proposed to her the life of a minister's wife. To Clovey, product of a union that had shocked the sensibilities of a community, the proffered position had held a certain redemptive appeal. She had eagerly said yes.

Her vocation as an artist had accommodated his need to move—first to Philadelphia, where he had attended divinity school; then to Paterson, where Aldridge was to pastor a small and struggling church. Clovey had packed her supplies and portfolio, carrying with her from one city to the next her growing distinction as a perceptive, imaginative artist in virtually every media.

Aldridge did not understand his wife's art. Others did, and to Aldridge, this validated her work, as the appreciative stares of others validated Clovey herself.

The approval of others was important to Aldridge. He prayed, preached, and lived for the reverence of his parishioners. He built a home of impressive dimensions, situated upon a mountain, in order to impress his peers. The grocery store and old folks' home, created pursuant to his vision, had garnered the respect of the community—the respect that he required. He needed the adoration of his wife—his wife who perceived things; whose spiritual depth, some were persuaded, rivaled his own.

They remarked upon this with sincerity. The Reverend's laugh, nearly a cough, told them that they had made a mistake; not in their belief in Clovey's perceptive powers, but in the expression of that belief. Hastily, they reminded him, and themselves, that Clovey was a humble woman who knew her place. With this, the Reverend agreed, but halfheartedly, bedeviled by the sense that he had been outdone by his wife.

But the truth of this was in her painting: the women looking inward at their own souls; inward—their arms were not outstretched, their faces never upturned. Their hands were clasped beneath their chins or upon their laps, and they prayed inwardly, to a power residing not only in the heavens, but within, their supplication not to a shining and external light, but to a light that shined within, unseen, only now discovered.

And her sculptures. Inaccessible. Sold at posh galleries at a cost prohibitive to most. They came nevertheless, to see daring women; leaping women, their legs long and lithe, clothed in dresses like tulip petals, as vivid as marigolds; flying women resurrected from the grave, their eyes empty, the set of their lips intent, intractable; women dancing wantonly—you knew that they had pasts—wanton women, balanced precariously on one toe, one leg raised, both arms raised; women delicate and severe, both graceful and lewd. Ugly women, mutilated, blind; crazy women, their heads in their hands, their environs garish, swirling.

The people saw this. They had assumed that the Reverend honored these women in his wife. They had not understood the tenuousness of his love for Clovey, or his delicate rivalry with her. They did not know that he feared her knowing eyes, feared his own transparence before those eyes.

Clovey understood his fear, although she could not tell him so.

Just as she could not stop the inspiration that was born in her when she heard the simple, lilting speech of her mother, or other mothers weeping as they prayed; when she smelled potato pies baking; saw white sheets hanging from a clothesline, or young girls in choral lines in the vestibules of churches. Things stirred in her. She needed to interpret, to create. For this she had been ordained before her birth.

Her gifts were burdens to her. They woke her at night and sent her stumbling to the bathroom, a thing in her that threatened to be born. She sought to experience more fully the God she had caught glimpses of in her own work—not the patriarchal God of her husband's dogma, but the nurturing, all-embracing God he had failed to discern in the scriptures; the mother God she felt inside herself. And the man who wished to be her god could only watch her with chagrin. He began to criticize her work, tacitly at first—

"Honey, some people don't understand your art."

"Some people do."

And he would glare at her before descending the stairs of their exalted house. She would often find him, hours later, still brooding in his study.

Then he began to berate her.

"You know, people are getting tired of you doing nothing but women."

"I do other stuff."

"No. You don't. You do nothing. Just women."

"I do nature and God and—"

"And that dead white man."

Her lip trembled. "He was my father."

"He was a white man. 'S what he was." He waited. She did not respond. "And you think he's God."

Months passed. Their bed became a battleground, in which he engaged in a unilateral war against her. And Clovey submitted to his gratuitous assaults for as long as she could keep silent.

"Aldridge, that hurts."

"You ain't hurtin'."

"Aldridge . . . that *hurts.*" And she tried with all her might to push him away. But he ignored her pleas, and her tears. She bit her lip and dug her fingernails into his back until he collapsed on top of her, breathing heavily, his breath like that of the wood-burning stove at Aunt Suzanne's house, like fumes from the hell into which she had descended—not the infernal pit of writhing reptiles, but the hell of understanding. She had been here before, when she was a small child. She was back.

Sobbing, Clovey pushed again at Aldridge.

He rolled away from her like a stone.

She stood and stumbled toward the bathroom. Across the dark corridor that separated them, Aldridge was speaking. Sickened and hurt, Clovey was not aware that she was hearing.

She painted a confusion of red labyrinthine tissue, its walls curved like the petals of a massive rose in bloom; and sodden velvet vulvae the color of pain. **oh and you think that white man *loved* your mama? you got no idea what *love* is** snaked its way through a tiny opening in the subtle folds, and slithered through the tiny corridors. **you got no idea who god is (i am god)** A bolt of steel, solid and black, forced its way through a narrow corridor of red hot ferrous, the walls glowing. Sparks flew. **love you i don't love you? what you think *this* is**

Later, these paintings would be hailed as the foretelling of a yet unborn and feminine consciousness, distinctively black in complexion. Colored women would bite their lips but would not speak.

Aldridge did not attend the exhibit.

No one asked.

To have left her would have confirmed what they all no doubt believed.

Aldridge set up a narrow cot and began to sleep in his study.

The urge to consume red clay moved Clovey to the fields of North Carolina, from which she had come.

Little had changed since her last visit. Tobacco still waited for harvesting in June. Potted geraniums still graced the windows of the house on Chestnut Street—her mother's house now. And although he had been deceased for some time, her father's love still made her feel particular, as her mother's understanding spoke to her of the mother god who waited for reaffirmation in Clovey. She spent idle days outside the house in Henderson, drinking the sun, attentive to the buzzing of bees.

Jewell had been licensed as a midwife. She counseled Clovey to rest, to avoid confrontation and to eat no salted pork. And she lay beside Clovey in the bed in the upstairs room, holding her as she had been held, rocking her as she had rocked Jessie; humming the tune that her own mother had known, when upon a raining night in a never-slumbering city, Vyda Rose had begun to hum—a tune she could not recall learning, or associate with a person or place or experience.

But Clovey seemed to recognize it, and succumbed to peaceful sleep. Time passed. And still, her mother hummed, murmuring, rocking Clovey uneasily.

She did not ask of Aldridge.

But she told Clovey to go home.

"Your adversary has surrendered," Jewell said. She paused to smooth back the copper hair, and to squeeze reassuringly Clovey's hand. "Your moment of glory awaits you," she said. "Go home."

chapter 14

> *Then shall the dust return to the earth*
> *as it was: and the spirit shall return*
> *unto God who gave it.*
> —*Ecclesiastes 12:7*

they whispered of her in ladies' bathrooms, in the clammy cold basements of Methodist churches. They dared not pronounce her name aloud, even those who knew it. She had been, they knew, appropriately ashamed, or at least discreet. So they spared her, to the extent they could, the humiliation of open scandal. Jewell had not, after all, been a whorehouse wench.

And he—the white man—had treated her well. She lay for two days in a fine polished casket, in the parlor of the house that he had left her. In her own name. And in her own name she lay sedately; the name unknown to many. Ashamed of this, they sneaked glances at her name as they fanned themselves with programs printed on heavy paper. 1902–1965. She had lived among them for more than sixty-two years. And they had denied her name.

But what else could they have done?

The husband had been dead for years. And the children had moved. To Philadelphia. And New York. Away from the shame. Even the youngest one—especially the youngest one, they had whispered—the one who was *his*, had moved away.

But they had come. The dark-skinned girls had become sturdy women, serious, settled, their manner as firm as their broad buttocks, their husbands solemn. They had made arrangements, as was expected of them, efficiently, prudently, nodding approval of the body, the yellow gown and strand of pearls, ordering the removal of the heavy powder from the face. Respectable women.

The boys had become silent men, their heads bowed, their hats in their hands, respectful if not respected.

And the youngest one had arrived on the day of the service. After the plans had been made, the work done. Smiling. Cordial. Pregnant, her black dress a tent draping the protruding belly that preceded her into the parlor of the house on Chestnut Street. She spoke softly, a catch in her voice occasionally as she dabbed with a tissue at the corners of her eyes. Proper, she spoke, like white folks, as did the husband of thunderous voice who was a preacher. *Hmph!* they snorted. And his wife in a dress above her knees! They stared at her, their brows knit, their lips turned down at the corners.

But Clovey was not unnerved. Her gaze was steadfast upon the tithes box at the New Bull Swamp. It was nothing in particular. But she stared at it as they stared at her. And she did not, would not apologize. She crossed her thin legs clad in sheer black leggings, and she looked them full in the face for a long, defiant moment.

Secretly, men dreamed of her. As her husband spoke, passion in his thunderous voice, they parted the proper black-clad legs. She looked at them in surprise. Their wives touched them, discreetly. They were brought back to reality. But they knew that she knew—had known in that moment between her legs and reality—that she was to them what her mother had been: black, but less so by association with her father; desirable because she belonged to the white man they supposed to be their oppressor. They would not have been surprised, they mused, if Clovey had married a white man—too good for their boys, as her grandmother had been for them.

They had forgotten their long-ago rejection of Jewell.

But they remembered the whispers of their wives. The touching, discreet, when her path crossed theirs. *Evenin', Miz Fanny.* Or *Mo'nin', Miz Rose Lee.*

Mo'nin', their wives had replied, and smiled falsely, thinking that they recalled her name, but not certain; grateful for her never lingering, but hurrying on, crossing the street, her basket full of geraniums that spilled over the sides, or cornmeal and flour, en route to the house on Chestnut Street, where it was said that they lived together in sin. It was said. It was not seen. Until the day that Clovey had been born, and the sun had hidden it's face in shame. And they had completely forgotten her name.

They burned the body after. Blue flames leapt and murmured. And Jewell's ashes were placed in an urn. The youngest—the one who was *his*—had insisted upon this. Miraculously, the sisters had relented. The black-clad Clovey sealed the urn and placed it in a safe deposit box in Henderson. As if the ashes were precious stones. People shook their heads. *She sho' got white folks' ways.*

But they lusted for her still, those men rejected and of dream-filled eyes. They lusted for Jewell despite her passing—the woman who was of them, and they of her. Mother. Sister. Would-be lover. But never truly theirs. She belonged, they supposed, to their master. They did not know that she belonged, had always belonged, to herself.

The ashes rested, nameless in their urn.

To the women, this was just as well. They had neither needed nor desired her.

But the spirits that had lived within her returned to the places from which they had come. They did not rest. They returned to come again.

BULL SWAMP CREEK, WARREN COUNTY, NORTH CAROLINA
AUGUST, 1965

> *And the graves were opened; and many bodies*
> *of the saints which slept arose.*
> *—Matthew 27:52*

The pains had begun at the scattering of ashes—weeks later, when Clovey had resolved to set her mother's ashes free. *Drive me to the bridge over Bull Swamp Creek,* she had said, because it had seemed as good a place as any.

Aldridge had worried about her health, her far-advanced pregnancy. But she had insisted upon the trip, and Aldridge, not wishing to upset her, had set out on the nine-hour return drive South, dutifully, though not without reservations.

He had stopped the white Lincoln at the edge of the bridge, and stood with her to whisper a prayer.

And there at the bridge over Bull Swamp Creek, her swollen fingers still wrapped around the empty, downturned urn, Clovey folded herself in pain.

The tearing at her womb had begun without warning. It stopped just as suddenly.

And a dark child was born without labor as the ashes sailed away in a flurry.

Clovey looked down at the thin black face, the sharp black eyes wide open beneath a cap of dark satin hair, and she knew that this was no ordinary child; knew that in the blood and the spirit and the person of this child lived all of the ancestors; and the child's own spirit, rising, on great black wings bearing without shame the scarlet past. Clovey stroked reverently the small velvet face, the skin soft like down against her knuckles. When she asked for a name, her heart whispered *Rae'ven*. She whispered this in Aldridge's ear.

Rae'ven, she whispered, *our mothers returned in spirit.*

And Aldridge agreed, though he did not understand: *Surrender*, Clovey had sought to call her, conjuring images of the letting go, the spreading of beveled wings in surrender. *Freedom*, she had meant to convey, the shame and the secrets that remained of the ancestors made incarnate, set free. *Triumph*, she had meant to say, the bearers of those secrets releasing shame, releasing bridled anger and tears, unburdening at river banks to dance beneath feathered wings spread like a canopy over the diaspora.

Back home, they dressed the baby in celebratory red, and debuted Rae'ven at church.

But some looked warily upon the chiseled dark face, so unlike her mother's. Lifting the thin blanket to peer at the tiny visage, some shrank back, discerning in spirit a warrior woman; and three small, angry girls who could not cry, at a grave near the edge of a wood.

Some knew of, but could not name, the woman said to have been buried there.

Rae'ven, Clovey whispered, when they asked the baby's name, and kissed the top of the bonneted head.

But those not ashamed to recall their mother's name; those who knew her whispered, *Sapphire.*

epilogue

she preached vindication, redemption.

She danced as if possessed across daises. Her feet bare, her head thrown back, she sang with the voice of rapture. She spoke in another tongue. When she parted her ceremonial robes, women rediscovered themselves beneath, neither angry nor mournful, but beautiful, graceful, human.

She preached freedom, salvation from the god of Judgment, the god of Propriety. When she opened her long and obscuring white robes, women discovered the distortions of their pasts. They saw their grand-

mothers' silences explained, their characters recast. They heard their fore-
mothers' stories retold with compassion and love.

Time magazine called her Fresh. New. The face of the future of min-
istry. But Rae'ven smiled knowingly, her teeth bright white against blue-
black skin. She was the past, and she was not ashamed.

Tall and arresting, proud and defiant, she paced the pulpit as though
it were a runway, arms spread wide, head held high, with the grace of her
forebears advancing a gospel infused with self-love. *Lesbian,* they called
her. *Heretic.* Shedding the mantle of silence. Baring her soul. Honoring
her mothers. Kneeling to mourn at the grave of Sapphire, extending her
hands, letting the mourning go.

Her sisters-only colloquiums drew millions from worldwide. The
doors closed in the faces of her critics. Cameras flashed.

Regal wraps and the skins of animals came to life on her slender
frame, something primitive, elemental in her wearing of them. Jewels
dangled from her forearms, her ankles—topaz, ruby, emerald—her eyes
onyx, her skin blue flame like sapphire. The paparazzi loved her. In New
York and Chicago, in Atlanta and L.A., they asked her to pause and to
posture, her head wrapped in the colors of the earth, or piled high with
serpentine braids. *Flamboyant. Ostentatious,* the faultfinders said. When
she parted the robes of ignominy and shame, they looked away. *Shameless,*
they said, drawn in spite of their discomfort. *Scan'lous.*

But Rae'ven laughed, as wanton women laugh. *I am my mother's
daughter,* she proclaimed, *and the daughter of her mother; sister of all sisters.*
People drew back, nervously. Fearfully, they moved away.

She spoke in mysteries: *Relinquish the gods constructed by others, fashioned of fallible things.* Rapt audiences stood mute in contemplation, their

mouths open, their eyes wide, not a sound in the mammoth hall but the voice of the messenger. Ushers left their posts, drawing nearer to hear the soft and commanding voice. *Serve God only. Love is the only true power.*

Newsweek named her THE MOST CHARISMATIC MINISTER IN AMERICA. But Rae'ven shook her head. She was not a "minister." She was the past, releasing the present.

The presbyters sought to revoke her license. She had none. The establishment disparaged her. She would not be silenced:

Lift your heads. Wipe your tears. Do not appease those who would see you craven and remorseful. Do not bow in humility before their gods.

When she opened again the long and obscuring white robes, the graves were opened. The departed arose.

From Maine to Texas, women discovered the dead in their mothers' pasts, in the shame and the silence and rejection of themselves, their judgments of each other. They woke up to find bones and teeth and hair in bed with them, the stench of an open grave polluting their nostrils, unacknowledged pain and guilt eating at their entrails, boiling their blood to a pressure unbearable. Ghosts and secrets with their chains and dust mimicked silently their every motion, every step. And they had not known that they were there.

In Miami, Seattle, they finally understood who they were and what they had done and why. And throughout the diaspora, they loved and forgave themselves. In Spain and Haiti and Brazil, they loved and forgave Sapphire.

In Charleston, the dying embers of a woman's rage evaporated her tears, and she sighed with relief.

And Sapphire, satisfied that they understood, began the slow journey back to her grave. Perhaps, she thought, she could begin the process of finally dying. Perhaps the shame would die with her. The sting of death was anticipated from Sierra Leone to Warren County to Paterson. The waiting grave prepared to share its victory.

God and Self were exhumed to make space for Sapphire—celebrated at last, no apologies offered.

once
we understood
it was neither the Lord's doing
nor our own

now
we have worn the scarlet garment
far too long
danced the dance
as the daughters of Herodias

and as unnamed sinners
who cry at the master's feet
we have emptied our basins
to sin no more

but we are the daughters of Hagar

who shameless knew

it was neither the doing of Sara's God

nor her own

and she wore the scarlet garment

as did Rahab

whose faith saved a people from ruin

as our faith has brought us to this place

once

we understood

but they took away our God

gave us others to impress

and a robe of pure white

they asked us to deserve

no saving grace

for the daughters of Sapphire

no flowers for her

grave

no mourners there

but a contempt-laden epitaph

to young women buried beneath the loam

her sons did not understand